Early Praise for Twelve Months

"Move over, Nicholas Sparks! Steven Manchester's *Twelve Months* is a book that will stay with you long after you've read the last page. Its story offers the reader a precious peek into heaven and will make you want to live better and love more. Steven Manchester is my new favorite author!" – Susan Farr-Fahncke, Author & Editor, 2theheart.com

"Steven Manchester doesn't just write books; he authors life lesson plans. *Twelve Months* is a powerful work of fiction." – Heather Froeschl, Reviewer, Quilldipper.com

"*Twelve Months* is a story that acts as a medicine for the desperate mind and is definitely worth the read." – Liana Metal, Book Reviewer, Rambles.net / Midwestbookreview.com

"Steven Manchester manages to pull on the heart strings – each one. *Twelve Months* can make even the most cynical reader pause to examine how one should live one's life." – Elizabeth Ross, Publisher, *River Walk Journal*

"It's not really what we did in our life but how we gave of ourselves, how we shared, and how deeply we loved that really matters. Perhaps that is the greatest legacy of Don DiMarco and *Twelve Months*." – Tami Brady, Book Reviewer, TCM Reviews

"You won't want to skim-read Steven Manchester's *Twelve Months* because you won't want to miss a word of the delightful prose. This poignant, yet humorous story will lead you to question your spiritual beliefs, reconsider your own life, and determine what is of value." - Linda Pynaker,
Author, *Messages of Hope & Healing*

"From the very first page, Manchester's mastery of descriptive language propels the reader into the life of Don DiMarco, a man given twelve months to live. *Twelve Months* is a joyful story that lays tribute to life. Throughout the book, the words attributed to Abraham Lincoln kept crossing my mind. 'And in the end, it's not the years in your life that count. It's the life in your years.' I rate it 5 stars." – Angie Mangino, freelance book reviewer, former book reviewer at *Inscriptions Magazine*

"*Twelve Months* gives readers the ability to step above the daily chaos that prevents them from asking the important questions. Readers will be encouraged to answer the questions instead of avoid them in fear; a relief that is rarely experienced, but will be after reading this book." – Krissy Brady, Editor, *Brady Magazine*

"Steven Manchester has created another heartwarming and thought-provoking masterpiece in his latest novel, *Twelve Months*. It is a book that needs to be read by anyone who has allowed themselves to take the gift of life for granted. I whole-heartedly recommend it!" – Diane Kozak, Author, *Full Circle 911* and *Exposing Eurabia*

"In *Twelve Months*, from the first page, I was genuinely impressed with the quality of the narrative and the integrity of the language. As readers, we are taken through the whole gamut of emotions as the novel's protagonist embarks on a journey of self-discovery, of introspection, of reminiscence, of gradual acceptance and above all – of bountiful love. This is a very spiritual and uplifting book." – LP King, Publisher, Mountain Mist Productions

"Like the pieces of a puzzle being brought to life, author Steven Manchester tells a fantastic, mesmerizing story of a life lived with no regrets." – Albie Cullen, Author, *Drown*

"Steven Manchester is proving to be one of the strongest voices in literature. With elegant simplicity, his latest offering, *Twelve Months*, is humorous, inspiring, and absolutely memorable." – William A. Kooiker, Author, *Knight of the Dove*

"In *Twelve Months*, Steven Manchester masterfully crafts the experiential elements of normalcy into the art of remarkable, and inspires us to seize every moment in this vivid picture of a life – celebrated rather than succumbed." – Buck Young, Author, *Arrows*

"Steven Manchester has written a winner! *Twelve Months* is yet another tearjerker; a truly inspirational story. Steven Manchester combines real life into fiction in the most amazing ways imaginable. *Twelve Months* is a must read!" – Noonie Fortin, Author, *Memories of Maggie*

Twelve Months

Twelve Months

A novel by

Steven Manchester

THE
STORY PLANT

The Story Plant
The Aronica-Miller Publishing Project, LLC
P.O. Box 4331
Stamford, CT 06907

Copyright © 2012 by Steven Manchester
Jacket design by Barbara Aronica Buck

Print ISBN-13: 978-1-61188-053-3
E-book ISBN-13: 978-1-61188-054-0

Visit our website at www.thestoryplant.com

For information, address The Story Plant.

First Story Plant Printing: August 2012

Printed in The United States of America

For Russell McCarthy, Stephanie Grossi & Robert Denson – whose lives exemplify the goal: *leave more than you take.* I am eternally grateful for their friendship, their support, and their determination to make a positive impact upon the world.

Acknowledgments

First and forever, Jesus Christ, my Lord and Savior.
With Him, all things are possible.

To Paula, my beautiful wife,
for supporting my every step.

To my children – Evan, Jacob, Isabella and Carissa –
for inspiring me beyond my greatest dreams.

To Mom, Dad, Billy, Randy, Darlene, Jeremy, Jenny,
Jason, Philip, the DeSousas – my beloved family and
foundation on which I stand.

To Lou Aronica and Peter Miller, for giving me the
amazing opportunity to share my stories with the
world. I am eternally grateful for Lou's keen eye,
determination and generous mentoring.

"Twelve months more valuable than the fifty-seven years that preceded it…who knew?"
- Don DiMarco, Puzzle Maker

Prologue

They say – whoever _they_ are – that every story has to start at its beginning. I'm not sure that's true. Maybe the best place to start with any story is the here and now. And that's exactly where we'll begin.

~ ~ ~ ~ ~ ~ ~ ~ ~ ~ ~ ~

Let me paint a picture for you: My name's Don Di-Marco and I live at 55 Summerfield Avenue on the outskirts of Pilgrim Hill. It's a small, residential neighborhood that sits beside a giant field of white and yellow daisies. And it's become the perfect place to enjoy my once-dreaded retirement.

In the mornings, even though I swore I'd never own another dog, Foxhound – named after my childhood companion – and I go for our daily walk and take it all in. It's like living in the middle of a Thomas Kinkade original.

Colonial, Cape Cod, and ranch style homes line both sides of the street, each one betraying the unique character befitting its owner. Brick driveways, laid out in a herringbone design, are guarded by statues of grinning lions or laughing cherubs. Faded cedar shingles are offset with cranberry or forest green shutters. Striped awnings hang above each window, while multi-colored petunias fill each box beneath. Open porches with rocking chairs lead to inviting front doors, their flowered wreaths matching the hanging potted plants that drip with warmth. Red brick and black wrought iron complement the sparkle of glass and richness of mahogany. In the rear, Connecticut stone patios host sturdy picnic benches and swinging hammocks.

Most of the yards are meticulously landscaped. Rhododendrons and azaleas burst with color, while apple and cherry blossom trees weave a carpet of pink and white petals beneath their twisted branches.

While Foxhound pulls at his leash, I prefer to maintain a leisurely pace. It's amazing the details you can pick up if you just stop long enough to pay attention.

To the harmony of singing birds, a tiny peeper calls out from a moss-covered stonewall. I like to stop for a moment and feel the tingle of a gentle breeze and the sun's warm hands on my skin. Suddenly, the powerful aroma of fresh-cut grass grabs my senses and I breathe it all in.

As we travel on, red maples and giant sycamores dance with the white birches and mighty oaks. If you follow their branches to the top, you'll find melted marshmallow clouds traveling a slow and easy pace against a sky of blue that's indescribable.

Though Foxhound and I enjoy our time alone, I also like the occasional exchange of a warm smile or friendly wave. When we're lucky, we'll catch Sarah pushing her newborn in an open antique carriage. When we're not so lucky, we'll come across another dog walker and his four-legged friend. Though I've tried to teach him better manners, Foxhound suffers terribly from an only child syndrome.

When you put all the pieces together, I guess Summerfield Avenue is my true refuge. For me, everything is at peace here. That, coupled with the fact I've finally managed a perfect lawn, how could I ever complain?

~ ~ ~ ~ ~ ~ ~ ~ ~ ~ ~ ~

As I think I've mentioned, I retired early – at fifty-seven years old – which allows me lots of time to spend with those I love and to think about the paths I've traveled. Family, of course, comes first.

Isabella – my beautiful Bella – is my true partner and wife. She's a great cook and from what I can tell, while I'm out cutting the grass or changing the car's oil, she's always loved playing the traditional role of homemaker. Through the years, she's insisted on very few things, but the one thing she's asked for is that the family eat together at the dinner table each night. Bella and I have been together so long it's tough to tell the differences between us. I guess you could say we more than complement each other. She laughs when I say it, but I believe we're two halves that make up a whole. A firm but compassionate soul, Bella has worked with mentally disabled children for the better part of four decades. We're holiday Catholics and for years, she took care of her ailing mother – her cross to bear – and had a difficult time letting go when the old woman finally passed. Bella can't sit still. She's constantly cleaning. And my wife, I've learned, has never been wrong – which might honestly be her only true flaw.

At thirty-six, our only child, Riley, is still Daddy's little girl. On the morning we were blessed with her company, I remember thinking, *In my daughter's face, I have seen my grandmother's smile.* With my brown hair and her mother's hazel eyes, she turned out as pretty as she is kind – which is most important, if you ask me. To the applause of thunder and torrential downpours, Riley came into the world without wanting to cause anyone any trouble. I sensed she was an old soul and we clicked right away. I suppose she had a normal up-bringing; from tomboy to boy crushes to college, where she eventually followed in her mother's footsteps and became an advocate for disabled children. Through the years, she became a gifted softball player – which I think was equally considerate of me, as I had no son – and an avid cyclist; a passion that has carried on through her adulthood. Riley and I have also shared an undying love for the Boston Red Sox. However, she did go through a rebellious stage I tried to ignore as much as humanly possible. With a back tattoo, belly button ring and a few nights where she had too much to drink and needed to call me for a ride (I never made a big deal about it at the time, preferring that she call me rather than drive home intoxicated), trust me when I say we've had our moments.

I thought I was lucky to have had two loves of my life – that is, until the grandkids came along.

After testing a string of potential suitors, Riley finally settled down with Michael. Even if I'd want-ed to dislike him like some of the others, there's no way I could have. He was respectful to me and Bel-la, but more importantly he was good to Riley. Before long, our daughter became Riley DiMarco-Resonina, a name I've never stopped kidding her about. "Wanna buy a vowel?" I'd ask, but she's always been a good sport about it. Riley and Michael waited quite a while, but they eventually gave me and Bella two beautiful grandbabies. The first was Madison Ruth, named after Michael's mother. Then came Michael Donald, which honored me beyond words. And with these children, I've been completely blessed. Grandkids are the perfect payoff for any life.

Ms. Madison, the oldest, was tough stuff from the start. With rosebud lips, a potato nose and her grand-ma's eyes, the gap between her two front teeth makes her smile contagious. The word determined can't even begin to describe this child. Of course, she looks like a living doll in her flowered dresses and fancy bows, but in reality she's all tomboy like her mom. Her relation-ship with her baby brother is reflective of the tough love my brother Joseph and I shared when we were coming up. "No one's going to mess with this kid," I've boasted time and again.

Michael Donald, the baby, was the chubbiest new-born I'd ever laid eyes on, so I nicknamed him Pudge and have never called him anything else since. With his dad's dimpled smile, he's a mix of mama's boy and the kind of rough and tumble lad that any man would love to have for a son. Before he could walk, this inquisitive little grubber was throwing baseballs and testing out different wrestling moves.

Madison and Pudge have always called me Poppa and I could not be any more grateful to their dad for allowing me to share in their love and adoration. As if it were possible, I've spoiled both of them even more than I did Riley. And the truth is – I've never once felt guilty for it.

Forgive me for going on like this. Though I always swore I wouldn't, it seems I've become the stereotypical grandfather.

Let's see, we were talking about the joys of retirement. Well, I still work – or volunteer, I should say. After years spent in a woodworking shop, I now volunteer in a children's hospital, transporting kids. I love it. I do. There's no pressure, better hours and I'm not killing myself any more because I've learned everything I need to know about money. The way I see it is – when you don't place so much value on something, it's not as important as it once was. Believe me, there's great freedom in that.

Before turning in each night, I like to sit on my deck in my Adirondack chair with my musty-smelling stray lying by my side. Prayer, meditation – whatever you'd like to call it – I now enjoy getting in touch with my spiritual side. At first, going within felt very strange, but the more time I've spent in the stillness – not thinking or doing anything, just being – the closer I've felt to myself; to the essence of who I truly am. To me, sitting on that deck at the start of a silver-lined dusk is like hosting a family reunion with my soul.

Like some unfinished masterpiece still in the process of creation, on most nights the light is bent to create the most magnificent colors, unnamed and infinite. Midnight blue poured onto black velvet; the ordinary is turned mysterious. Like a snow-covered mountain range, billowy clouds crawl by. The dark silhouetted tree line against a steel gray sky leaves me with the illusion of solitude and I am grateful for the opportunity to appreciate the light. Then, a giant curtain is drawn and the light announces its final surrender. As promising as the dreams of a child, though, it will be back. The world closes in all around me, allowing me the time I need to recharge my batteries. By now, the eye can only pick up movement. Sounds and smells become much crisper. The scent of moisture settles in and then burnt hardwood from a distant fireplace. Twinkling specks of light, of pure energy, are gradually scattered across the firmament, and I stare until I can see depth. All sounds are heightened beyond a whisper; the steady beat of a whippoorwill, the rustling of a skunk foraging for a late dinner, the patter of a moth's wings on glass. Even in the moon's halo, the clouds are no more than wisps of smoke drifting by. Like tiny magicians, the fireflies disappear and reappear until the cool air ushers them off to some hollowed-out log. Before long, all things are tucked away into their rightful place.

And though I must do so through the innocent eyes of a child, I can witness this most nights. If Foxhound and I are real lucky, on special nights we'll catch a lightning storm on the deck. Hearing the echo of rolling thunder and seeing the flash of lightning only reminds me that God never sleeps. "The angels are bowling," my mother used to say. Grandpa, however, preferred to capitalize on fear whenever he could. "God is angry with us!" he'd swear. Either way, it was a childhood fear that I'd never internalized or had to overcome. Like a mosquito to a bug zapper, I was drawn to these dangerous storms. To me, it's like being stuck in a car wash that comes with a very cool light show.

Stormy or clear, any night is ideal for thinking about those paths I mentioned. I'll spend hours just sitting there, searching my memory. It's funny the things you pick up along the way; the things you can share with your grandkids if you're smart.

I've learned that anyone can change the world; you just have to start with one person at a time. I've also learned that not caring what other people think of me has allowed me the energy to focus on what I think of myself. For me, life is like looking through a kaleidoscope. With every turn, a different view will be brought to light.

I've taught my grandkids that good things come to those who wait, but great things come to those who go after it; that a gift within is meant to be shared or else it wouldn't be a gift; and no matter how large or small, everybody's problems are enormous to themselves. Though the list goes on, the most important thing I've passed on is that life can be a beautiful dream, or a living nightmare. It's all about your attitude – your perspective.

But I didn't always see things this way...

Chapter 1

I hadn't been feeling well for a while; a change in bowel habits, unexplained weight loss and terrible cramping in my lower abdomen. When I started to find blood in my stool, I knew I had to see the doctor. "You stupid man!" Bella scolded. I thought she was going to kill me for waiting so long.

Together, we visited one doctor's office after the next, while I was subjected to a battery of intrusive testing. Most diseases were immediately ruled out – at least all the livable ones.

While Bella sat by my side, Doctor Olivier conducted his line of questioning. "Family history of intestinal polyps?" he asked.

"Not that I know of."

"History of an inflammatory bowel disease?"

"Nope."

"Any possible genetic factors?"

I cringed. "Yeah, both my parents died from cancer." I looked over at my wife. Her eyes were filled with worry.

After giving samples of every bodily fluid you can imagine and enduring the most God-awful probing, I was sent to the hospital's radiology department for a CT scan.

~ ~ ~ ~ ~ ~ ~ ~ ~ ~ ~ ~

As I recall, it was the final days of a long, harsh winter. The wind banged on the window, while the last remnants of a blackened snow bank stood off in the distance. Though Bella was worried sick, she reluctantly agreed to let me return to Doctor Olivier's alone because Riley needed someone to watch the kids. "But please come straight home after you're done," she requested.

As I sat half-naked on the exam table, I couldn't help but take note of the meaningless details that surrounded me; a water color painting hanging crooked on the wall, a glass container that needed to be refilled with tongue depressors, an extra chair that didn't belong, making the room feel cluttered.

The door opened and Doctor Olivier walked in, holding a yellow folder under his arm. It was my entire medical history. His face looked somber.

This can't be happening, I thought. *I never smoked, rarely drank and I'm only in my fifties.*

Doctor Olivier was a white-haired gent with a moustache trimmed a half-inch off his top lip, betraying his military background. With a white coat to match, his stethoscope swung freely from his thick neck. He had large hands with perfectly manicured fingernails. It's strange the things you pick up when somebody's about to invade your private parts. "Don," he began in his calm, no-nonsense approach, "I'm sorry to be the bearer of bad news, but…you have colon cancer." He opened the folder for more details.

I felt like he'd just punched me in the gut. "I what?" I asked, one octave higher than normal.

"The rectal bleeding, weight loss, abdominal pain and the fact that your stools have become longer and more narrow are all symptoms."

"But it hasn't been going on all that long," I argued. He only shook his head. Now I definitely felt like vomiting.

"Sometimes colon cancer fails to produce any symptoms until the cancer has grown very large and even metastasized, or spread to other parts of the body. This is why the identification and removal of polyps through regular screenings play such an important role in prevention."

"Spread to other parts?" I asked.

The man's green eyes peered up from behind narrow reading glasses. I knew right then and there that I was in serious trouble. "The cancer's already spread to your liver," he said.

A bolt of panic, generating from my core, shot out and filled every cell of my body. My extremities began to tingle and my breathing turned shallow. There was a sudden pain in my chest and I knew intuitively that this was felt for my wife. *What's Bella going to do?* I wondered, and a wave of dizziness nearly pushed me off the table. Then, I must have gone into some kind of shock or something. I kept eye contact, but for a while all I heard was a hum; the occasional phrase dancing in and out.

"...trace amounts of blood. Blah. Blah. Blah. ... blockages preventing bowel movements. Blah. Blah. Blah. ...consumption of red meat, obesity, smoking. Blah. Blah. ...stage four. Blah. Blah." There was a long pause. "Do you understand what I'm saying, Don?" he finally asked.

I don't know how long we stared at each other before I answered. "Yes, I heard you. I have cancer."

"That's right. You have stage four colon cancer which has started to spread to other organs. At your age, I strongly recommend we pursue aggressive surgical treatment to remove the cancerous tissues. We'll also want to consider chemotherapy and radiation therapy." From his tone, this wasn't so much a recommendation as it was an order.

Along with oxygen, my wits were returning to me. I understood the words he was saying, but they were still difficult to register. "But I've always been more of a quality guy…not so concerned with quantity," I blurted.

He folded his arms, awaiting an explanation.

"What kind of life will I live…even if it's extended?" I asked.

"We won't know that until we begin, will we?"

"Maybe I should get a second opinion?"

"By all means, please do. It's important to…"

"I just don't want to cut myself short by living a few more months hooked to tubes," I interrupted.

He nodded once. "I understand," he said. After explaining a few more details I was too overwhelmed to comprehend, he left the room. There was clearly nothing more he could do for me.

Minutes later, I was dressed and walking down the icy sidewalk toward a frightening future that had just shrunk by decades. It was as if adrenaline forced me to move, one foot in front of the next. I felt numb, high on the fear of losing my life. And then I pictured Bella's face and stopped. I must have dry-heaved for a solid five minutes.

~ ~ ~ ~ ~ ~ ~ ~ ~ ~ ~ ~

My pretty, light-haired wife met me at the front door, shivering. I looked into her hazel eyes and attempted a smile. Before I said a word, she already knew. "Oh, dear God..." she gasped and pulled me to her.

As we stepped inside, I told her, "Stage four colon cancer."

"I thought it was..." she began. "But it can't be..." Her voice began cracking like warm water on ice.

Although we both suspected the same prognosis, there was no real way to prepare for it. We held each other for nearly a half hour and cried. Although I was already worried about having to leave her, I tried to console her. "We'll be fine," I whispered.

For a moment, she pushed away and peered into my soul. "We'll be going for a second opinion," she confirmed.

~ ~ ~ ~ ~ ~ ~ ~ ~ ~ ~ ~

While a late-night hailstorm threatened to shatter the living room windows and Bella tossed and turned in bed, I fumbled on the Internet and conducted my own research:

> It is estimated that fifty-seven thousand Americans will die from colon cancer this year; the second leading cause of cancer death in the nation and a disease

that it is completely preventable. Prevention and early detection can mean the difference between life and death. Colon cancer forms from non-cancerous polyps on the wall of the small or large intestines. Polyps can eventually increase in size and turn cancerous. If polyps are found during a routine test, a biopsy may be done to determine if cancer is present and to which stage it has advanced. Women are usually diagnosed with colon cancer in its latter stages because many believe this disease only affects men. Unfortunately, this disease affects people of all genders and ethnicities. There are five stages, zero through five.

I stopped reading. *I'm already nearing the final stage*, I thought, and for the first time I felt guilty about not taking better care of myself.

I was preparing for bed when I looked up from the sink and surveyed my face in the mirror. I still had most of my dark hair. My brown eyes were filled with life. *Dying can't be what I'm in the process of,* I thought. Besides the pockmarked cheeks from a cruel case of pre-adolescent acne, I looked as healthy and unscathed as the day I was born. I washed down two pills with a gulp of water and shut off the light.

As I headed for bed, it suddenly dawned on me: *All the things I was planning to do when I finally had the time…I may not actually have the time to do!* I snickered at the thought of it. *Shoot, I was gonna go fishing and travel the country with Bella in a motor home, where we*

*could rekindle our romance…which took a backseat to too
many other things.*

I lay down in bed, placed my hands behind my
head and stared up at the ceiling – haunted by my un-
realized aspirations. I was hoping to do some writing,
maybe even for the newspaper, and beg the boys down
at the local race track to let me go for a spin. I even
thought about talking Bella into doing some horseback
riding…

I turned to my side and watched Bella's eyelids struggle with another bad dream. *Now what?* I
wondered.

~ ~ ~ ~ ~ ~ ~ ~ ~ ~ ~ ~

It's funny how the mind works. Besides making Bella
promise not to tell anyone until we were absolutely sure,
I honestly cannot tell you what my feelings or thoughts
were between doctor's visits. I remember going to work
in the cold and coming home to watch Bella pray each
night, but most of that time remains a complete blur to
me. I vaguely recall the desperate phone calls and hours
of research my frantic wife conducted, and her sudden
outbursts of grief. I stayed out of it – all of it. I wasn't
ready to consider death. It wasn't part of the comfortable routine I'd spent decades perfecting.

~ ~ ~ ~ ~ ~ ~ ~ ~ ~ ~ ~

For whatever reason, I was surprised to find that Dr.
Rice was a woman. She was too thin and pale, but
she had kind eyes and a soft tone to her voice. "Colon

cancer is one of the most common types of cancer," she explained to Bella and me. "And treatment usually depends on the location, size, and spread of your cancer at the time of diagnosis. When colon cancer is detected at an early stage, surgical treatment is very effective. We also use chemotherapy or radiation with surgery to reduce the chance that the cancer will return."

Seated by my side, Bella couldn't wait to ask. "And Don's…do you agree with the surgery, chemotherapy and radiation in his case?"

The doctor hesitated. It was slight, but she hesitated, and as plain as day, I could see that she was too kind for this aspect of her profession. Without a word, she confirmed our dreaded suspicions. "It was caught too late, Mr. and Mrs. DiMarco," she explained. She looked at Bella and then back at me. "Your cancer is inoperable, and although radiation is an option, the diagnosis is still terminal."

"How long?" Bella asked, her voice cracking.

"Twelve months…at best."

"Now what?" I asked. It was a stupid question, but I still hoped for an answer.

"Go…and *really* live the time you have left."

Like a puppet that had snapped its strings, Bella collapsed into a chair and began to sob. "Oh, dear God," she cried.

"My father didn't raise a quitter," I said, surprised at my last-ditch effort.

"That's admirable, but you can either spend your remaining time fighting or enjoying it," Dr. Rice advised.

I felt devastated, but when I found her eyes again I also felt a brief moment of peace. It was unexplainable.

To the beat of Bella's heavy sobs, the doctor took out her prescription pad. "I'll give you all the medication you'll need to manage the pain."

"Thank you." I took the two scripts and helped my wife to her feet. It was time to go home and face Bella's unanswered prayers.

~ ~ ~ ~ ~ ~ ~ ~ ~ ~ ~ ~

As the days threatened to turn into weeks, I moped around in a silent state of numbness. Life was a fog and I was traveling aimlessly with no light to guide me. I prayed harder and with more frequency: *God grant me the serenity to accept the things I cannot change, the courage to change the things I can and the wisdom to know the difference* – but serenity and courage were nowhere in sight. Instead, as though I was competing in the emotional Tour de France, I cycled through denial, anger, depression and negotiating with God – again and again.

"Talk to me!" my wife pleaded, trying everything to include herself in my secret mourning. But I was too selfish to let her in. For whatever reason, I needed to sit with the misery for a while longer before sharing it – with anyone.

It didn't take long to run the full gamut of darkness – anger, sorrow, fear – and then run through each of them again. *WHY?* I screamed in my head. *WHY ME?* But there was no answer. Eventually, I was only left with the stinging realization that on many levels, it didn't matter that there were people who loved me and didn't want to lose me. In many respects, my dying was the perfectly natural thing to do. Still, I wasn't ready to surrender to it. For the time being, I preferred to stay within my shell and simmer in a bitter rage.

Bella, on the other hand, was more than happy to express herself each day. I never realized my gentle wife could be so angry and sad – all at the same time.

~ ~ ~ ~ ~ ~ ~ ~ ~ ~ ~ ~

After canceling my next dentist appointment – I figured, *What's the use, right?* – I finally called for a family meeting with Riley and Michael. It was time we broke the terrible news. I didn't want anyone outside the immediate family to know, though. You see, I've always believed that positive thoughts and actions bring about positive results, with the same holding true for the opposite. So, with the negative hens in our extended family, I figured if they caught wind of my illness, I'd be dead in a matter of weeks. Besides, the fuss would be too annoying.

We were at the kitchen table for a few terrible moments before Bella began to explain exactly what Doctor Rice had said.

Before she was through, Riley screamed, "No, Daddy…NO!"

I honestly thought I was going to be strong for everyone until she did that. I looked up to find Bella sobbing and Michael looking away to wipe his eyes. I couldn't help it. I joined the family for a good, long, healthy cry. When I finally composed myself enough to speak, I said, "Okay guys, this is the last time I want to see anyone mourning for me while I'm still alive."

Everyone reluctantly nodded.

"What are you going to do now that..." Michael stopped himself and looked away again.

"I'm going to run a marathon."

No one laughed.

"I'm going to *live*," I said and meant every word of it. "I promised Pudge a couple years ago at his sister's kindergarten graduation that I'd be there at his, and I fully intend to keep my word."

Riley peered into my eyes. "There's always a chance for a miracle, right?"

"I'm expecting it!" I told her.

She jumped into my lap and hugged me for a long while. It was the type of medicine that could heal anything.

Bella barely excused herself and hurried out of the room. Even through my own haze, I knew she was furious with God; a rage that lasted longer than I would have ever expected.

~ ~ ~ ~ ~ ~ ~ ~ ~ ~ ~ ~

Right from the start, everything changed.

After Riley had flown the coop, for years Bella and I would go for a ride in the car every Friday night with the windows rolled down and the music playing. Nine out of ten times, we'd end up at Flo's on Island Park. Flo's served the best clam cakes and fried clams anywhere. Bella and I would sit together on the sea wall and share our feast with the seagulls. But Bella had a different idea now. "What about taking me to Venus for that baked stuffed lobster we always talked about?" she asked.

I had to smile, thinking, *She is a clever one.* For years, I'd wanted to try that lobster but never thought we could afford it. We finally went.

I was stunned. Venus's baked stuffed lobster wasn't nearly as good as I thought it would be, nor was it all that hard to shell out the cash for it. *After all these years of fantasizing*, I thought, *and we should have gone to Flo's for the cakes.*

~ ~ ~ ~ ~ ~ ~ ~ ~ ~ ~ ~

Thanks to a vested retirement plan, I was able to retire early from McKaskie's. This money was sure to carry me through to the end. For Bella's well being however, I was thankful for the large life insurance policy I'd complained about paying on for years. From the moment I'd signed the papers, I thought we'd overpaid, but he was a good salesman. "We don't need it," I complained again and again to Bella, but once we started making payments it seemed foolish to stop. I've never been so happy to stick with something I didn't want. Now, not only would my wife be able to survive on the money, she'd be able to live quite well – long into her own retirement. On one hand, it was strange to be worth more dead than alive. On the more important hand, I was thrilled that Bella would be able to live better than she ever had.

With no intentions of sharing the truth about my impending doom, I walked into McKaskie's for the last time to take one final stroll through the grease and wood shavings. It felt so surreal. Here I was, the foreman in charge of quality assurance of this giant woodworking shop, taking one last look around. I didn't expect it, but it hurt. I'd been at the same job forever. It was the place that had provided purpose for my entire adult life and the reason I'd gotten up every day – five days a week – at five o'clock in the morning. It had offered just enough overtime to put my daughter through college and now I was never going to see it again.

Bobby, Marty – even the Smeaton brothers, who were supposed to be identical twins but looked nothing alike – came over to shake my hand and wish me luck on my early retirement. "We'll be seeing each other soon," they all promised

I knew better.

I sat with them on the loading dock for the day's final break and listened to Adam go on about his ex-girlfriend. "We were together through most of Tractor Trailer School," the young smartass joked, creating just enough laughter to get him rolling. "God, did I love her. She was so big, though, that you could have put a swing set in her backyard."

Everyone laughed.

"I think she snacked between meals. For whatever reason, what really turned me on was walking behind her when she climbed stairs. It was like watching two baby pigs fighting under a blanket."

Even I laughed at that one.

"When we went out dancing, I couldn't tell whether she was doing the electric slide or having a seizure. And she used to have me shave her back in the shower

– that is, until the weed whacker nearly electrocuted us."

We shared one last laugh and the whistle went off. It was perfect timing. The guys each got up, dusted themselves off and went back to work. I took one last look around, grabbed my timecard and – for old time's sake – punched out.

~ ~ ~ ~ ~ ~ ~ ~ ~ ~ ~ ~ ~

While Bella wrestled with the reality of my early departure and the sharp pains that went with it, I watched in agony as she stumbled through the same dark valley I was traveling in. She snapped at the slightest annoyance and cried at the most random times. Days fit slowly into weeks.

I slept in one morning but it wasn't easy to break old habits. For decades, I'd gotten up before the sun. Now, all I could think was to take my coffee to the deck where there wasn't much to do but sit in the Adirondack chair and listen to the birds gossip.

Idle time can be a killer. I started thinking too much about where I might be heading. I wasn't sure about heaven and hell, but I eventually pictured my Nana. *Wherever she ended up is good enough for me,* I thought. *And if she didn't make it to heaven, then I don't have a snowball's chance in hell.*

One night, I got up from bed and went into the living room away from Bella's sensitive ears. I cried for a long while – not for myself, but for the love I was going to have to leave behind – for Bella, Riley, Michael and the kids. Before long, I heard some rustling around

in the kitchen. Bella's angelic silhouette suddenly appeared in the doorway. Without a word, she joined me
on the couch where we cried together. When we'd had
our share of grieving, she turned to me and asked, "Are
you ready to share this with me now?"

"Yeah. But I..."

"No buts," she said, "for better or worse, remember?" She rested her head on my chest. "In sickness and
in health...you big oaf."

"Okay," I said. "In sickness and in health."

~ ~ ~ ~ ~ ~ ~ ~ ~ ~ ~ ~

The following week, after my bi-weekly visit with Dr.
Rice, the blue-collar stiffs from McKaskie's threw me
an impromptu retirement party in Jimmy Smeaton's
frigid backyard. It was half-assed at best, but they did
the best they could. It was an off-season cookout, with
burgers and dogs, a full keg of beer and a beat-up radio playing country music. From this jaded crew, the
thought really was all that mattered. I found out later
that Bella funded the majority of the shindig. It didn't
surprise me. I did my best to enjoy the celebration, but
my mid-section throbbed in pain the entire afternoon.

Suddenly, I had all the time in the world to do
whatever I wanted. Besides my wife, though, there was
no one else around to do it with. Everyone was either
working or taking part in that thing I used to know as
life.

Five weeks to the day I'd received the bad news,
Bella and I took in a movie. The smallest details seemed
to mean everything; the smell of new carpeting mixed

with buttered popcorn; the young, inattentive ushers with their roving flashlights. The entire experience was so different from anything I'd ever known; much different from the days not so long ago when I took everything for granted.

Like a switch that had been turned back on inside of me, as I walked out into the sun it hit me. I had already lost fifteen pounds and was now fitting into my skinny jeans. If my attitude didn't change, I wasn't going to last six months. *You'd better accept this dying thing before you waste the rest of your life*, I told myself. *Besides, you've been a pain in the ass since you were a kid. What's more appropriate than going out with colon cancer?*

I turned to Bella. "I need to stop pouting, we both do, before we waste the time we have left."

She grabbed my arm and kept walking. "I know," she said. "I've been thinking the same thing."

From that very moment on – with the filters turned off, the walls torn down and all the defenses lowered – we stepped back into our life together, or at least what was left of it.

~ ~ ~ ~ ~ ~ ~ ~ ~ ~ ~ ~

Michael popped over on that next weekend to help me carry my worn recliner out to the sidewalk for the junkman.

"But you love that chair," Bella said.

"But I love you more," I told her and then turned off the TV. "As far as I'm concerned, you can get rid of this, too. I don't have time for it anymore."

She was shocked. She'd always called that TV my soul mate.

It took some searching, but I finally found the jigsaw puzzle on the top shelf of the hallway closet. It was a five thousand-piece mural of angels ascending into heaven, a gift that Riley had gotten me many Father's Days ago. The picture on the box showed shades of blue and green so close that they were guaranteed to make me pull every remaining hair out of my head. Puzzle making was a simple task of such complexity that I couldn't help but embrace the torment. This one wasn't going to be a one-nighter, but if I had to fill my time I wanted it to be with the pastime I loved most. *A picture of angels can't hurt either,* I figured. "It's going to help relax me," I told Bella when I showed her the box.

"Sure it will," she snickered. "Just make sure you watch your mouth in front of the kids."

I laughed. "Those days are done," I promised.

For as long as I can remember, I've always loved putting together puzzles. I think I was six years old when I got my first puzzle for Christmas. I don't remember how long it took me to put together or how many pieces it was, but it looked like a lot. I guess it must have been about a hundred pieces.

As I got older, during the long New England winters my mother would set up a card table where I'd chip away at three hundred-piece Whitman puzzles, or the more expensive Wysocki's. Back then, the average puzzle was around two hundred fifty pieces and a large one was no more than five hundred. The pieces were at least three or four times thicker than they are today.

I've tackled two giant puzzles in my time. One was eight thousand five hundred pieces, cost eighty-nine dollars and took nearly three months to complete. There were three of us doing it on the weekends – Bella, Riley and me. Every time I passed the puzzle, I'd have to stop and put in a piece or two. When adding up the cost of soda pop, beer and snacks, that puzzle ended up costing us around five thousand dollars. The other monster had twelve thousand ninety-six pieces and was four and a half feet wide by nine and a half feet long. I gave them both away after we finished them.

Over the years, I must have put together at least a thousand puzzles, maybe more. Per Bella's orders, many of them were laminated and framed and now hang everywhere throughout our house. I really enjoyed making all of them. I'll tell you, though, sometimes I'd get so involved that I'd call McKaskie's and tell the boss something important had come up and I'd be to work a little late. I did that more than once.

I can remember staying up late some nights, getting only two or three hours of sleep before having to go to work. I'd wait until the last possible moment so I could put in a few more pieces. There were even days when I'd get to work and tell them I wasn't feeling well and had to go home. Crazy, I know.

For a one thousand-piece puzzle, it would take Bella and me a month or so. There were others, though, that took longer. Though I wouldn't admit it to my wife, there were definitely moments when I'd get pretty steamed.

I was really looking forward to getting back into one.

~ ~ ~ ~ ~ ~ ~ ~ ~ ~ ~ ~

We were working on the angel puzzle after dinner one night when Bella blurted, "We need time for us. So, where's your favorite place in the whole world?"

I didn't need to think. "Martha's Vineyard," I replied. We'd only been there three times in all the years we'd been married. It seemed odd to me now. A rush of memories came flooding back. I could picture the narrow cobblestone streets, the quaint shops, water views from anywhere, elephant grass blowing in the stiff sea winds, the beautiful sunrises and sunsets...

"Then Martha's Vineyard it is," she said. "When do you want to leave?"

"How 'bout in a week or two?"

Her raised eyebrow requested an explanation.

"Before I go anywhere, I'd like to take some time and go back...to remember how I got here."

The raised eyebrow remained.

"I've been thinking about visiting the old neighborhood," I explained. "I'd like to spend a few moments with my memories...at least the good ones. They seem to deserve at least that much."

The eyebrow surrendered and was quickly replaced by a smile. "Then that's where you should go," she said.

I gave her a kiss, and with a grateful nod, returned to the puzzle.

Chapter 2

Before being able to go anywhere, Bella and I kept my appointment with Dr. Rice. As she reviewed my latest blood work, the doctor asked, "How have you been feeling?"

"Like hell," I blurted, honestly.

Her head flew up. "The pain's bad?" she asked.

I half-nodded. "I don't know what to compare it to, but yeah…I'm not thrilled with it. But it's more…" I stopped, searching for the right words.

"More what?" she asked, putting my folder down and giving me her undivided attention.

"Right now, I'm more interested in doing what I can to prolong my stay here." I glanced at my wife before locking eyes with Dr. Rice. "Are you sure there are no medications that can…" Again, I stopped.

She took a seat and explained to both of us, "Sorafenib and Cisplatin are both chemotherapy medications that have been shown to slow advanced hepatocellular carcinoma from progressing for a few months longer than with no treatment. Basically, it interferes with the cancer's ability to generate new blood vessels." She paused, acknowledging the hope in my eyes. "But the side effects are pretty serious…chest pain, difficulty breathing, loss of balance, skin rashes, abnormal bleeding…on top of what you're already starting to suffer."

"All of that for a few more months, huh?"

While Bella shook her head, Dr. Rice nodded. "There's also Doxorubicin, which is an antibiotic drug administered by injection. But its side effects are just as bad…trouble swallowing, fever, blistering of the mouth and…"

"Not a chance," I interrupted, feeling just as defeated as my wife.

"But there are ways you can slow the cancer down."

My raised eyebrow asked that she embellish.

"A good diet is more important than you realize. You need to incorporate a variety of fruits, vegetables and whole grains into your daily diet. They each contain vitamins, minerals, fiber and antioxidants, which can play a role in slowing down the cancer. Next, if you have to drink alcohol at all, no more than one drink a day. A good night's rest and exercise are also very important."

I tried not to snicker, but some sort of negative grunt still came out.

She smiled. "Nothing too intense with the exercise, of course. Just take a walk every day…for as long as you can."

"That'll also take care of my weight problem," I teased, poking fun at my shrinking size. No one laughed, but Bella did slap my arm.

With a final recommendation that I begin taking calcium and Vitamin D supplements, Dr. Rice handed me another script for pain medication.

"Thanks," I told her, and had just reached the door when I turned back to her. "So you really think the change in diet and daily walk might sneak some more sand into my hourglass?"

She smiled, gently. "The more you do, the more you can extend your life."

"Consider it done," Bella told her.

~ ~ ~ ~ ~ ~ ~ ~ ~ ~ ~ ~

I never imagined wanting to return to my past, but I also didn't want my life to just flash before my eyes when that fateful moment came.

"You want me to tag along?" Bella asked, as I packed a small cooler for the trip.

"Aren't you supposed to have lunch with Riley?"

"Yeah, but I can reschedule. She'll understand."

I shook my head. "No, don't reschedule. She needs time with you right now...to help her accept this thing. I only planned on spending the day anyway."

"You sure you don't mind me staying here?" she asked.

"I'll be fine," I said, "Go help our daughter. I'm sure I can find my way back all by myself."

She kissed me. "Just make sure you find your way back home when you're done." She patted my backside and handed me my jacket and gloves. "And don't be too long."

"I won't," I promised and returned her kiss.

~ ~ ~ ~ ~ ~ ~ ~ ~ ~ ~ ~

As I drove two towns over, eating my lunch – an apple and two granola bars – it struck me that I'd never traveled all that far in my life. I'd never really gone anywhere or saw all that much. On the way, my mind began to create random glimpses of many yesterdays…

~ ~ ~ ~ ~ ~ ~ ~ ~ ~ ~ ~

I could picture myself standing on the back stairs of my childhood apartment, one arm wrapped around my mother's leg, the other holding the toy-of-the-day. Sunlight filtered through the banisters like a sign of freedom from outside the prison walls. My brother, Joseph – older by one year – was allowed to go with my father, as long as he "held onto the railing and watched his step." As he walked away, I didn't wonder where he was going, but whether or not he'd ever return. The life of a young child sure is a simple one.

And his name was Joseph – not Joe and never Joey – but Joseph, as my father had named him. It was a name he would strictly enforce throughout his life. Built like a fire plug, my only sibling carried a concrete head atop a set of broad shoulders that allowed no room for a neck. He had raven-black hair and walked with the swagger of someone who knew his own strength. Even as a kid, he spoke like my father with a mob-style accent and wore long sideburns. Though we shared the same prominent nose, his dark eyes were more beady and set together, giving him the look of a Bowery Boy. He was naturally strong, loyal and took his job as my big brother very seriously – though he had no choice with my old school father watching. And though I honestly never envied him for it, he was my father's pride.

I then pictured holding my Nana's hand, as we trudged through the fresh snow on Pleasant Street. It was my turn to go with her and it beat waiting for her to return, even though she always came back with a surprise. The great unknown might have been a lot more frightening than sitting at home, but it was also much more exciting. Men tipped their hats to her and she smiled in return. She always dressed pretty and smelled just as nice. Even as a young boy, I had a keen sense of who this matriarch was and the many important roles she played within our family.

Me – I was called the runt. Lanky or "scrawny," as Dad put it, I also had dark hair and brown eyes. Tall and awkward, I was destined for a deep voice.

Going for a ride with my father was a real treat until I discovered that most of the people he came into contact with wore the same look on their faces that I felt inside. I would later know that feeling to be fear.

Standing taller than six feet on a large, sturdy frame, my father was a real bastard. Though I wondered why, he had religious tattoos on both arms. He chain smoked unfiltered cigarettes and liked to drive his black Cadillac with the windows rolled up. His music alternated between Sinatra and Dean Martin to country and western, which I also thought was very strange. He looked like Elvis to me, with his greasy black hair and long mutton chops to match. The man's temper was legendary. Just his voice instilled panic in most people. He was quick with his hands and even quicker about using them to exact his judgment – or "discipline," as he called it. Though no one really knew what he did for work, when people mentioned his name they cringed and said he was "good at his job." Years later, I discovered that most people knew him as Gino Stefinelli. I don't know what you call a creature that feeds on sharks, but that's what my father was.

Not all my early memories are bad. With little money from my dad, my mom once took a cardboard refrigerator box, cut out holes for a door and windows, and then used old markers and crayons to draw in the rest of the clubhouse. It was the best gift I'd ever gotten and I'm pretty sure Joseph felt the same, though he was less apt to express how he felt.

Mom was also a chain smoker, but hers were the long, filtered ones. She wore a beehive hairdo that Dad insisted she keep up. Per Dad's orders, she was always "well maintained" with make-up and jewelry. She wore horn-rimmed glasses to read – which I believed to be her escape because she sure did enough of it. Even when she smoked, she snapped her chewing gum. Her job was me and Joseph, and she also took her work very seriously. She was a spiritual woman and a wonderful mom, though even when I was young I sensed she was a very unhappy person.

I recall my parents taking Joseph and me into Pleasant Drugstore at Christmastime. I can still see the gifts Dad bought on "his tab" at the drugstore, as well as at Jack & Harry's Department Store. Then we moved from the city to the country because Dad "didn't want us to grow up around violence." That irony still baffles me.

Youth can be filled with such incredible hope, and as is often the case, I didn't fully understand the value of it – of all the possibilities at my feet – until it was too late. One day, like low-hanging fruit, the world was all mine. The next, I looked up to find the orchard gates closed.

~ ~ ~ ~ ~ ~ ~ ~ ~ ~ ~ ~

It wasn't long before I reached Swansea. I parked the car alongside the railroad tracks and got out.

A natural tunnel of oak and maple trees formed a thick green canopy overhead, while the sun occasionally forced its way through, creating dancing shadows. It was dark up ahead and I nearly jumped when I heard a stick snap in the wood line. I could also make out the faint smell of wet, musty hair. *I'm not alone,* I thought. For some strange reason, I looked down expecting to find my best friend, Foxhound, standing by my side. But my childhood dog wasn't there. *And why would he be?* He'd died when I was twelve and broke my heart. It hurt so bad, in fact, that I vowed I'd never own another. With my steamy breath leading the way, I started off on the second leg of my journey.

One sweat ring later, I reached the old clubhouse. There wasn't much left, except a pile of mismatched boards and planks, a tangle of frayed ropes; discarded pieces once brought together to create a haven from authority. I took my time and climbed up into my past.

Under a damp swag of red carpet, Miss November waited with a smile. Her breasts were faded from the elements, but not so blurred that I couldn't remember she'd once provided a wonderful starting point for my pre-adolescence. With Miss November back under the rug, I spent the better part of the day reminiscing. I took a couple deep breaths, closed my eyes and went back…

~ ~ ~ ~ ~ ~ ~ ~ ~ ~ ~ ~

I could still see it. It was the last house at the end of Oliver Street. They called it "The Biggins's Place," and since as far back as I could remember, it was completely abandoned. My brother, Joseph, used to tease me that I didn't have the guts to jump the fence and walk through its yard on our way to school. For years, Joseph was right.

The Biggins's Place was an old Victorian house taken straight out of a horror movie. Blanketed in overgrown trees and lurking shadows, it was quite a scary sight and I hated it. From the first time I set eyes on the place, I hated it.

The city's hearsay historians claimed that the house was built on an old Indian burial ground. Whether this was true or not, there was a graveyard just to its east. And with each year of small town rumor, the place took on a more haunted appearance.

Legend had it that Mrs. Loretta Biggins had lost her husband, a sea captain, to the frigid depths of the Atlantic. Shortly thereafter, she lost a good part of her mind. They say she paced upon the widow's walk for weeks after he was lost at sea, screaming his name in a shrill voice that would weaken the spine of the strongest man. Her only saving grace was her young son, Charles. Half out of her wits and with the intention to protect the boy, she locked him in the house like some common criminal. They say he slept in a closet and ate with the family pets. She never let the boy out of her sight. But this only lasted until the disturbed woman grew weary and rested her penetrating gaze.

Charles was ten years old when he escaped his mother's twisted bastion. They say he ran to the dock where his father had shipped out to eternity. Deciding on one parent over the other, the boy jumped into the icy water and pumped his arms as fast and as hard as he could. Once they tired, he turned back and bobbed in the water, quietly awaiting his fate. Even if he had wanted to change his mind, he no longer had the strength to return to land.

There was a scream. He looked up to see his mother standing on her widow's walk, her arms outstretched and her voice shrieking his name, "CHARLES!" Some claimed to have seen him smile when he went down. The rest of the city, however, braced themselves against the most horrid pitch a woman had ever released. She wailed, "CHARLES! CHARLES!" but young Biggins was not to return. Preferring to embrace his own death, he'd finally escaped her torment. Tragically, his mother was just sane enough to understand that she had killed her only child.

From that point on, there was no question that the old lady had completely abandoned her mind. Neighbors soon complained about losing their pets, only to discover the butchered carcasses lying in the street in front of the Biggins's house. No one dared question her on it, though. Those who even considered it got only as far as her porch before they heard the demented shriek of a banshee. They'd look up and find her half-concealed behind a broken window, gesturing wildly that they come in. No one ever did – ever.

The place deteriorated as fast as she did. She became a recluse and lived that way for two decades. No one ever knew the exact day she died. Her body was discovered from the rancid odor it omitted. They say that the man who removed the body could feel her presence in the room and vowed, "She was there." In fact, just as he closed the front door, he heard her laugh insanely and release a high-pitched scream.

As the Biggins's only heir had drowned and there were no living relatives, the city eventually auctioned off the place to a family from out of town. The Densons were the first of two families to reside in the place, but moved in to discover that they were unwanted. Fixed objects moved around the house under the power of something angry and invisible. Doors opened and slammed shut throughout the night. Then, to insure their prompt departure, something began to physically strike out; something that couldn't be seen but felt to the point that it bruised. The Denson's quickly sold.

The next courageous clan, the Letendres, wasn't there a month when the patriarch of the family was badly beaten and rushed to the emergency room. "Who did this to you?" they inquired.

Covered in cuts and bruises, he vowed he honestly didn't know but believed, "It was some vile ghost who wanted to kill me." He spent a good stretch at Corrigan Hospital, committed for mental health reasons.

The city boarded the windows and shut off the power to the house. Still, the exterior light came on randomly. Some reported seeing a young man – dripping wet in turn-of-the-century clothing – beckoning for his mother from the deserted widow's walk.

Old Loretta was feared more in death than she was in life. Everyone stayed clear of the Biggins's place. The only true adventurers of the neighborhood, the kids, used to break in. On one such daring night when the tide was high, two children broke in to prove their courage, while a third kept watch on the porch. They say that the porch lookout never saw Old Lady Biggins standing on her walk until it was too late. When he ran inside to warn his friends, to his horror he discovered one had died. In shock, the second remained catatonic for several weeks. When he finally came around, his child-like babble reported that the old lady had approached them, turned to his friend and whispered, "You're home now, Charles. And I'll never let you go again." At that very moment, the boy choked to death.

That legend witnessed many seasons and outlived many people who tried to dispel it. It undoubtedly grew larger through the ages, so by the time my brother and I caught wind of it, it was bigger than our own lives. It was rumored that the place was going to be a funeral home, but the window boards never came down. Instead, the eerie house continued to serve as a test of courage to adolescents who were chased off the property by town police.

For years, I sprinted past the place on my way to and from school. And though it witnessed all of my childhood woes and triumphs, most of the time I never spared the place a look. As my courage grew, though, so did Joseph's challenges.

On one late September night when I was ten, I decided to take my brother up on his dare. After all the years of harboring fear of the place, I was finally willing to face the demons of Loretta Biggins – and perhaps even my own.

It was autumn in Massachusetts and there was no prettier place on Earth. On this night, the whole world was perfect – except for the Biggins's place. It loomed over me worse than my overactive imagination. I'd agreed to the wager only if I could take Dewey, my best friend, along. Joseph agreed.

Peter Duhon, or Dewey, was a heavy-set kid who was a bit too jaded for his age. Though cocky, it was only a defensive trait to combat his low self-esteem. His overprotective father was the complete opposite of mine and showed me what a good dad could be. As a result, Dewey was hell-bent on being somebody; being successful and having money, which he was convinced would bring him all the happiness he'd ever need.

Donned in our hooded sweatshirts, Dewey and I started for the house. I doubted that Old Lady Biggins's laughter would be any match for that of my cynical brother's. Under the faint light of a crescent moon, like Marines hitting the beach, Dewey and I approached the place on bicycles. There was never a shortage of drama in our neighborhood. I was just nearing the overgrown yard when I actually felt a presence – an invisible, unfriendly presence. I looked over at Dewey, but my best friend was already high-tailing it home. He'd obviously felt the same thing. Unwilling to face Joseph's ruthless teasing, I gritted my teeth and willed myself closer. It was then that I heard it. Though faint, it was the distinct sound of a sea captain's whistle. I expected to find my brother in wait and squinted hard to search the yard for the shoddy ambush. Joseph was nowhere to be found. And then I felt something; it was like a patch of cold air traveling straight through me. I gasped, and at that instant, felt a tormented solitude well up inside of me. I was suddenly lost and alone. In one spine tingling moment, I honestly believed I'd just met the anguished spirit of young Charles Biggins.

The boy's energy was wandering aimlessly, unaware of the great sin he'd committed; unaware of his natural place in the universe. Although the experience reached beyond bizarre, for reasons unknown I did not feel afraid. Instead, it seemed that all of the fear in the world belonged to Charles. The boy was trapped, imprisoned, without knowing any means of escape. Surprising myself, I called out, "Charles?" I saw and heard nothing, but the stiff hairs on the back of my neck announced that the boy was nearby. I could think of nothing but trying to help. "You no longer belong here, Charles," I told him. "You must go." The spirit's feelings of despair only increased. Nearly paralyzed, I realized that this boy was in hell; the very hell he'd created when he'd tried to cheat nature by cutting his time short on Earth. He was still connected to this earthly dimension and would probably serve his remaining time alone – lost and scared. I had to get out before it was too late; before I was forced to share in the boy's horrid grief. I pumped my legs and prayed hard all the way home. When I reached safety, I drummed up the courage to look back. There was nothing there.

Joseph was waiting on the porch, smiling. "Told you there was nothing to worry about," he said.

I calmed my quick breathing and looked into my older brother's eyes. "Nana was right," I said, panting. "Nobody can punish us more than we can punish ourselves." With that, I pushed my rubbery legs into the house.

Joseph followed me in. Before the door closed behind him, his words echoed down the street. "Come on, Donny. It couldn't have been that scary. Are you really that sorry you went?"

~ ~ ~ ~ ~ ~ ~ ~ ~ ~ ~ ~

A shiver traveled the length of my spine. This time, it was from the falling air temperature. I looked up to see that my trip down memory lane was losing light. *Where are you now, Charles Biggins?* I wondered. Turning up the collar on my jacket, I half-stood, stretched out my aching back and eased myself out of the clubhouse. As I started down the tracks, I looked back once and had to smile. When you're a kid, it's so foolish to think that life will remain the way it is forever; that nothing will ever change. But maybe that's the true gift of innocence. Good or bad, I'd survived my childhood and was exposed to just enough to choose the life I wanted. I suppose when you add up those two factors, it was a success.

When I reached the car, I popped a pain pill and called Bella on the cell phone. "Miss me?"

"Before you even left," she said.

"Listen," I told her, "I think I'm going to spend the night at Joseph's, so I can spend one more day with my memories. You okay with that?"

"That's fine. But are *you* okay?"

"Yup."

"The pills helping?" she asked.

"I'm a little tired and achy, but yeah – they're working. How's Riley?"

"She taking it rough, but she'll be fine." There was a brief pause. "I love you, you know," she said.

"I know. Me, too," I said and was starting to learn just how much.

Chapter 3

Sometimes, the memory is too kind. Take high school, for example. Most people claim, "I wish I could go back." But if you recall high school – I mean, really remember it – you'll probably remember it the same way I do. It sucked! There were bullies, peer pressure, acne and girls – a terrible mix. Folks go through their whole lives without having to face a fraction of the rejection they faced in high school. But when we recall it, the only things we remember are the prom, graduation – all the good stuff.

Adolescence and the few years that led up to it are still a bit hazy to me…

The customers who didn't tip on our paper routes got hit hard on Halloween. Weeks before the big night, Joseph, Dewey and I bought dozens of eggs and hid them so they'd go rotten. We also used soap, lipstick and shaving cream – anything that would allow us to express our creativity. We thought we'd done it all one year before we saw Ronnie Forrester, the neighbor bully, throwing small pumpkins off the highway overpass onto passing car windshields. I'll never forget it; the cops thought we were responsible and everyone scattered for cover. But we weren't complete lunatics. We were only egg pitchers.

I remember going to a slaughterhouse with one of our Portuguese neighbors. The pig squealed something horrible until they slit its throat. Once they drained all of its blood, it was my job to stir the big red pot all the way home so it wouldn't clot.

The drive-in theater saw a few empty quarts of beer and once we even smuggled in a mayonnaise jar full of moonshine. As I recall, the security guard couldn't place the odor, and Dewey and I weren't about to stick around until he did.

The older I got, the more I realized that the generations who passed before us were just as screwed up. Though they criticized and judged our every move, they'd also indulged in alcohol abuse, domestic violence and infidelity – my dad more than most. If anything, the one thing that had changed was that there was less hiding it.

~ ~ ~ ~ ~ ~ ~ ~ ~ ~ ~ ~

The one person I'll never forget from my childhood is Mr. Duhon, Dewey's dad.

Mr. Duhon worried terribly over his son from the moment his boy was born. And for years, the worries were justified; the trials and terrors of toddlers, the daring dangers of youth. Even the quirky quests of adolescence were very upsetting to him; us borrowing his car without permission or licenses, and so on.

Then Dewey grew up. He was all done jumping from roofs and eating hard candy while lying on the couch. But his dad still couldn't adapt. Whether it was the years of conditioning, or his own internal wiring – or a combination of the two – he just couldn't let his guard down. He was a bundle of nerves.

For as long as I knew him, I thought the man's twitchiness was no more than his poor attempt at humor. Years went by before I realized he wasn't kidding at all. He was always overly concerned, without being able to conceal his fears.

Once, the old man sprinkled rat poison under a porch that stood no more than a foot off the ground. When Dewey and I returned home from school, his father was frantic. "Have you boys been playing under the porch?" he asked, as Dewey and I walked up the driveway.

"Huh?" Dewey grunted.

"Have you eaten any of the white powder under the porch?" he asked, his voice high-pitched and anxious.

Dewey just walked away, with my grinning face in tow.

The old man called out behind us. "Because it's rat poison…"

We never looked back.

"You know that holly berries are poisonous, too… right?"

I thought I was going to pee my pants from laughing so hard. "It's not funny," Dewey said and slammed the door behind us.

But it was funny. The best, oddly enough, was the morning Mr. Duhon buried his mother.

~ ~ ~ ~ ~ ~ ~ ~ ~ ~ ~ ~

After a life filled with shared misery, Dewey's grandmother gasped her final complaint and left the world bawling as loud as she had coming in. "She's no longer suffering," Father Grossi sighed. The young priest ran his hand across her wrinkled face and closed her distant eyes on his way.

"Sure," the family mumbled under its breath, "and neither are we."

At fifteen, I was honored with being chosen a pallbearer. It was my first assignment as such and I welcomed the opportunity to help my best friend.

It was a cold morning when Aldina Duhon – or Grandma – was laid to rest. Dewey, his father, and his Vovo – Dewey's other grandmother, the Portuguese one – swung by to pick me up. Dewey gestured his hello and then smiled wide, motioning his eyes over the front seat toward his strangely clad father. In one quick moment, I took it all in: Vovo was snoring like a bear. Mr. Duhon, however, was awake and ridiculously out of style. He wore a brown corduroy sports jacket, one size too small, over a white button down shirt. The slender Western rope tie matched perfectly with a pair of black snakeskin boots. To top it off, a belt buckle the size of a hubcap reading, "If It Ain't Country, It Ain't Music," held up a faded pair of blue khaki slacks. He smelled of cheap cologne and he was smiling.

I nodded and returned the smile. "Mornin', Mr. Duhon," I said and then glanced back at Dewey. My friend winked. I choked on the laugher that clawed to break free. "This oughta be one hell of a funeral," I whispered to Dewey.

He grinned. "You have no idea."

~ ~ ~ ~ ~ ~ ~ ~ ~ ~ ~ ~

From the outset, it was clear that Mr. Duhon had honored his cherished mother with the pauper's package. With a comical rudeness, the funeral director hurried the handful of mourners along. The priest sensed the urgency and spoke like an experienced auctioneer. Upon his blessing, the pallbearers were asked to "report to the rear of the parlor."

I did as instructed.

One couple after the other was called to pay their last respects. I stood shocked. Not one moist eye passed me by on the way out. *Old Grandma's cruelty must have touched everyone*, I decided.

"Will the pallbearers please remove the flowers," the director called out, startling me from my morose thoughts.

I approached the blue velour casket, mouthed one final prayer and grabbed two of the cheap carnation arrangements. As I reached the sidewalk, I discovered that Mr. Duhon had opted to skip on the flower car. The frugal man waved me over and opened his trunk. "Throw'em in here," he said.

I was taken aback. *For a man who just said goodbye to his mother, Mr. Duhon doesn't look all that sad*, I thought. Rather, he looked impatient, as if he were running late for his tee time.

When I returned to the funeral parlor, the coffin was already sealed closed. Under the director's frustrated direction, I grabbed one handle and assisted Dewey's grandma into the black hearse for her last car ride. The morbid job absolutely dumbfounded me. Even when carefully carried by six able-bodied men, a corpse was so much heavier than most people would guess.

Worse yet, it seemed to have a mind of its own, shifting its weight wherever it wanted within the closed casket.

On the way to the church, the smell of flowers was nauseating. Dewey's half-deaf Vovo threatened, "I'm gonna pass out. I swear I am!" Her tone was ear piercing. I struggled not to laugh.

When we arrived at St. Anthony's, I took note of the steep stairs awaiting us and hurried to the hearse. I grabbed my assigned handle, grunted once and marched. Not three steps up, the cardboard casket moaned and creaked like a sea vessel preparing to capsize. I could feel the weight shift, but there was nothing I could do. The box was so cheap and flimsy that I was just hoping we could get Grandma to the altar before all four sides blew out and the old lady performed her last cartwheel. Suddenly, we were stopped. I looked beyond Mr. Duhon for a reason. There was none. *Father Grossi isn't ready,* I assumed.

In the cold air, all six of us waited, arms locked and throbbing. I looked up again, just in time to see several bird droppings hit the back of Mr. Duhon's gaudy jacket. I snapped back to Dewey. My friend had obviously witnessed the same and was already laughing. Vovo took notice of the white wad of bird poop and rushed over with her kerchief. With a sense of purpose, the old hen began wiping, startling Mr. Duhon who'd been oblivious to the aerial attack. I had to look away. It was too much.

By the time I composed myself enough to look back, Vovo had smeared the mess like marshmallow fluff all over the poor man's back. When she pulled her kerchief away to survey her handiwork, another bird hit its target – then another, and another. As if sent by some angelic comedian, the bird crap machine-gunned Mr. Duhon's back. The casket rocked back and forth from the stifled hysteria. *Grandma's saying good-bye the only way she would have,* I thought.

Mr. Duhon was a mess. His entire back was covered in bird droppings. Vovo looked over and shook her head, disgustedly. "To hell with it," she muttered. Not even she was willing to tackle the job again. It didn't matter. The kerchief was already saturated. Father Grossi waved everyone forward.

I helped place the makeshift coffin onto the aluminum dolly and then darted for the back of the church. Out of respect, I fought desperately to contain my laughter. I couldn't. I was too human. The last pew shook violently.

Before long, Dewey slid in beside me and wiped his crying eyes. I struggled to apologize when I realized my friend wasn't wiping away tears of sorrow. "My father can't get over how broken up you are over Grandma's passing," he whispered, his last words drifting out on sheer will. He laughed so hard from his belly that it was easily confused for wails of grief.

I tried a few times to answer, but couldn't. "I swear that your grandmother must have had this whole thing planned," I whispered. "There's no way so many pigeons could have crapped at once and hit only your father."

Dewey nodded. "She was a mean old coot, but she had a twisted sense of humor…and she constantly screwed with him for being so cheap."

I came up for air. "Your old man should have used that belt buckle as a shield."

We laughed until there was nothing left but aching belly pains and mourners who nodded their understanding over our incredible grief. In the end, we were both grateful for the strange sign from above. *If Grandma made it upstairs, then the heat was off for the rest of us.*

~ ~ ~ ~ ~ ~ ~ ~ ~ ~ ~ ~

For a moment, my mind raced back to the present. *Even my childhood memories are obsessed with death,* I thought. But death wasn't so far away now, nor was it nearly as comical. *Maybe it wouldn't be such a bad thing if folks had one last laugh on me?* I pondered. But picturing Madison and Pudge's innocent faces, I quickly reconsidered. *Shoot for something more meaningful,* I decided.

~ ~ ~ ~ ~ ~ ~ ~ ~ ~ ~ ~

Returning to my childhood, death was a joke – until it became personal.

A year after Dewey's grandmother bid her final farewell, my mom suffered the same fate. At sixteen, I took care of her while she died. I changed her, fed her and did what most good sons do when they're middle-aged.

I held her the morning she died and it broke my heart when she whispered, "I'm sorry I can't stay longer with you boys." Her premature death haunted me with a strange mix of love and pity. My mother had never lived her life. She'd lived each moment for my brother and me. She loved us completely – so much so that I can still feel it today.

Once she was gone, there was no reason for me to stay at home. I rented an apartment from my Uncle Benny and quickly flew the coop. You know how it is. When you own a fast car, you have all the answers.

~ ~ ~ ~ ~ ~ ~ ~ ~ ~ ~ ~

My first and last roommate was a drummer, so our one bedroom pad only worked with bunk beds – this way, Matt's drums could fit, too. We paid much more rent than we should have. The only benefit was that the heat was included. With a keen sense of fairness, we used this benefit any chance we could. When the rest of the world was frozen under a sheet of ice, we were prancing around in boxer shorts, our front door opened wide. The place was furnished to the taste of people without money. The only decent thing in the apartment was the new hi-fi stereo system. By the end of the first week, I'd convinced Matt he could build his credit by renting one. He'd excitedly agreed.

It was a test right from the start, with no more mothers taking care of the menial details known as survival. I suppose it was a matter of give and take; we had to learn to do laundry, but there was no longer a need to make a bed. It didn't make sense, anyway – straightening something you were only going to mess up again hours later. Cooking was a real treat. A frying pan lined in crusted lard sat atop the stove. We only needed to heat it and drop whatever we dared eat into the brown, bubbling oil. Beer became a staple in our diet and I felt it just as important to learn the lessons of overindulgence; bed spins, projectile vomiting and waking the following morning with vise-like headaches. Youth can be so cruel to itself.

Like it or not, we had to take jobs. Matt worked at an Indian restaurant, washing dishes for twenty dollars a night. After his first shift, he awoke to find his brand new sneakers infested with ants. He was already behind the eight ball. I chose a different occupation. I began at McKaskie's, a woodworking shop that made giant wooden spools for wire companies. My third day there, I was sanding a reel on a belt sander when I heard a grown man scream out, "Mommy!" I wiped the sawdust from my goggles and saw Tommy Bigelow, the table saw operator, holding his arm. He'd run his hand right into the saw, cutting one of his fingers down the middle like a peeled banana. It was gross. There was blood everywhere. The foreman called the ambulance, offered the paramedic a piece of Tommy's fingertip and then turned around and barked at everyone to "get back to work." As I returned to the sander, the foreman tapped me on the shoulder. "Get on the table saw, Don," he said, "We have an order to get out." I always hated that man. Even still, I cleaned off the blood and did as I was told. All the while, I prayed that OSHA would show up and shut the place down.

When not sleeping from sheer exhaustion, Matt, the boys and I played poker. We had tournaments that sometimes lasted right through the night. While the wind and snow pounded off the windows, we stripped to our underwear, cracked open the front door and dealt cards until the sun burned away the black horizon.

In two months, Matt was twenty pounds lighter and broke. I knew it was the end of the line when two repo men arrived in trench coats to pick up the stereo. Matt's parents begged him to go home. He never argued. He owed me for a few outstanding bills. "Just sell me everything," I told him and he did. The odds and ends that he'd begged, borrowed and stole were left behind and the debt was returned to scratch.

~ ~ ~ ~ ~ ~ ~ ~ ~ ~ ~ ~

And then I met Bella.

It was a typical Portuguese feast with all the spicy food you could dream of: roast pig-cacoula, chourico and pepper sandwiches, codfish, baked beans, favas, kale soup, stuffed quahogs, grilled sardines and spit-fire chickens. For dessert, there was molassades, rice pudding, custard cups and sweet bread – all washed down with jugs of sweet red wine.

When a dozen little girls dressed in angel's wings delivered a golden crown to the priest, the band struck up the first notes of the night. The Holy Ghost Procession was done and the celebration had begun.

The streets were cordoned off, with strings of bare bulbs zigzagging across the block party. With several large tents in the middle, a mass of people moved in circles to enjoy the festivities.

At the first drop of rain, I saw her and lost my breath. She had sandy blonde hair with hazel eyes and a smile that could forgive you for your greatest sins. I drummed up all the courage I could muster and asked her name.

"Isabella," she said, smiling.

I knew right then and there I was in love.

While we pretended to dodge the rain, we spent the better part of two hours talking and getting to know each other. Her scent was distinct – a mix of Ivory soap and fabric softener.

Darker clouds rolled in, attacking without warning. It started to rain hard and the first bolt of lightning crackled in the dark sky. There was a certain authority and strength that came with the downpour, while a series of close rapid-fire bolts had everyone running for cover. As Bella started to back peddle, I asked, "Will I ever see you again?"

She hurried back to me and took off one of her pearl earrings. "These are my favorite earrings in the whole world," she said, "and having just one of them would ruin the pair." She handed it to me. "Let's stay in touch, okay?"

"Okay." I swallowed hard.

"The number is 555-8374 and call before five," she whispered. "That's when my dad gets home from work." With an amazing smile, she hurried off.

Soaked to the bone, I stood in the street repeating 555-8374 in my head until it became a song. I knew in my heart this was the woman heaven had delivered to me on a bolt of lightning. After striking a few more random targets and forcing the trees to dance, the dark clouds suddenly dispersed. As if the entire world had been cleansed, a fresh perspective was left behind. I loved lightning storms. If you endured the trouble long enough, the peace it brought was indescribable.

~ ~ ~ ~ ~ ~ ~ ~ ~ ~ ~ ~

And we did stay in touch. Her dad was very strict, so we dated whenever we could sneak away. I was never sure if the pearl was real or fake, and I didn't care enough to ask. The real jewel was Bella.

Chapter 4

Upon returning home from my visit to memory lane, I was met with a kiss from my wife and three enormous suitcases sitting at the door. "We're leaving for the Vineyard at first light tomorrow," she informed me.

"Will I have time to shower and shave?" I teased.

She grinned. "As long as you can make it quick."

~ ~ ~ ~ ~ ~ ~ ~ ~ ~ ~ ~

Even though it was still off-season and we'd left the house in the early morning light, the traffic down to the Cape was thick. The shuttle bus from the parking lot to the dock was packed. As we pulled up to the Steamship Authority terminal, I leaned over and kissed Bella. The excitement was building and I wondered again why we'd only been a few times to my favorite place on Earth. It was only a few miles down the road and a chilly ferry ride away.

Bella hung over the side of the boat, but I couldn't take the rolling waves and rocking handrails. I stayed inside and tried to meditate the time away. When that didn't work, I read one of the island brochures:

> More than a century ago, Martha's Vineyard was home to nearly half of the world's whaling fleet. Sons and husbands left their families and boarded

giant wooden ships to find their for-
tunes. As petroleum became a popular
use of fuel, however, whale oil was no
longer needed. Vineyard Sound and
Nantucket Sound became the highways
for the great Atlantic coastal shipping
fleet. Many ships anchored in Vineyard
Haven harbor, awaiting a high tide and
a fair breeze. For three centuries, Vine-
yarders have looked to the sea for their
livelihood. Where once whaling and
shipping had been the backbone of the
economy, it has since become travel and
tourism…

I looked up. The harbor's distinct skyline was dominated by church steeples and a fleet of wooden vessels.
As if I were ten again, I felt a celebration try to break
free from my throat. I hurried to the outside deck to
find Bella.

We docked in the very same harbor where Spiel-
berg had filmed the movie, *Jaws*. Among the masses,
we walked down a bouncy metal ramp to join the on-
slaught of weekend tourists that came to spend money,
make memories and join the mass exodus on Sunday
evening – tanned, smiling and carrying bags of souvenirs home. Most people, generations of them, came
back year after year. "We must have been too busy with
work and keeping up the house," I thought aloud and
shook my head at our foolishness.

"But we're here now," Bella said.

It was a different world, long removed from cor-
porate America. From the largest and busiest harbor

on the island, I could feel the ocean breezes on my face and taste the salt on my tongue. "It's like heaven," Bella added.

I hope so, I thought.

~ ~ ~ ~ ~ ~ ~ ~ ~ ~ ~ ~

The Kinsman House was only four blocks from the dock and town center. It was a beautifully restored 1880 Victorian, a former sea captain's home that had been converted into a quaint Bed & Breakfast.

Three ancient oak trees shaded the front lawn. After stopping to catch my breath, we stepped onto the full-length porch through an archway of thick vegetation. I opened the door for Bella. A grand piano, antique roll-top desk and French doors dominated the entrance and stairway. "Hello?" I called out, but no one was there.

"Doreen said she might not be here," Bella explained. "She said to get comfortable and leave the door unlocked, if we step out."

There was a note at the top of the stairs, directing us to one of the three bedrooms. Bella opened the door and sighed. "Definitely heaven," she said. It was a little girl's dream, with a queen-sized bed, antique chests and floral prints from floor to ceiling.

As we'd arrived early enough to salvage some of the day, I paced with an energy I hadn't felt in weeks. I helped Bella unpack our bags, while she began making the cozy room our home for the weekend.

Once finished, Bella turned to me and smiled. "All settled in," she said.

I nodded. "Good…so let's go have that walk Dr. Rice prescribed."

~ ~ ~ ~ ~ ~ ~ ~ ~ ~ ~ ~

Hand-in-hand and dressed in thick sweaters, we took our first stroll down Main Street in Vineyard Haven. Shops, untouched by time, lined both sides of the narrow street; art galleries, sellers of home accents and furniture, antiques and collectibles. We walked by a French restaurant. I looked at Bella. "Maybe tonight?"

She shook her head. "I was hoping for something a little more casual."

"And healthy?" I teased.

She nodded.

There was another B&B beside a gourmet shop that Bella stepped into. They had all the ingredients she needed to make bruschetta. "Now we're talking," she said, "We'll be back for some things tomorrow."

We took our time and looked at everything. There were nostalgic candy stores that still twisted saltwater taffy – in every pastel color imaginable – right in the front window for everyone to see. Fudge was also made by hand; most things done like days of old. We bought a half-pound of chocolate walnut fudge and took turns with the small white bag as we went along. There were jewelers, gift shops and clothiers. Led by my curious wife, I poked my head into each and wasted the afternoon away. Past the goldsmith, photographer and realtor's office, we made it to the Mansion House Inn on the corner. And then it was time to make our way back up the other side of the street.

The Island Theater, closed for renovations, was a definite glimpse of yesterday. I dragged Bella back across the street to check out Bunch of Grapes Bookstore.

It was a busy, independent shop that seemed to capture the spirit of the island. We browsed for a while. They had a wide range of island books, from local hiking-trail guides to cookbooks and collections of poetry by local artists. The atmosphere was personal and made book shopping a pleasure, something the major franchises had long abandoned. I walked upstairs to find a small parlor where they hosted local authors and poets. Unfortunately, there were none scheduled for the weekend. I bought a copy of Roland Merullo's *Revere Beach Elegy* and followed Bella out into the early spring sun.

We spent an hour or so comparing prices at a few of the mom and pop souvenir shops. Each one had an abundance of similar items to tempt buyers: scrimshaw jewelry and other imports from Cape Cod (most including cranberries), seashell wind chimes, old lobster pots converted into tables, and buoys for sale in every primary color. I considered buying a puzzle of the island, but thought, *I doubt I'll have the time to finish it* — and quickly pushed the thought out of my head. Even if I hadn't known, I would have been able to tell we were at an artist's colony. There were sculptures, watercolor paintings and beautiful pieces done in metal. Nantucket lightship baskets and gold charms led me to the white braided bracelets that children soaked and let shrink to their skin. They were the same ones that turned black by the end of summer and had to be cut off before school, leaving behind a white ring around the wrist where the sun hadn't touched. I grabbed two for the kids. "Let's pick up the rest of the souvenirs before we leave, so we don't have to carry them around," Bella said.

I paid for the white bracelets and put them into my pocket. "Let's go eat," I said. "I'm starving."

We walked the two blocks to The Black Dog, the historic and legendary tavern whose world-famous ambassador represented the easy Vineyard way of life. It was a big tourist draw, but I was happy to find that the specials featured freshly caught fish and a collection of delicious desserts. After we ate our clam cakes and chowder by an empty fireplace, I ordered apple pie with vanilla ice cream. Cashing out, Bella bought us two matching sweatshirts and one bumper sticker.

"That's going to be heavy to carry all the way back," I teased.

She made a funny face. "I'll be fine."

As we made our way back to our room, the air temperature dropped and the streets began to fill with people coming out for the night. There were plenty of interesting characters and I'm certainly not shy, but this was a time for just Bella and me. So we kept to ourselves, held hands and walked along in comfortable silence.

After watching a magical sunset, on bended knees I prayed. *Father, bless my family – Bella, Riley, Michael and the kids – with good health, both of mind and body. Shroud them in the safety of your angels and allow them to live in a world of peace and harmony. Bless those who have passed from this world. May they live in Your presence for all eternity. Forgive us of our sins and help us on our daily path back to You – Amen.*

I realized that for the first time since I'd gotten sick, I'd prayed for only those I loved and not for myself. It felt good. "Good-night," I said.

"Good-night…and don't forget to take your medicine before you fall asleep."

There's no way I could, I thought. *I've been in pain all day.*

I grabbed an extra blanket from the closet for Bella so I could keep the screen windows open. I took my pills and turned in early for the night. I loved the smell of the ocean and its music lulled me to sleep.

~ ~ ~ ~ ~ ~ ~ ~ ~ ~ ~ ~

The next morning, after two bowls of fresh melon and some wheat toast, we rented a candy-apple red convertible. It was Bella's idea – *thank God for her.*

It was still too early in the year for a ragtop, but we didn't care. Right away, it took me back to my youth. The first car I'd owned was a '65 Buick Special, powder blue on blue, with a Wildcat 310 under the hood. And it was in that very car that I discovered the true sense of freedom.

With the top down, the front seat pushed close to the windshield and the music playing a little louder than normal, my girl and I cruised the land of mopeds and bicyclists. There was nothing more exciting than the freedom of the open road without worrying about your brains being splattered in a helmet. While we stopped for the things Bella needed to fill our picnic basket – bread, cheese, a jar of mild salsa – I noticed that everyone was looking. I couldn't wipe the smile off my face. Bella got back in the car and looked at me. "What?" she asked.

"No apple pie?"

"There's a little bakery on the way," she said and grinned. "And we should also pick up some fruit and vegetables."

I never replied. Leaning back on my headrest, my face pitched to the sun, I pointed the car north.

On one of the back shady roads, I pressed the accelerator to the floor and could hear the four-barrel open up and guzzle down a gallon of gas. The exhaust was throaty and sounded mean. I looked over at Bella. With her hair whipping around in the wind, she shook her head and giggled. There was a blanket and picnic basket on the backseat, the love of my life in the passenger seat and the gas needle was on full. *Life can't get any better,* I thought.

The further inland we went, the more rural charm we experienced. I was surprised to see deer in the open pastures and horses at play. With the Atlantic Ocean as a backdrop, sheep farms and rolling hills were greener than I remembered. The sea breeze stinging my face made me feel young again. We stopped once at a roadside fruit and vegetable stand that still worked on the honor system. It sold jars of rose hip jelly and beautiful dried sunflowers. A coffee can was set up to receive payment. I dropped in a ten, grabbed a jar of jelly, two dried sunflowers for Bella and a colorful mix of fruit and vegetables for me.

As we drove the winding roads, I couldn't remember feeling more alive or carefree. With the sun beating down, though, I did remember we had to keep moving or we were going to bake.

We finally reached Aquinnah, better known as Gayhead, and parked the car. We passed the Native Wampanoags selling their wares at cliff-top and headed for the lighthouse. From atop the hundred foot cliffs, the winds shrieked and we could hear the waves crashing into the rocks below. The foul odor of low tide took hold. I couldn't help it. I turned to Bella and pinched my nose, "Geeze, Babe."

She slapped me.

The red cliffs were smothered in thick vegetation. Fragrant rosa rugosa and beach plums grew just above the rumbling surf. It was a great spot to see lobstermen and fishing trawlers at work. I threw a quarter into the magnifying viewer and watched as a shriveled old naked couple strolled along the beach. Bella whacked my arm again. "You pervert."

Just then, a chubby tour guide hyperventilated his way up the hill that led to the lighthouse's overlook. There were at least two dozen tourists in tow. Before melting into the rear of the pack, I nudged Bella and gestured that she join me. I was surprised when she did. As the man's bus idled on the road, he explained, "Gay Head was named for the brightly colored rock formations on the one hundred-foot scenic cliffs. Home of the Wampanoag Tribe, it has also been witness to some terrible maritime accidents. Today, the grandiose lighthouse at Gay Head is still an active guide to navigation. Besides ensuring safe passage, Gay Head

Lighthouse features one of the most picturesque loca-
tions on the East Coast, offering an awe-inspired view
of the sound."

People started snapping pictures. I looked at Bella
and shrugged. "I left the camera in the car," I said.

"Of course you did." She laughed. "I'll get it."

"On a clear day, you can see for miles," the guide
explained. "Just below, there are several rocky coves and
inlets where bass and bluefish hide. This part of the island is also one of the best places to watch the sunset
on the water. This lighthouse is one of five on Martha's
Vineyard and one of three currently maintained by the
Historical Society."

Bella returned to the group and began taking pictures. Once she'd had her fill, we headed to one of the
shops and bought two tall glasses of tea that had been
brewing in the morning sun. It was delicious. Bella ordered a dozen clam cakes for the ride back. They didn't
touch Flo's.

~ ~ ~ ~ ~ ~ ~ ~ ~ ~ ~

It was early afternoon when we reached Vineyard Haven. We pulled into one of those gaudy souvenir shops
where things aren't so cheap anymore. Everything had
to be shipped over to the island, so everything was considered imported – and they charged for it. We bought
two giant overpriced beach towels and headed for the
shore.

On a stretch of beach between Oak Bluffs and Edgartown, I pulled over. Driftwood, broken shells, old
fishing line and tattered nets that covered a cluster of

rocks led us to the ideal spot. Children with their shovels and pails, and mothers with their paperback books watched as we spread out the towels and set up camp. The horizon was peppered with weekend sail boaters. *Bella's right,* I thought. *This is heaven.* "Thank you," I told her.

"For what?" she asked.

"For having such a great idea."

She grabbed my face with both hands. "There's more where that came from," she promised. The sun was warm, the rhythm of the waves mesmerizing. It must have only taken seconds before we both fell asleep – side-by-side, holding hands.

~ ~ ~ ~ ~ ~ ~ ~ ~ ~ ~ ~

By dusk, the air got colder, but we were rested and ready to ride. We put the top down on the convertible, turned on the heater and steered back onto the street. I was suddenly aware that the gift of life is offered in every breath we take.

As the darkness crept in, Bella slid closer to me. I put my arm around her. With an unobstructed view of the moon and stars, we reminisced about our life together. *Sometimes it doesn't take much to experience perfection*, I thought. *The simple things may actually be the greatest of all.*

We spent the next hour debating whether we should get a clam boil for dinner or go for the baked stuffed shrimp. In truth, I didn't care. My stomach was churning something awful, so wherever we ended up I didn't expect to eat more than a few bites.

~ ~ ~ ~ ~ ~ ~ ~ ~ ~ ~ ~

On Sunday morning, we decided to spend the second half of our getaway in Oak Bluffs and Edgartown. My wife insisted, "We have to visit the gingerbread houses in Oak Bluffs first." Known by the locals as "the Cottage Colony," this cliquey community is famous for its storybook gingerbread cottages, three hundred thirty in all, encircling Trinity Park. With rocking chairs on the front porches and candle-lit Japanese lanterns glowing at night, names such as Time Remembered, Rose Crest and Alice's Wonderland made Bella coo. Many of the gothic resort cottages – adorned with their ornamental scroll work, decorative shingling, porch aprons, arched double doors and candy cane colors of pink, blue and green – contained miniature gardens behind white picket fences.

"They look like doll houses," I said.

She nodded. "They're wonderful."

Rising out of the center was the Tabernacle, an open-air cathedral with dominant wrought iron arches, colored windows and an octagonal cupola. The Trinity United Methodist Church was just next door. It had a classic New England spire that had been hit three times by lightning. With blown-glass windows and a stamped-tin interior, I remembered visiting it as a kid. "It's still my favorite," I told Bella.

Beyond the summer cottages that rented for more than it would have cost us to put both Madison and Pudge through college, the Annual Oak Bluffs Harbor Festival beckoned.

It was a junk-food junkie's paradise. The air was thick with the distinct aromas of cotton candy and fried dough. While a live band played on the dock and young children competed in a chalk art contest on the cement walkway, we ate as we walked along and looked at the boats. I'd given my belly a rest, so we shared a pulled pork sandwich from a local Bar-B-Q smokehouse, and then an expensive lobster roll overflowing with claw meat. *I'm dying*, I figured, *but I'm not dead yet.* At the end of the dock, a heavy-set woman dressed like a rag doll yelled out, "Strawberry shortcakes! Get your strawberry shortcakes here!"

We stopped and I turned to Bella. "Oh, good... fruit!" I said, excitedly.

She laughed, and we bought one and split it. It was made with fresh strawberries, a real shortcake and sweet whipped cream. Two bites in, I almost told Raggedy Ann that I loved her.

As we strolled further down the pier, I stopped and gave Bella a hug. I was starting to understand that it wasn't so much about doing anything; about feeling or even thinking anything. It was about *being*; being who I was, and being with the woman who owned my heart. I looked into her eyes and kissed her again.

"What is it?" she asked.

"Nothing," I said. "It's just that I love you."

We hugged for a while, swaying together on the dock, while the crowd milled around us. *Sometimes all we have to do is breathe*, I thought. *The rest is out of our hands.*

~ ~ ~ ~ ~ ~ ~ ~ ~ ~ ~ ~

The Flying Horses Carousel was the nation's oldest operating platform carousel. In 1884, this treasured merry-go-round was brought to Martha's Vineyard and placed right in the heart of Oak Bluffs where it could be enjoyed for more than a century. I bought two tickets for four dollars and tried my best to catch the brass ring and win a free ride. It never happened. Instead, I shelled out a few more bucks for a cone of cotton candy and an iced-cold bottle of water. I grabbed Bella's hand and headed back to the convertible.

When we reached the car, I looked at her and couldn't help but laugh. She had a wad of the pink cotton candy stuck to her chin. "What now?" she asked.

"Nothing," I said again and opened the passenger door for her. "I was just thinking that sometimes the silliest things make for the best memories…even though no one ever realizes it at the time."

She nodded, her cotton candy beard still intact.

~ ~ ~ ~ ~ ~ ~ ~ ~ ~ ~

Everything tucked away into back alleys and unassuming little neighborhoods, Edgartown was another national treasure. The quiet streets were lined with large elegant homes, many crowned with widows' walks built by wealthy nineteenth century whaling captains. I parked the car on South Water Street where we had to walk around the roots of a huge pagoda tree breaking through the slate sidewalk. It had been brought back from China in 1843 in a tiny cup by Captain Thomas Milton to decorate his home.

Edgartown was home to many of the Northeast's most elite. With their boat shoes and sweater-wearing dogs, most of them reeked of money. They weren't any better or worse than the rest of us – just experiencing a very different reality.

As we navigated the red brick sidewalks and marveled at the amazing architecture, two women in big flowered hats happened by. If I didn't know better, it would have been difficult to identify the exact era we were in – that is, until a guy walked by, wearing two earrings and holding hands with his tattooed girlfriend. The tiny shops and cafés were a delight, each one a glimpse of Norman Rockwell's inspiration. Bella finally broke the silence. "We were crazy to stay away from this place for so long," she admitted.

I agreed, and as we made our way toward the Edgartown Lighthouse, the sun glistened off the water, its light dancing on the waves. A foghorn sounded in the harbor and the taste of salt grew stronger on my palate.

The colonial-style homes, sitting almost flush with the quaint street, flew American flags in the stiff Atlantic winds. Most were covered in white cedar shingles stained driftwood gray, trimmed in white and offset with a red front door. Though the lawns were no larger than a postage stamp, some had anchors in the front yard; others had sheds decorated with colorful buoys and fishing nets in the back. The white Adirondack chairs reminded me of home.

We finally reached land's end where the Harbor View Hotel overlooked the lighthouse. While Bella chose to wait on the sidewalk and take in the harbor, I stepped onto the massive wraparound porch and told her, "I'm going to check out the place."

Built in 1891, the hotel was credited with beginning Edgartown's climb to fame as a summer resort. Built on a generous scale, the advertisements boasted, the hotel offered comfortable bedrooms, gaslights in every room and large public parlors. Guests, however, were lured most by the gorgeous panoramic views promised from its front porch.

Today, the hotel's sprawling veranda was lined with rocking chairs, inviting guests to take in the sweeping views of the sea and yachts of Edgartown Harbor. I took a seat and then a deep breath.

"Don...look," someone called out in a strained whisper.

I glanced up to see Bella waving me over. I walked the length of the porch and when I reached its end, I spotted a young couple exchanging vows before a hundred family and friends beneath the hotel's gazebo. I'd crashed a wedding and didn't even know it. As I sneaked off the porch, I had an idea – as well as most of the details figured out by the time the evening ferry docked back at the mainland.

"What's that smile about?" Bella asked, as we searched for our car in the giant, dirt parking lot. "You've been wearing it all afternoon."

"Nothing," I said, giving her a kiss. "It's just that...I really love you."

Chapter 5

"So the pain levels are the same, but the fatigue is getting worse?" Dr. Rice asked.

"Yes," I said. "I get so exhausted from the smallest things sometimes."

"Well, as the cancer progresses, the fatigue will get worse. The trick is to save your energy for when you really need it…like dipping into your savings for a rainy day." She smiled and raised one eyebrow. "How has your diet been?"

"Much better," I said, with a grin. "I'm eating my veggies and my grains…and *some* junk food."

She nodded. "That's fine, but all things in moderation, right?"

"I know."

"The old saying 'garbage in, garbage out' is still true."

~ ~ ~ ~ ~ ~ ~ ~ ~ ~ ~ ~

Although spring was upon us, my poor lawn, which I'd slaved over for years to get just right, was abandoned. The smell of fresh-cut grass, the pride of reaching perfection – it no longer meant as much as it once did. Even my weekly car waxing had come to an end. Instead, if I could have, I would have taken every class available to man. As my appetite for food decreased, my hunger for knowledge became voracious. But there was so little time left. In my sudden quest to learn as much as I could, I picked up a *South Coast Learning Network* catalog.

According to SCLN's diverse catalog, all courses were short-term and non-credit, held in local libraries, workplaces, churches, museums, schools, public buildings and even private homes. Instructors were experts in their fields; artists, business people, cooks, computer specialists, craftsmen, health experts, historians, scientists, woodworkers and writers. "Real learning for real life," they called it. "Besides being fun, every new learning experience improves the quality of life, while helping you to succeed in a world of constant change."

From Food & Wine and Home & Garden to Liberal Arts and Nature & Science, there was something to spark the interest of those who had not stopped learning – the curious, the adventurous; people who were still looking to stretch their personal horizons – me. Yoga and meditation; American Sign Language; Acting 101; it was an inexpensive invitation to become a more cultured and well-rounded human being; to become a true Renaissance person. Like a fat man reading through a Chinese menu, I flipped through its pages.

There were classes on painting, pottery and photography. One could learn Tai Chi and how to invest money one term, and then take classes on stained glass and scrapbooking the next. There were belly dancing lessons, or beginner guitar. Languages such as Japanese, Spanish and Scottish Gaelic were offered, as were courses on fencing, kickboxing and chess. For the aspiring writers, SCLN hosted several classes from creative writing to a popular workshop on how to get published.

There'd be no scrolled diploma, or cap and gown received at the end of the class. Instead, I'd get a fresh perspective and some valuable knowledge to carry with me for the rest of my days. I circled the one that interested me most.

~ ~ ~ ~ ~ ~ ~ ~ ~ ~ ~ ~

Though I believe it was only one of two things she'd always wished for and never received from me, I'd never cooked dinner for Bella. So, as the first half of my ingenious plan, it was time to do just that. And if I was going to successfully turn my grand idea into action, I needed a diversion.

~ ~ ~ ~ ~ ~ ~ ~ ~ ~ ~ ~

After coming to the United States from Portugal, Master Chef Antone Carvalho worked in New York as a chef and magazine food editor. He apprenticed at several New York institutions, including the Waldorf Astoria, before being appointed Executive Chef at Bittersweet Farm in Westport, Massachusetts. Teaching was a lifelong dream that became a reality in 1999 when he joined forces with SCLN.

For four hundred dollars, his class looked great. I had a few questions, though, so I called him. "I'd like to learn how to cook dinner for my wife…for the first time in thirty years," I told him, "and I have some specific dishes in mind."

"And what are those?"

I read from the paper in front of me. "For the hors d'ouvres, I'd like to serve coconut crusted shrimp with a soy dipping sauce. We'd start with a traditional minestrone soup and tomato & mozzarella salad with an olive oil drizzle." I waited for a reaction. He was still listening. "Just in case, I'd like to serve two entrees; chicken stuffed with spinach and feta cheese, as well as tenderloin of beef in herb garlic butter. For dessert… chocolate cake."

"Plain old chocolate cake, huh?"

"Yup. That's what she loves. How much will it cost me to learn all this?"

"I'm impressed," he said. "You've done your homework." He paused. "Let's just say it'll cost you more time than money," he finally answered, clearly moved by my gesture.

"How much time?" I asked, brutally aware that I had much less time than money.

"I can teach you what you need to know in three weeks, two nights a week, two hours each night."

I was thrilled. "When do we begin?"

"Tomorrow night, six o'clock sharp."

"Perfect! I'll see you then."

I hung up the phone and called Riley. "I'm planning to take a culinary class and cook dinner for your mother, but…"

"Oh, Daddy…"

"Yeah, I know. It's long overdue. Anyway, I need your help to throw her off. When she asks, tell her that I told you I'm taking some writing class for a few weeks."

"I will," Riley promised.

"That's my girl."

~ ~ ~ ~ ~ ~ ~ ~ ~ ~ ~ ~

I had no choice. Though I didn't like it, I had to fib to Bella. "I'd like to be able to capture a few of my stories on paper, so I'm taking a class."

The next time they spoke, Riley corroborated the story. The heat was off for a while.

~ ~ ~ ~ ~ ~ ~ ~ ~ ~ ~ ~

By the second week of fumbling around in Chef Carvalho's kitchen, he pulled me aside and reluctantly told me, "Some people have a knack for cooking and some people... well...some people don't."

"And I'd be in the second group, right?"

With a gentle grin, he nodded.

"Be honest...do I have any chance of pulling off this dinner for my wife?"

"Sure, if you can smuggle me into your house and hide me in your kitchen for a few hours," he joked.

I laughed. "Although that sounds tempting," I told him, "I need to do this one by myself."

"Then follow each recipe to the letter and take your time!" he said, stressing the last few words with the same effort that a father instructs his six-year old son.

I didn't take offense, though. I completely understood where he was coming from. "I will," I promised, thinking, *I wonder if he makes emergency house calls.*

~ ~ ~ ~ ~ ~ ~ ~ ~ ~ ~ ~

It was a Friday morning when I sent Bella shopping. She knew something was up, but humored me and didn't ask. No sooner had she pulled out of the driveway than I began cleaning the house, top to bottom. I spent hours cleaning. Once I finished, I dragged myself to the market for all the ingredients I needed to make dinner. Two pain pills later, I started cooking. Each tiring step was a lesson in appreciation for all that my wife had done for me through the years. I tried to follow Chef Carvalho's instructions and take my time, but my nerves were driving me and I knew it. A few times, I looked at the telephone and considered calling him. Pride stopped me.

Severe fatigue had me by the throat and was choking the life out of me. But if there was ever a rainy day to spend my energy on, it was today. Bella deserved at least that much.

~ ~ ~ ~ ~ ~ ~ ~ ~ ~ ~ ~

As quickly as it had started, it was over. "Oh, my God!" she gasped. Through her look of astonishment, I served dinner and even threw on an old Sinatra album for us to dance afterward.

If it weren't for healthy, active taste buds, the meal would have been delicious. Bella tried her best to conceal it, but by her second bite, her face contorted. The dinner was nearly inedible. By my third bite, I threw my fork into the plate and shook my frustrated head. Bella smiled at me from across the table – and kept smiling. Eventually, I joined her until we both began to laugh. "I'm so sorry," I said, thinking, *I should have called Chef Carvalho.*

"Don't you dare apologize," she said, her face growing serious. "This is the sweetest thing you've ever done for me." Her smile returned. "The thought means everything."

It took a moment before I surrendered to her wisdom. *I guess she's right*, I pondered. *Results mean so much less than effort.* I stood to clear the plates. "So what'll you have on your pizza?" I asked.

"Mushrooms and onions, please," she answered with a beaming smile.

I nodded and, as I walked past her to grab the telephone, she grabbed my arm and pulled me to her.

"I love you so much," she whispered into my ear. "And I loved your surprise. Thank you!"

I hid my smile in her shoulder. The first part of my plan was complete; my wife's curiosity to uncover my secret had been quenched. I now had a decent shot at surprising her for the first time in my life. I struggled not to giggle.

~ ~ ~ ~ ~ ~ ~ ~ ~ ~ ~

From the moment I'd met Bella, I loved her and she knew it. But life – work, a child, bills, and a thousand responsibilities – all jockeyed for priority and fought for our attention. We did all we could to keep the romance alive, but both of us wished there were more.

I decided that she'd waited long enough to be properly courted. It was time to guarantee the rest of our precious days together by returning to where it all began. For me, the joy was all in the planning. While Madison and Pudge helped me by pretending to be working on the puzzle, I schemed and planned and had the time of my life.

~ ~ ~ ~ ~ ~ ~ ~ ~ ~ ~

I secretly met with Vic at Sagres Restaurant on a random Monday night, exactly one week before the big night was to take place. Sagres sat on the very location where Bella and I had our first date; the same spot I'd proposed to her thirty-one years before.

"The most important thing is that the timing be right on," I told Vic.

My friend winked. "I'll make sure the entire night goes off like clockwork."

On Tuesday morning, I called nearly a dozen acoustic guitarists before I found one who would also sing. "To play for three hours?" the musician confirmed.

"Or until she runs out the door, crying."

The man laughed and promised he'd be there, awaiting our arrival.

That afternoon, Riley and I stepped into a jewelry store on Washington Street in Boston. "What exactly are we looking for?" the stuffy clerk asked.

"A diamond engagement ring," I answered. "Princess cut…something around a carat."

With a wave of the hand, we were escorted into a locked room where the clerk poured out a velvet satchel of glittering rocks and then began a brief class on the four C's of the diamond world – cut, color, clarity and carat. By the third diamond he touched, I'd discovered the one. "She'll love it!" I said and handed him my credit card.

On Wednesday, I contacted Bella's favorite flower shop and ordered a dozen long stem red roses with baby's breath and greens, boxed and scheduled for delivery to Vic at Sagres for Monday afternoon.

Thursday had me on the phone again, confirming a white stretch limo for Monday night, as well as ordering a half dozen of Bella's favorite chocolate covered strawberries from a gourmet sweet shop. "At three bucks a pop," I told Riley, "she'd better love them."

The entire day Friday was spent finishing up the poem, *Moments of Destiny*, which had taken me weeks to craft. It had to be just right.

But the toughest days of all proved to be Saturday and Sunday. I thought I was going to burst. Instead, I reserved my fleeting energy and acted like nothing was going on. I spent my time eating wholesome foods, getting plenty of rest and taking a walk each evening.

On Monday afternoon, I rushed to Sagres Restaurant with a half dozen chocolate-covered strawberries and a scrolled sheet of tan parchment tied in red ribbon. "The flowers should be here in an hour or so," I told Vic, "and the guitarist says he'll be here by six o'clock."

With a promise of success and a pat on the back, Vic sent me on my way. "It's going to be unforgettable."

At the car, I flipped open my cell phone and dialed Bella.

"Hello?" she answered.

"Hi, it's me. Just make sure you're ready for seven, okay?"

"Okay," she promised. "Is there something going on?"

"Yeah. I'm already starving."

~ ~ ~ ~ ~ ~ ~ ~ ~ ~ ~ ~

Though there were empty tables up front, Vic escorted Bella and me to a darkened back room where no one else was seated. The table sat in the center of the room and was very nicely decorated. I could tell by Bella's face that it seemed peculiar to her. As we took our seats, Vic lit a candle. "I'll right back," he said.

Bella started to question it, but I shrugged it off. "There must have been reservations for the other tables up front?" I suggested.

She nodded, and then noticed a man seated on a stool a few tables over. He was holding a guitar and squinting at some sheet music.

He looked over and smiled. "I hope you guys don't mind, but I'm trying out tonight for a weekend gig at this place."

"Oh, that's great," Bella said, with no idea Gary had already landed the job.

"Not a problem," I added, acting as though I'd never spoken to the man. And through an acoustic set of love ballads, Gary was just as convincing.

Bella had no idea but the order had already been carefully spelled out – drinks first, Pinot Grigio for her, beer for me, and the itinerary would begin. Vic approached with both drinks on a small round tray. "Appetizers tonight?" he asked.

I smiled. "Why don't we start with an order of little necks in garlic and oil?"

Vic nodded once and headed for the kitchen, while Gary swooned, "You say it best when you say nothing at all…"

Bella leaned into my ear and whispered, "How did he know I wanted white wine?"

I was into my second shrug when Vic returned to the table with a gorgeous arrangement of long stem red roses. Without a word, he placed them in front of Bella and rotated the vase until the card faced her. "Your appetizer should be out in a few minutes," he said and strutted away again.

Gary was already on his second number when Bella plucked the card from the arrangement. It read: "Bella, I love you, forever – Don." She looked up to find the entire restaurant staring at us.

"And always will," I whispered when she leaned over and kissed me.

After the steaming appetizer and another round of drinks, Vic placed a silver platter before my glowing wife. It held a scrolled sheet of parchment secured by red ribbon. She looked up at him, but he never let on. She glanced over at me. "What…"

"Open it," I said, while Gary strummed away in the background.

She did. It was the one thing she'd always wanted from me, but had never gotten – until now.

Moments of Destiny

From the moment I met you,
I knew there was a fire between us

that even hard, driving rain could never put out.

From the moment we spoke,
I knew I'd spent my entire life
in search of your deep and passionate love.

From the moment we kissed,
I knew my heart was no longer mine
and I'd finally found my future.

From the moment we laughed,
I knew there would never be enough time
to share all the things I needed to share with you.

From the moment we danced,
I knew, at last, what the phrase 'better half' meant
and surrendered to your gentle touch.

From the moment we walked hand-in-hand,
I knew I'd discovered my partner
and that my dreams were suddenly within reach.

From the moment we lay together,
I knew I'd made it to heaven
and thanked God for blessing me with you.

From the moment you agreed to be my wife,
I knew my journey was now worth taking,
through days of sunshine –
or nights of hard, driving rain.

As her watering eyes read the final verse, the musician stopped playing, the restaurant went silent and I went down to one knee. I opened the ring box.

"Isabella," I said, "I want to spend the rest of my life with you. Will you be my wife...again?"

She never hesitated and dove into my arms. For a while, we just hugged.

"I love you so much," she cried into my shoulder.

"I know," I said. "But..."

She pushed away from me and looked into my eyes. "But what?"

"But I need your answer?" I said, grinning.

"Yes...the answer is YES!" she gasped and jumped back into my arms.

The crowd shared a collective sigh, and everyone was clapping when Bella and I returned to reality. It took a few moments before each table returned to its own conversation and half-eaten meals.

Chuckling, I introduced my beautiful wife to Gary, the musician. As they shook hands, Gary admitted, "I was so nervous."

I bought the man a beer when Vic delivered two previously ordered dinners to our table. Though Bella couldn't touch hers, I ate and listened to Gary fill the room with a soothing melody. By the time the chocolate covered strawberries arrived for dessert, Bella was emotionally spent. She grabbed me once more for a kiss. "This has been the perfect night," she whispered.

"And for all these years...you've been the perfect wife, my dear."

As we left the restaurant, another round of applause carried us to the front door. I opened it for my new fiancé – only to discover a white stretch limousine idling at the curb. She quickly turned to me. "It's not over?"

I shook my head. "It'll never be over for us." As we made our way to the limo, waves of nausea threatened to drown me. *This is Bella's perfect night*, I told myself, *our perfect night. Whatever you do...do not throw up now!*

~ ~ ~ ~ ~ ~ ~ ~ ~ ~ ~ ~

A few short weeks later, the wedding ceremony was held outdoors in the presence of family and a handful of close friends. As the Justice of the Peace recited his spiel, I gazed into my fiancee's eyes and felt like crying. We shared so much love, but had so little time left. She was everything to me. "If I could live a thousand lives," I told her, "I would choose you as my partner each and every time."

As a final surprise to my beautiful bride, the reception was catered by Sagres Restaurant. We dined on the same Portuguese food we'd eaten all those years ago; roast pig-cacoila, chourico and pepper sandwiches, codfish, baked beans, favas, kale soup, stuffed quahogs, grilled sardines and spit-fire chickens. For dessert, a tray of malasadas, rice pudding and custard cups were washed down with jugs of sweet red wine.

Though there were no large tents, or strings of bare bulbs zigzagging across a wet glistening street, Gary made magic on an acoustic guitar and we danced to Keith Whitley's classic, *When You Say Nothing At All*. At one point, Riley, Michael, Madison and Pudge joined us to create a circle of love on the dance floor. We had the night of our lives.

~ ~ ~ ~ ~ ~ ~ ~ ~ ~ ~ ~

As our guests finally dispersed, we returned home with the moon. In the driveway, I pulled my new wife into my arms. "I know we haven't talked about it, but what do you say we go some place tropical for our honeymoon…like Barbados?" I waited for an explosion of joy. Bella had talked about going to Barbados for years. It was her dream.

She squeezed me tight and shrugged. "I was thinking tropical, but someplace different."

I was stunned. "Where?" I asked.

"I was thinking about the only place that ever came between us; the one place that you still need to make peace with, Don."

A sudden wave of sorrow rolled over me. She was talking about Vietnam. The thought of it still caused me to lose my breath – and not the same way I did when Bella and I exchanged vows. "But…"

"Barbados is a sweet gesture," she interrupted, "and I appreciate it, but I think it's more important that we face some old demons and finally put them to rest… together." She was right.

"Okay," I agreed. "But I'm not sure 'Nam's gonna be the best honeymoon spot."

She kissed my cheek. "As long as we're together, who cares where we are?"

I kissed her back, and was instantly filled with equal amounts of excitement and fear – and nausea, caused by the cancer that was gnawing away at my insides.

Chapter 6

After an exhaustive night of consummation, I awoke early and left Bella to her dreams. In the early morning light, I fumbled in the hallway closet until I found the old shoebox. It was the box that held everything that meant anything to me – a silver dollar, a pearl earring, a colored drawing of me and the kids, a white rabbit's foot, and a small wooden box that contained my greatest secret: a message intended for Madison and Pudge when I was gone. And there were also two letters, the one I'd written to Marc Suse many moons ago, and a letter I'd received from Dewey quite a few years back. I shook my head and put Dewey's letter back in the box with the rest of it.

From my dew-covered Adirondack chair, I read the yellowed letter I'd written my fallen comrade:

Dear Marc,

It's hard to believe, brother, but it's been ten years since we served together in 'Nam...a whole decade since you died. As Infantrymen, we shared every horror imaginable. They labeled us the Dream Team, though our experience was more like a nightmare. When I got home, I learned that our perspective of Vietnam was very different from everyone else's. I'm sure few people know of the children we saw slaughtered, while even fewer people understand the real price of freedom. I envy them. And I also wish we could have talked about the pain before you left for good.

During the fighting, so many friends were lost and so many promises were broken by those who sent us into the jungle. Though I returned home visibly whole, what I brought in pent-up rage was more than any man should ever be asked to carry. Some said, "You were serving your country." I still wish folks saw what really went on.

When I got home, I carried a souvenir called PTSD, with nightmares, flashbacks, depression and insomnia. I also suffered from blinding headaches and some mysterious digestive problems. But, according to the VA, my problems weren't service-connected, so I couldn't get any help. And then I thought of you and felt guilty that I'd even complained.

Before that fateful afternoon, I sensed you had a tough time in the jungle...trying to patch up some of the Vietnamese kids who never made it. Those gory pictures have haunted me for years. I pray that they don't still haunt you.

When we got home, the rest of the Dream Team parted ways and saw each other only at special events. It actually became less painful to avoid faces that served as reminders of a difficult time – no matter how much we loved the people behind those faces.

Marc, trust me, it's taken me years to realize that I was never alone in that damn jungle. This is probably the greatest tragedy to come out of Vietnam. Not one of us had to suffer alone. Yet, that's all any of us have done for years.

I still pray that your death brought you peace from your demons. I'm writing you now to let you know I haven't forgotten you, that none of us have.

I love you, brother, and I'll be seeing you soon.

Your eternal comrade,
Don DiMarco

I folded the letter and thought about the devastating effects of Vietnam. Although the shiny medals had lost their gleam, the war was still far from over. I'd done my best to ignore it, but that one year of my life so long ago had carried me away in the eye of a terrible storm; the type of storm that rages out of control deep inside, tearing at the spirit.

I looked up to see my new bride standing there, watching me. "You're right," I told her. "I do need to go back to 'Nam and make peace with it." Unhealed pain stunted growth and stifled the spirit, and it had gone on much too long. "I'll go check for flights," I told her.

She nodded once and started for the house.

I got up after her, but before heading for the computer, I went to the hallway closet to grab the luggage we'd taken to Martha's Vineyard. *Though I doubt this trip will be as relaxing*, I thought.

~ ~ ~ ~ ~ ~ ~ ~ ~ ~ ~ ~

The flight took even longer than I remembered – New York to Anchorage Alaska in seven hours. From there to Taipei in eleven hours. And then into Vietnam, which took five more anxious hours. The only ray of sunshine throughout the entire trip revealed itself when we boarded in New York. I spotted three American soldiers dressed in desert camouflage uniforms sitting in coach. By the time we were a half hour in the air, three passengers seated in first class offered to swap seats in a show of gratitude. Each time one of the soldiers made his way to the front of the plane, my chest swelled with a newfound pride.

"Looks like some things have changed since you returned from war," Bella whispered.

I nodded. It was hardly the welcome home I remembered.

"It's about damn time!" she added.

~ ~ ~ ~ ~ ~ ~ ~ ~ ~ ~ ~

On the final leg of our journey into 'Nam, my thoughts drifted back to places in my mind I'd vowed to never visit again.

Bella nudged my arm. "You can share it with me, you know."

I smiled at her.

Her eyes bore into mine. "Talk to me, Don. You don't have to do this alone."

I felt a weight lift off me and I was surprised at how quickly I jumped at the opportunity to open up and share the hell I'd experienced all those years ago. "As you know, my decision to join the Army was more my need to become the opposite of my father than anything else."

She nodded, wrapped both her hands around my arm and left them there.

With little coaxing, I began explaining it to her and my mind went back…

~ ~ ~ ~ ~ ~ ~ ~ ~ ~ ~ ~

It's funny the things you share in common with people when you take the time to get to know them. Seth Cabral also had a bastard of a father, while Cal Anderson loved a woman as deeply as I loved Bella.

And with Suse, it was nothing more than a twisted sense of humor that brought us as close as brothers. Other guys joked that Suse, Cal, Seth and I were the awesome foursome – together from boot camp through advanced infantry school right to deployment in Vietnam.

We'd been trained by the government to kill and there was no better place to fine-tune our skills than in the jungles of Southeast Asia. We never slept in the hooches. The rats were as big as dogs and they nested just beneath us. Most of us had crotch rot from our knees to our nipple lines because we could never get dry. So, we stripped buck naked, climbed up on top of the hooches and called in artillery fire for entertainment. It was like the Fourth of July every night. And while we slept up there, three well-trained dogs patrolled our barbed-wire perimeter. There were two shepherds and a Doberman – and they saved our hides more than once.

They knew every gap in the perimeter and could get in and out with ease. On several occasions, we'd wake to the sound of some Viet Cong screaming. The dogs would catch them in the concertina wire and gnaw on their flesh like they were slabs of prime rib. They'd eat them alive. The K9 Officer purposely didn't feed them a whole lot and we were told not to throw them anything, either. This kept them hungry enough to hunt. Every morning, Sergeant Ruggiero would walk out and finish the trapped Viet Cong with a .45 round into each head.

One of the saddest days in 'Nam was when the K9 Officer wrapped up his tour and was preparing to ship back home. Sergeant Ruggiero told him that he couldn't take his dogs with him. He said they'd tasted too much human blood – lived off it for twelve months – and there was no way they could be trusted back in the real world. As there was no way they'd take to another master, Ruggiero offered to shoot them. The K9

Officer thanked him. "But they're my animals," he said, "I'll do it."

I walked over and watched. I felt like I was eight years old again, standing there with tears in my eyes. The man lined up his three loyal friends and fired the first round into the Dobie's head. The shepherds never flinched. Then, one-by-one, he popped them off. I walked away, feeling horrible for the deaths of those animals. I was grateful for their service and believed then that I cared more for them than I did for most people. Dogs were different. They never chose to hurt a man. They did as they were told and never let us down…

~ ~ ~ ~ ~ ~ ~ ~ ~ ~ ~

I stopped there. Dead dogs were one thing, but the slide show in my head was starting to show human faces.

Bella tightened her grip even more, but never uttered a word.

For a while, I thought about the lunacy of Vietnam; skirmishing eventually grew into a full-scale war, with escalating U.S. involvement. The most savage fighting occurred in early 1968 during the Vietnamese New Year known as Tet. Although the so-called Tet Offensive ended in a military defeat for the North, its psychological impact changed the course of the war.

We'd shipped in at the tail end of 1968 when President Johnson ordered a halt to U.S. bombardment of North Vietnam. In 1969, as President Nixon began troop withdrawals, Ho Chi Minh, the North Vietnam president, died. Massive demonstrations of protest were in full swing at home when we finished our tour of duty. By then, according to us, the war had claimed the lives of 1.3 million Vietnamese and fifty-eight thousand American troops. If there was a winner, somebody forgot to tell us.

I looked up to find Bella smiling at me. Only she could give me the space I needed and still be right there by my side. Mentally and emotionally, I felt a little better about the trip, thinking, *I'm in good hands this time.* Physically, however, I couldn't imagine anything but jagged knives causing the kind of pain that shot through my upper abdomen. *I need to take some pain meds now,* I thought, *or I won't even make it off this plane.*

~ ~ ~ ~ ~ ~ ~ ~ ~ ~ ~ ~

When we touched down at the Ho Chi Minh City Airport, Bella and I were met by several greeters who bowed in traditional Oriental greeting before us. It was unexpected and felt awkward. *Where there were once rifles pointed at our heads, now we're embraced?* I turned to Bella and shrugged. Something deep inside felt very different and it didn't take long to figure it out. I was no longer filled with hate, an all-consuming feeling that had been fueled by my fear of losing my life in the war, as well as having to take the lives of others for a cause I didn't believe in, nor truly understood.

We gathered our bags and stepped outside of the airport terminal to hail a taxi. It hit me. The heat and humidity were downright oppressive, nearly unbearable, and I was reminded of the endurance it took to survive in this climate. *Some things haven't changed,* I thought.

As we drove through the city toward our hotel, though my heart remained in my throat, my eyes took in every detail.

Vietnam was an ancient land, struggling to catch up with the modern world. Even with their massive population, there was a significant lack of technology. There were more bicycles and mopeds on the road than cars. What struck me most, though, was that these people were happy; most of them smiling, others waving. A slight grin made its way into the corners of Bella's mouth, as she watched my reaction. She could tell I was dumbfounded.

Hundreds of people stood along the roadside; some even outside their homes, selling chickens, liters of gasoline, soda and cigarettes. "For a non-capitalistic country, everyone's selling something," I whispered to Bella.

"It's the way of the world, I guess," she replied.

The taxi driver jerked the car to a stop and jumped out to grab the bags from the trunk. As I opened the door for Bella, I felt something take a good bite out of the back of my neck. I swatted hard. *The bugs haven't changed, either. 'Nam's still infested with them.*

For sixty-three American dollars per night, we checked into a four-story, French colonial-style hotel called The Continental. It was located in the hub of the business and commercial district, adjacent to the famed Municipal Theatre. When we opened the door to the room, I was baffled again. Considering my previous accommodations, it was no wonder. The room was an old mansion style, with a beautiful city view, a nice double

bed and a bathtub with overhead shower. As Bella unpacked, I skimmed through the hotel's impressive list
of amenities: air conditioning, gift shop, several restaurants, laundry service, car park, lounge bar, business
center, fitness center, spa and sauna. "Wow," I muttered
and got up from the bed to take in the view. There were
two young prostitutes peddling their goods on the corner just below our window. I shook my head. From this
perspective, it could have been 1968 all over again.

Bella took a nap to recuperate from the long flight,
but – surprisingly – I was too wired to sleep. I flipped
through some magazines and got caught up on my
history:

> Ho Chi Minh City, located on the right
> bank of the Saigon River, population
> 5,250,000. It is the largest city, the great-
> est port, and the commercial and indus-
> trial center of Vietnam. A modern city,
> laid out in rectilinear fashion with wide,
> tree-lined avenues and parks, it enjoys
> a reputation for its beauty and cosmo-
> politan atmosphere. Today, the U.S. is
> Vietnam's largest trading partner, buy-
> ing seven billion dollars in Vietnamese
> goods each year. This includes the man-
> ufacturing of home appliances, clothing,
> shoes, as well as automobile parts.

I put down the magazine and walked back to the
window. From what I remembered, this city was the
military headquarters for U.S. and South Vietnamese
forces, and suffered considerable damage during the
1968 Tet offensive. Throughout the 1960s and early

70s, at least a million refugees from rural areas poured into the city, creating serious housing problems and overcrowding.

Just as Bella began to snore, I decided there was no time like the present to face my demons. I pocketed two pain pills – *just in case*, I thought – and headed for the street.

~ ~ ~ ~ ~ ~ ~ ~ ~ ~ ~ ~

Unlike Hanoi, where the temperature could dip into the fifties, the city I once knew as Saigon enjoyed summer year round. The streets were bustling with bike bells, car horns and people talking to each other in their native tongue. As I walked, I searched their faces. Most appeared genuinely happy to see me. Music played in the background and I heard a child's laughter. I stopped. The little people who were once sent to booby-trap us were now nothing more than children, playing and having fun. I scanned the streets, searching for danger. There was none. Those who would have pulled a pin on a grenade and thrown it into my sleeping bag were now shining shoes or peddling their goods in some back alley. The changes took some time to process – laughter instead of screams; aromas of street vendor delicacies instead of rotting flesh; the sight of people smiling, not grieving in some village over a corpse I might have been responsible for.

I walked for a while. To tell you the truth, I'm not sure how long. As I entered one of the shoddier markets, I noticed an older man selling American dog tags. For a moment, I lost my breath and felt an old rage begin to surface. But I stopped myself and walked away. *Bella and I are here to put the pain behind us, not create more. It's no longer my fight,* I told myself and felt relieved. Even in my diminished condition, I made record time back to the hotel.

Bella had been waiting, worried.

"Sorry..." I began.

"No," she barked. "You had my stomach in knots. And besides, I thought we were supposed to walk this one together?"

"I know, but…"

"But nothing," she interrupted, her voice finally returning to normal. "This is my honeymoon, too, so promise me we won't spend another moment apart."

"I promise."

~ ~ ~ ~ ~ ~ ~ ~ ~ ~ ~ ~

I kept apologizing through the first half of dinner and spent the second half explaining what I'd experienced. My obvious relief removed the nervousness in her eyes.

The hotel advertised dinner in a romantic and stylish atmosphere, which provided good dining options at reasonable prices. I hardly touched a bite and even stayed away from the water and ice. To be on the safe side – and still holding on to some old, misinformed beliefs – I drank an expensive imported beer. Bella reluctantly followed my lead. Though driven by the American dollar, the wait staff was doting. As I played with my chopsticks in a bowl of white rice, Bella asked, "Is that all you're going to eat while we're here?"

"No. I spotted those blue tins of Swedish butter cookies in the gift shop. I plan to pick up a few before we turn in tonight."

She shook her head and started to chuckle, but stopped. Her face changed. "Is it your stomach? Are you feeling ill?"

"No, no. It's definitely the food," I confirmed. "The Vietnamese cuisine has never agreed with me." But it was a lie. The cancer was doing a tune on my entire digestive system and it didn't matter what the cuisine was – I wasn't going to dare take another bite.

~ ~ ~ ~ ~ ~ ~ ~ ~ ~ ~ ~

The next morning, we headed north to Danang by car. Even with Bella's soothing words, it had been years since I felt that scared. In fact, I didn't remember Dr. Rice's prognosis causing the bone-chilling panic I now felt.

"I'm right here," she whispered, and I could feel her trying to offer whatever strength she possessed behind her nervous mask.

On the outer edges of the city, the landscape of the countryside was green and calm. There were no explosions, no smoke; no impending doom waiting around the next corner. Once a living hell, the jungle was now a place of beauty and serenity. There were children playing, men and women tending to their rice fields and livestock. Dressed in their cone-shaped peasant hats, sarongs and bamboo sandals, they worked the same way they had for centuries – with oxen-drawn plows.

We passed one small village after another, each populated with stilted one-room huts. The driver went slow – so slow, in fact, that I wondered whether Bella had given him instructions before we left. The people were no longer in hiding, but coming out into the open to greet us. A few times we even stopped to say hello. Several of the locals met us on the roads; others, in the middle of their tiny villages. I tried desperately to look at this world with a different set of eyes, and for a while, I was doing well.

We were just outside Danang when the faint sound of a bell coming through the village startled me. I tried to conceal my anxiety, but Bella's hand tightening in mine told me she knew.

"Remember, I'm right here with you," she said.

Then I saw it. The bell was tied to a goat's neck. I took a few deep breaths and a long hard look. I needed to brand a different perspective into my psyche. This was my last chance to make new memories and recall this land in a totally different light. I was here to create a different picture, a kinder perspective, and I wasn't about to waste it. Although many of my feelings were engrained, there was also a chance to release some deeply disturbing feelings; feelings that served no purpose but to silently gnaw away and continue to destroy any real sense of peace.

As we made our way into another village, the smell of damp earth and the sun on my face pushed me back into 1968. A pig snorted in a nearby pen. A woman, washing clothes by hand, sang while she did her chores. Our eyes met and she smiled. I smiled back, but felt like puking.

Another hundred yards and we were standing on the very spot where my best friend had lost his life. For whatever reason, I thought I might actually feel the presence of Marc Suse when I reached it, but my friend wasn't here and I was grateful for it.

A small dog scampered out from beneath one of the huts and my stomach turned. I gasped for air twice and felt the world start to spin when Bella grabbed my shoulders and peered into my eyes.

"It's okay, hon," she assured me in her sweetest voice, "nothing bad is going to happen. We're here to make peace."

I think I smiled at her, but my mind was reeling out of control. Like a well-planned ambush, it all came back to me in one sudden and violent moment. Once again, I could picture everything as clearly as I did back in '68…

~ ~ ~ ~ ~ ~ ~ ~ ~ ~ ~

Wet – everything was wet, which is pretty ironic considering it was hell on Earth. The fear was nearly paralyzing, fighting an enemy that looked no different from our ally. Women and children were as lethal as any man; people fighting for their survival, while we simply fired at anything that moved in front of us. We were boys who were called forward as men by a country that would later despise our every move. Our greatest fear was that the twelve months spent in the bush would become who we were and not just what we'd been forced to do.

The tastes of sulfur and mud came back, as though they were still packed in my nasal cavity. The disturbing sounds of shelling pierced the air; grown men screaming, calling for "Mommy," while the color in their faces drained out of them and the world turned cold. The horrid sights of healthy men cut to pieces by machine gun fire, or vanishing by taking one wrong step, appeared before me once again. But the worst were the smells. The smells of charred human flesh were so vulgar that it made my skin crawl; a nightmare made complete by the rancid odors of a smoking corpse, its eyes open and teeth bared.

My buddies – men I'll never forget, faces I wish I could – the best of them perished in a dense patch of jungle that no one ever cared about. Like me, those who made it out might have been tasked with the hardest mission of all – living with all we saw; all we suffered; all we caused.

And then it came into focus, the day that had tormented me for my entire life.

Led by our platoon sergeant, Ruggiero, we were humping through the bush one morning, just talking and laughing. Suse was smoking a butt, his sleeves rolled up revealing his tattoo; a U.S. flag crossed with the flag of Italy, the word "Goombah" etched beneath it. Cabral was going on about fast cars and how he was going to race when we got home. I looked over at Cal. As usual, he was silent and distant. He'd gotten his girlfriend, Karen, pregnant before we shipped out and it haunted him something awful. He probably endured more pain than any of us. And when Karen had their daughter, it was even more difficult for him.

We were strolling along, when all of a sudden a single shot rang out. A sniper!

Suse was my best friend, something any rational man should avoid during war. And he paid back the favor exactly the way I should have expected. He died a quick and violent death. He took that sniper's round right in the forehead and that was it. Such a death wasn't as dramatic as most folks imagined. We were talking and laughing one second, and an echo later, he collapsed onto the red mud like a dropped bag of bricks. The moments following this played out, and still do, like some psychedelic slide show – our squad firing wildly, the vegetation all around us flying into the air, as though some demented sushi chef had been cut loose from the asylum…

~ ~ ~ ~ ~ ~ ~ ~ ~ ~ ~ ~

I could no longer hold back. I dropped to my knees and mourned my friend's useless death. In the distance, I could hear Bella crying with me. While my body convulsed, I cried so hard and for so long that I believe I might have actually made peace with the same patch of earth I'd once helped destroy. *How could we have committed such horrors against each other?* I questioned. Four decades later, the answer seemed so obvious. *Because we thought we were separate. We thought we were superior.*

I remained on my knees for a while, paying homage to my deceased comrade. I pictured Suse's face one last time; his forehead tanned and smooth, his cocky smile juggling a cigarette. *I'll be seeing you again soon, buddy,* I silently promised. *Real soon.*

While my wife waited patiently for me to return to the present, I considered the price my friends and I had paid. The effects of Vietnam had been devastating.

When I got home, life was nothing more than another test of survival. I married my sweetheart, Bella, and returned to work at McKaskies, but I was lost.

For five solid years, though I tried like hell to hide it, I felt so guilty for coming home unscathed – which I now know couldn't have been any further from the truth. I felt incapacitated for years. There was a force that pulled at me and though I didn't want to go, my tired mind gave in. The tunnel of depression was so dark that I could see no end. Carrying a tremendous weight upon my shoulders, I only wished to rest, perhaps sleep forever, but the fear of staying made me forge ahead. I sensed there were others in the tunnel, but a vicious loneliness tore at my soul. Each step was agonizing, as I went nowhere. I wondered if anyone even knew I was lost; if anyone even knew how to pull me out. Many times, a tormenting fear welled up inside of me. I'd reached despair and questioned whether it was the end. But I also wondered, *What if it's one more step?* But it was more than one more step. It took years of small, cautious steps and the love of a compassionate, understanding woman to finally guide my heart and mind back home.

"You okay?" I heard someone ask.

I looked up to find Bella standing by my side, as she had throughout our entire life together. Her face was pale and drawn. She looked like she'd been through a war of her own. I grabbed for her hand and kissed it. "It's finally over," I told her, "let's go home."

"Thank God," she said and melted into my arms to finish healing my soul.

~ ~ ~ ~ ~ ~ ~ ~ ~ ~ ~ ~

The following morning, as we made our way back to the airport, I glared out the taxi window as intently as I had when we'd arrived. From the vegetable peddlers to those who slaved in the rice paddies, there was no hatred or blame felt by these people; a truth found easiest in their eyes. Even their native tongue – a language I quickly grew to despise during my last visit – appeared friendly in tone. The Vietnamese were an honorable people, treating each other with mutual respect; something many of my own countrymen now lacked.

When we reached the airport, the cramps in my abdomen threatened to bend me in half and I realized my pain was no longer emotional. It was now just physical. I tipped the driver, forced down a pain pill and grabbed our bags. The man smiled at me and bowed longer than he needed. I wasn't sure whether I deserved the respect or not – I even felt a pang of guilt because of it – but this was a new generation. Though their country sustained far more damage – physical, emotional and psychological – these people had forgiven the sins of the past and put it all behind them. *It's a lesson I should have learned long ago*, I thought, *but at least I learned it before it was too late*. I felt blessed for the trip and turned to my wife. "Thank you," I told her, as we entered the terminal.

"You don't have to thank me," she said and searched my face. "Feel better?"

I nodded. "I do. But the food's still horrendous," I fibbed.

She laughed all the way to the plane.

~ ~ ~ ~ ~ ~ ~ ~ ~ ~ ~ ~

Riley, Michael and the kids greeted us at the airport. I was never so happy to be tackled to the ground. "Get off of Grampa," Riley scolded the kids.

"Don't you dare," I told them, and accepting every ache and pain because of it, I tickled them both into a fit of hysterics.

On the ride home, I sat in the back of the van with my clingy grandchildren, while Bella filled Riley and Michael in on the details of our healing pilgrimage.

~ ~ ~ ~ ~ ~ ~ ~ ~ ~ ~ ~

After dinner, the kids and I began working on the puzzle. Before long, Bella entered the room with Riley and Michael. They were all smiling.

"What's up now?" I asked.

"I've been thinking," Bella said. "Why don't you make a wish list – a 'no regrets' list – of everything you've wanted to do in your life and never got a chance to?"

Instinctively, I shook my head. "I don't have the time for that."

She smiled at me, gently. "But you do, Don. You do have the time." She sat on the arm of the chair. "Pick the top five and let's go do them. What do you say?"

"We think it's a great idea," Riley chimed in and elbowed Michael to agree.

I placed another piece into the puzzle and looked at the kids, who were also nodding in agreement. "Do it, Poppa!"

They're right, I thought. *I never took the time to pursue any of my dreams. I was too busy working.* "I guess you're right," I said, realizing, *It's now or never.*

"Let's live life for all it's worth!" Bella added.

"This means you'll have to learn to relax and enjoy life, too," I said, half-teasing her. "No more cleaning the house every day. No more running around doing errands for hours on end. Can you do it?"

"I'll make her," Riley teased.

Bella nodded. "I'll learn."

At that very moment, a sense of urgency that came from somewhere deep inside of me – even deeper than the cancer – rose to the surface and screamed to be free. *Okay,* I thought, *it's time to get moving!*

~ ~ ~ ~ ~ ~ ~ ~ ~ ~ ~

Late that night after everyone had gone home, I sat down with a pen and paper. I gave some serious thought to the five things I would most want to do. It might sound ridiculous, but as a child my fantasy was to be a cowboy. As an adult, I dreamed of being a professional racecar driver. I fantasized about shagging fly balls in the outfield at Fenway Park. I even thought about trying to write a book, but quickly decided there were more important ways to spend my time. In the end, my no regrets list wasn't all that hard to draft. In no particular order, I listed:

> <u>No Regrets</u>
> (1) Take a Cup car 150 mph around a super speedway
> (2) Herd cattle on a real drive, cowboy boots and hat included
> (3) Get paid as a newspaper reporter
> (4) See the country from the tinted windows of an RV
> (5) Land a 40 lb. striped bass

I read the list over a few times and told Bella, "Maybe I can get it done?"

She plucked it out of my hand, read it over and smiled. "I have no doubt," she said. With a black magic marker, she wrote the words "HONEY DO" at the top of the page, posted it on the refrigerator and gave me a kiss. To Bella, it was going to be as easy as that.

I kissed her back. "Thank you," I said.

Chapter 7

I was looking forward to our weekly visit from Riley and the kids, and made my way to the dining room table to prepare. Though Bella cringed, our dining room table had been converted into the puzzle table where the family gathered to figure out which pieces fit where. For years, it was the center attraction and home to one puzzle after the next. And for years, Bella complained we could have found a more suitable location.

I remembered Riley and I sitting for hours, talking and working on puzzles. Now, it was with my grandkids, bringing the legacy full circle for me. I couldn't think of a better way to bond with them.

With little time left to accomplish a lifetime of dreams, I quickly jumped on the Internet to research what it would take to make one of those dreams come true. Just as soon as the Checkered Flag Racing School website popped up on the screen, my body tingled with anticipation. Even if I'd wanted to, I couldn't have wiped the smile from my face as I read:

> Checkered Flag Racing School will fill your need for adventure, excitement and most importantly – speed! We have assembled the finest and most authentic equipment available to most closely duplicate a true racing environment. Forget skydiving, bungee jumping, or scaling Everest. This is the ultimate stockcar

driving experience, taking you to the
edge of Nextel Cup racing most people
only dream about. Whether you're looking for the ride of your life or want to
test your nerves behind the wheel, we've
got a package to fit most sizes, egos and
budgets. No matter where you start, this
full-throttle adventure is guaranteed to
fuel your passion for speed!

The pitch definitely got my heart pumping. I read
on to find that the instructors had thirty combined
years of racing experience. They used NASCAR Winston Late Model stockcars. Skill levels ranged from
novice to intermediate.

There was a package available for any budget. They
had The Qualifier for one hundred twenty-five dollars.
This included a passenger seat ride at 170 mph. *I'm all
set with that*, I thought. The Season Opener cost a few
hundred more. It included a thirty-minute classroom
orientation, placement in a passenger seat for a ride
and then ten laps behind the wheel at 165 mph. There
was also The Rookie Adventure, Happy Hour and The
Advanced Stock Car Adventure – each package increasing in price, as well as in time spent on the track.
And then there was the dream package: The Champi-
onship Shootout. This was the most advanced Nextel
Cup driving experience available. It included all the
programs listed above, but you also experienced driving
two car groups side-by-side at two car lengths apart.
The final session of the program also simulated a ten-
lap race. The three-day experience came to a grand total
of two thousand nine hundred ninety-five dollars.

I was excited about the possibility, no doubt, but I'd always been hesitant about spending money on myself. I read on:

> The school's emphasis is on spending as much time as possible at the wheel. The three-day racing programs feature lots of track time in the racecars. The longer the course, the greater the speeds you'll reach and the more variety of exercises you'll experience.

I took note of the school's number and grabbed for my wallet. *What the hell*, I thought, *you only live once.*

I hated credit cards. Only in America could people buy things they couldn't afford, adding twenty percent interest on top of it – as if everyone expected to hit the lottery. I used them from time-to-time, but never charged anything I couldn't pay off at the end of the month.

The receptionist booked my reservation. "We look forward to seeing you on the 11th, Mr. DiMarco," she said and hung up. That's when it hit me. *I'm going racing!*

Just as I stood, the phone rang. It was Riley. "I'm going racing!" I yelled. "I just got off the phone from booking it."

There was a pause. "That's great, Dad," she said, her voice melancholy.

Ice water coursed through my veins. "I won't go then," I blurted.

"No," she sniffled, "you have to. And that's the point, isn't it?"

"It'll be okay," I whispered, but that wasn't completely true. The hourglass was emptying and there were no words powerful enough to freeze time. "It'll be okay, sweetheart."

~ ~ ~ ~ ~ ~ ~ ~ ~ ~ ~ ~

Rather than wait for me alone in some motel for three days, Bella insisted it would be better if she sat out this adventure at home. "You don't want me beating you on that track, anyway," she said. "It would be embarrassing."

I packed, swung by the pharmacy to pick up two refills Dr. Rice had called in, and headed home to try to get at least some sleep.

I awoke even earlier than usual. I didn't want to waste a moment.

On the flight, I reminisced about growing up feeding my need for speed.

~ ~ ~ ~ ~ ~ ~ ~ ~ ~ ~ ~

We were fourteen years old when Dewey and I took the old man's Cadillac. It was supposed to be a joy ride; only a childhood prank, but it turned into a nightmare.

With me behind the wheel, we headed down the road and took a right toward a private lane that ran the length of the pond. I punched the gas, squealing the tires, throwing up rocks and barreling down the narrow lane. As we turned around, we saw that a mob of unhappy neighbors had gathered at the beginning of the road to meet us. "Oh, crap!" I said, but drove back to face the jury.

I rolled the window down a bit. A man with bulging eyes approached. Although his anger was understandable, the rage in his voice seemed inappropriate. I was terrified, but stayed calm. The man placed both of his massive hands into the window. "Get out of the car… NOW!" he barked. "We're going to call the police."

"Go ahead and call," I told him, "but we're not getting out."

The man freaked out, screaming, "GET OUT!" His huge hands pulled on the window, trying to break it in half.

I punched the gas, but the man never let go. We dragged him over several bushes before he was thrown from the car. I panicked, took a quick right and started for his back yard. We looked back. By now, he was up and running. "The whole neighborhood's after us!" Dewey screamed.

I had my foot to the floor when we hit the soft lawn and began to sink. As the car began carving a tank trench into the angry man's yard, grass and mud flew up from the rear wheels. Just when it looked like we were goners, the car swayed right, then left, then right again until it bucked itself free. I aimed for the road.

The mob was now screaming for blood. Dewey yelled "ROCK!" and took cover. A small boulder crashed through the rear window and landed on the back seat. We looked up. The giant was smiling. *He could have competed at shot put in the Olympics*, I thought.

We got to the end of the road, bailed out and ran for home. For once, my dad's snarling face, or even a talk with the police, seemed like child's play. We needed protection.

From the look on my dad's face after he saw the rock sitting on the Cadillac's back seat, I suspected my punishment was nothing compared to what he'd dole out to Mr. Bulging Eyes.

~ ~ ~ ~ ~ ~ ~ ~ ~ ~ ~ ~

One freezing November afternoon, my speed addiction also found Dewey and me out in a cornfield. It was an old Chevy and I was trying my hand at the art of the reverse donut. Essentially, I'd drive the car as fast as I could in reverse. Just before I lost control, I'd spin the wheel hard and go for the ride. As we rode the amusement park ride for the price of a gallon of gas, Dewey yelled in delight, watching the trees whip by his window. It was all about the thrill of feeling out of control.

On our last spin down the field, I put my foot to the floor. The car swayed to and fro, threatening to unhand the reins from me before I made the decision to give them up. At the last second, I turned the wheel and the car whipped into a violent spin. Suddenly, the driver's side door flew open. It felt like some invisible force plucked me from the interior of the vehicle, my foot still wedged under the dashboard. As gravity summoned us in the opposite direction, Dewey struggled to the window on the driver's side. He was just in time to see my body being dragged, while the front wheel missed my head by inches. My eyes were open, but I wasn't enjoying the ride. Shock had set in. Dewey finally grabbed the wheel and straightened out the car, managing his foot onto the brake. He waited to hear my groan and then burst into laughter.

I wiggled my foot free and gradually got to my feet. I felt sick. Without a word, I reclaimed my seat, slammed the door and turned the car around. "Let's try that again," I told him and tried to slam my foot right through the floor. Dewey held on. It was one of those 'back on the horse' kind-of-things.

As frightening as it was, it was still easier than staying home with Dad and Joseph.

~ ~ ~ ~ ~ ~ ~ ~ ~ ~ ~ ~

After a long flight delay and a lively discussion with an arrogant customer service representative at the rental car desk, it was nearly dusk by the time I reached Charlotte, North Carolina. Right away, the southern heat smacked me and reminded me of Vietnam. Instinctively, I waited for the heart palpitations and shortness of breath that always came with such reminders, but they never came. My body felt calm. I was completely relaxed. *I really have healed*, I finally decided, *and I have Bella to thank for it!*

Grateful and exhilarated, I checked into the motel and made a call home. I told Bella about my recent revelation and she was thrilled to hear it. She then silenced my guilt of being away from the family, saying, "You've put everyone before yourself for years. Right now…this time is about *you*. Now go enjoy it!"

I thanked her, hung up and took the rental car over to Lowe's Motor Speedway just off of Highway 29 in Harrisburg. The first class wasn't scheduled to start until the morning, but I couldn't wait to see it.

With the majority of NASCAR teams located within a short drive from Charlotte, Lowe's served as a home track for many of the stars. This 1.5-mile quad-oval was the showpiece of the Speedway Motor sports portfolio. It was also the annual site of NASCAR's longest race, the Coca-Cola 600 hosted on Memorial Day weekend, holding a capacity crowd of one hundred thousand screaming fans. With turns banked at twenty-four degrees and the straightaways banked at five degrees, Lowe's was one of the faster super-speedways.

As I circled the place in the dying light, I noticed there were rows of condominiums perched above Turn 1, the best place to watch the action. *What a cool place to live*, I thought.

~ ~ ~ ~ ~ ~ ~ ~ ~ ~ ~ ~

I was up with the birds. I ate a banana and some granola, swallowed two pills, and took my time getting to the track. When I arrived, I was surprised to find a heavyset guy with sandy blonde hair and a pair of brown eyes already waiting. I extended my hand. "Mornin,' I'm Don DiMarco."

"Billy Hutchins," he said and shook my hand. "Good mornin'." He looked me over a few times. "So how long you been teaching us speed addicts?"

"Not all that long," I answered and laughed. "I'm a student."

He did a quick double take. "I'm sorry, you looked…"

"Old?"

He shrugged. "Nah…like a teacher."

We spent the next few minutes getting acquainted. Billy Hutchins was from Huntersville, North Carolina, and was wise beyond his years. He'd raced short tracks throughout the south where he won Pro Stock Rookie of the Year and the coveted Sportsmanship Trophy. As more people joined our circle, Billy greeted his friend before introducing us. He said, "Ev, this is Teacher." He then looked at me and smiled. "Teacher, this is my buddy, Evan Jacobs."

I shook the kid's hand and laughed at the new nickname. He wiped his brow and said, "It's hotter than two mice going at it in a wool sock in August."

I laughed even harder. But he was right. The air was already so thick that I was covered in a film of sweat that wouldn't evaporate. It was definitely climbing into the 90's, humid, with no relief in sight. "I just got back from Vietnam," I told them. "It was hotter than Hades over there."

"I bet," Evan said and looked up to find Maia Julius, the only female student in the class, signing in. "Damn," he muttered, "a girl."

I chuckled again. "Good for her," I said.

We were greeted by an enthusiastic crew of three men; a student to instructor ratio of five to one. Jeff Bolduc, the head instructor, was no more than twenty-five years old – which down south equated to more than fifteen years of racing experience. He was squared-away, much like an army drill instructor, but with a more friendly temperament. "Our mission here at Checkered Flag Racing is to give you the individual attention you need," he began. "When racing, you will be in constant radio communication with your instructors, allowing us to correct mistakes as they happen, give advice and offer encouragement. I promise you'll get maximum seat time and obtain faster speeds each time out."

We were escorted into a classroom located a stone's throw from the pit lane area. Registration took place first, waivers were signed and we were invited to purchase a photo package produced by the photographer on site for the day. Bella would have been ticked had she known, but I passed and took a seat at the front of the classroom.

Once Maia and the other thirteen students settled in, Jeff got started. "The first thing we're going to learn at Checkered Flag is to look ahead," he said. "It's all about paying attention to the track ahead, which isn't easy when you're inches away from another car or a concrete wall, traveling at one hundred fifty miles per hour or more. Believe me, there's little a driver can do about things that happen within a hundred feet of the car and nothing he can do within fifty feet. The trick is to develop a constant scanning pattern, using your peripheral vision to note what's happening on the sides of your car, while constantly scanning your mirrors, the car's instruments and the track in front of you."

Though I didn't take many notes, I was impressed by our young instructor. He was informative and well spoken. The rest of the morning was spent on accident avoidance. "To finish first, you must first finish," Jeff explained. "Whenever a racer is driving wheel-to-wheel or nose-to-tail with another car, whenever he is about to pass another car or is being passed, some portion of his mind should be considering accident avoidance. 'Where will I go if.....? 'What will I do if....?'"

I nodded and looked back at my classmates. Most of the guys, to include Maia, were anxious to get behind the wheel and weren't paying complete attention. I found it disturbing.

"Accidents are avoided in the driver's head, not in his driving skills and techniques," Jeff went on. "It's imperative to look well ahead of the car and be aware of your surroundings at all times. It's about anticipating dangerous situations and responding to each of them, as needed. And remember, guys, the single most important element of accident avoidance is space."

The morning instruction didn't seem long enough. We were dismissed for lunch – which was comical considering that it was delivered to us in the form of a stainless steel roach coach. "Get whatever you want," one of the other instructors announced. "It's on us."

"Yeah…with the help of our three thousand dollar tuitions," one of the students called out.

The guy smiled and walked away to eat his sandwich.

As I picked at a veggie wheat wrap, I took a seat near Billy and Evan.

"What the hell…it's only money," Evan said. "We only go around once."

I started to nod in agreement when Billy drove the message home. "You got that right! We gotta drive this thing until the wheels come off and we head into victory lane out of gas, all banged up…the doors torn right off it."

I finished the nod and laughed to myself. Though I missed Bella and the kids, I realized my wife was right – as usual. *I'm exactly where I'm supposed to be.*

~ ~ ~ ~ ~ ~ ~ ~ ~ ~ ~ ~

The afternoon was spent on learning how to properly corner, braking to slow and braking to stop. When we wrapped up for the day, Jeff said, "Life is not a spectator sport, people. Starting tomorrow we're going to prove why."

Everyone stood and stretched. Billy approached me. "Me and some of the guys are heading out on the town tonight. You're welcome to come with us, if you want?"

I looked up to find Maia and a few of the boys waiting for my answer. "I appreciate it, but I'm really beat. I think I'm just going to head back to the motel and get caught up on my beauty sleep."

"So you'll be sliding into a coma then?"

I laughed.

He patted my back. "See you in the morning, Teacher."

~ ~ ~ ~ ~ ~ ~ ~ ~ ~ ~ ~

I bought a tuna fish sandwich from a convenience store near the motel, ate one bite and threw it up. For the next half hour, I sat on the toilet and tried to push out the pain in my guts. But nothing would come out – not even the usual pencil stools. *Great*, I thought, *constipation should be a real hoot.*

I then called Bella. We talked for most of the night like teenagers. The fact that all I'd done was sit in a classroom all day took nothing away from the excitement for either of us. Bella wanted every detail and I offered each one twice.

"The kids okay?" I asked. "Riley?"

"Everyone's fine," she said. "Stop worrying."

I chuckled. "That's something...*you* telling *me* to stop worrying."

"I know." She laughed. "I guess I'm trying to remind myself, too?"

"I love you, Bell," I whispered.

"I know. I can feel it."

~ ~ ~ ~ ~ ~ ~ ~ ~ ~ ~

As expected, Maia and most of the guys looked like they'd prayed for death the next morning. They were hung-over, the whole lot of them.

The morning briefing covered safety issues. Once completed, we left the classroom for the garage area where Jeff and his partners explained the controls, gauges and features of the Winston Cup style racecars. Each car was exactly how I'd imagined it – beautiful. They were designed to accommodate different student heights and weights, so we had to try out a few until seating became comfortable.

Once fitted properly, we took a track orientation ride in a long, white van. As we puttered around the track, Jeff explained the meaning of the orange cones as specific slowing areas. He went over establishing the correct racing line, as well as other reference points "to assist you in maximizing your track time." He then covered the rpm limits that would be used throughout the course. This took some time. Three of the four turns had different degrees of banking, while the front straightaway seemed to go on forever. We returned to the garage for another lunch on wheels.

As we ate, Evan turned to me. "Why are you here?" he asked. "I mean, aren't you a few years late to be trying out for the circuit?"

"It's never too late to try anything," I told him, "and if you ever get too old to think this way, then you're only waiting to die."

Billy listened attentively and grinned. "I guess it's not really about where we came from, but where we're heading that counts, right?"

As I nodded, the hair on my neck prickled up. I was going to respond when Jeff came back into the garage and announced, "It's time to draw your racing suits and helmets. Please make sure you find your right size."

In the early summer sun, the driving suit was warmer than I'd imagined. We stood around one of the racecars for a final explanation of the switches and fire suppression system. "Okay, people," Jeff concluded, "let's go have some fun!"

With all the classroom instruction behind us, we were finally ready to take our seats behind the wheel. My stomach turned once, but it had nothing to do with cancer or the medicine that sometimes numbed its pain. This was from nerves and it was astounding. The cars had already been warmed up by the mechanics and were ready to go. The exhaust fumes gave off the sweetest smell.

I jumped into my assigned car and headed out behind Jeff's lead car into the bright afternoon sun. My heart pounded hard in my ears. I'd never felt so alive.

The first session started out slow. We went around the gigantic track at no more than 140 mph which didn't feel all that fast in a professional racecar. By the time the second lap session was done, we'd already reached our top speed for the day. As we pulled into the pit, I realized that the practice was done. *Tomorrow's the big day.*

Before dismissing us for the night, Jeff explained, "Although everybody races under the same sun, not everybody enjoys the same horizon. If you're willing to learn, grow and overcome any obstacle in your path, the sky is the limit. It's just a matter of pulling it down and driving it home."

Everyone applauded and headed for the parking lot.

~ ~ ~ ~ ~ ~ ~ ~ ~ ~ ~ ~

Maia and the boys went out to drink whatever they couldn't finish the night before. Once again, I decided to stay in. Between the exhaustion and crippling constipation caused by the medication, I wouldn't have lasted another hour on my feet. Bella and I talked for hours. "Sweet dreams," she finally said.

"I'm living one of them, babe," I told her and could feel the warmth of her smile.

After we hung up, I laid in bed for the next hour, thinking about what I'd already experienced since receiving the devastating news – an unforgettable trip to Martha's Vineyard, our engagement and wedding; making dinner for Bella and peace with Vietnam – and not even the worst physical torment could have wiped the smile from my face. *I can't wait to experience what-ever lies ahead*, I thought, and dozed off excited about the immediate future.

~ ~ ~ ~ ~ ~ ~ ~ ~ ~ ~ ~

Morning arrived in a wink.

Anxious for the roar of racing motors and the smell of burning rubber, I donned my helmet and fired up the late-model Chevy Monte Carlo. In a line of other drivers, I sat in the belly of the fiberglass beast and adjusted my safety harness. On cue, I rolled out of the pit, allowing every horse under the hood to gallop into the concrete arena. A last minute check of the gauges made me smile. The hour of unbridled competition was at hand. Then, for whatever reason, Seth Cabral's face popped into my head; my old Vietnam comrade who did nothing but talk about fast cars. For a moment, I wished he'd been able to experience this day for himself.

The first lap was driven at 5000 rpm, allowing me and the car to get acquainted with the track. It was also an opportunity for the slick racing tires to heat up to their proper operating temperature. Our second lap was quicker at 6000 rpm. Our third lap was even faster at 7000 rpm, firing down the long front straightaway at 155 mph. Slowing to negotiate Turns 1 and 2, I juiced the throttle down the back straight. Turn 3 required an earlier lift off the throttle and a little patience, and then we were roaring down the front straight again. The car handled flawlessly.

After two separate sessions of ten laps each, we were instructed into the pit to receive our critiques and an early lunch. "Just get on the throttle earlier coming out of the turns," Jeff told me. "Trust the car and let it run for you. I promise, she won't let you down."

The afternoon format changed to two cars lining up side-by-side. The instructions were as follows: "If you're going too slow for the person in front of you, you'll be shown a blue flag with an orange stripe. This means you should move to the bottom of the track to allow the driver behind you to pass." He scanned our faces one last time. "Now let's go racing."

While imagining the roar of the crowd and the other engines waiting to jump, I stayed focused. From behind tinted glass, the last minute felt like an eternity. I calmly waited. At last, the green flag dropped. With lightning reflexes, my callused hands shifted through the gears. A lifetime full of anticipation was disappearing at every turn.

Within two laps, I passed the student in front of me. The speedometer wasn't working, but I could tell how fast I was going by the tachometer. A few laps later, Billy Hutchins, Evan Jacobs, Maia Julius and I were drafting past another group of four cars. I didn't know whether to soil my pants or scream out in joy. Thanks to the constipation, I let out a howl.

Toward our final track sessions, even though it felt like we were slowing down, our lap times started to decrease. Since we'd already conquered top speed on the straight-aways, we must have begun picking up time in the turns. The training was already paying off. I could hear Jeff say, "The faster you get through the turns, the less you have to accelerate coming out of the turns."

By the end of the day, the car and I came to a mutual trust. I got her up to 8500 rpm. Due to the restrictor plate, we weren't going to go any faster than that. We'd topped out at 170 mph. Jeff was right. She never let me down.

No matter how hard I tried, though, I couldn't catch the others in my pack and accepted my place in the rear. *There's no substitute for youth…or practice*, I thought. Even still, I imagined taking the checkered flag and slowing for the victory lap. I could picture the cheering crowd, smell the oil and burned rubber drifting north. It was an unspoiled moment of glory and I savored it; the thrill of a lifetime. *Yes…yes…yes…* I repeated over and over in my head.

Before I knew it, we were being ordered back into the pit. Exhausted and covered in sweat, I met Billy, Evan and Maia for a round of high fives. "Well done, Teacher," Billy said and then searched my face for a moment. "If I'm out of place, please tell me, but I have to know," he began, pulling me aside. "What in hell are you really doing here?"

I understood his curiosity. "I'm dying of cancer," I told him and explained my honey do list.

His forehead folded in wonder. "Then you're crazy…'cause this is the last place I'd be, if I only had a year left to live."

"Oh, really. Then where would you be?"

"I'd be out asking for forgiveness from some people and offering it to others." He shrugged. "It's all about karma, if you ask me. And you don't want to carry any extra baggage into the next world, if you don't have to. My daddy used to say, 'Always give someone the benefit of the doubt and never allow a suffering from the past destroy what could be.' I don't think he was only talking about this world."

"Your father was a wise man," I said.

He laughed. "Yeah, when he was sober enough to remember his own name."

I was astounded by the wisdom Billy showed for such a young age. I shook his hand for the last time. "Good luck on the upcoming racing season," I told him.

With a sincere smile, he nodded. "Thanks, Teacher, but I make my own luck." As he gathered his things to leave, he said, "You make sure you take care of yourself, okay?"

I promised I would and headed for the rental car. I couldn't wait to get home, kiss my wife and cross the first item off my list. Then I planned to sleep for a week. *It's gonna take at least that long to recover*, I figured.

Chapter 8

To Pudge's hanging jaw and Madison's loving eyes, I shared my tales of North Carolina and the pride of a dream finally realized. They listened in awe.

The words of Billy Hutchins, however, were already haunting me, and it wasn't long before the shoe box from the hallway closet called out to me again. I grabbed the letter I'd received from Dewey years earlier and brought it out to the deck.

Dewey and I had grown up together and were best friends since childhood. When I got his letter, it had been seven years since we'd talked. I remember thinking it was odd that he'd send a letter and not just call.

> Dear Don,
>
> I'm sure this letter may come as a bit of a shock to you. I realize it's been so long that even the craftiest excuse won't do. So I'll save it, grateful that there's never been a need for excuses or apologies between us. Consider yourself my New Year's resolution and trust that I forgive you for not writing...
>
> Kidding aside, I hope that you, Bella and Riley had your typical Christmas. Trust me, it's not the same outside of New England. The shallow pond I now

call home wouldn't know the difference between mistletoe and marijuana. It has its good points, I suppose. Even though Los Angeles is the land of the fake and superficial, all in all, it was a fine holiday; everything we ever dreamed for as kids – top-shelf liquor, good food, stimulating conversation and enough beautiful women to make even Santa forget his hectic schedule.

In any event, if I ever learned anything from you, Don, it's that truth has many perspectives. So, I'm looking for a different perspective from one of the few people in the world who truly knows me. The crystal on my moral compass is fogged from anger and bitterness, and I have some very important decisions to make that will affect many lives. But I don't have the slightest idea what to do. There are two options, and no matter how frantically I search for a third, I don't see it.

Two years ago, I met an attractive woman through some mutual friends. Her name was Maria and she was gorgeous. She was also enslaved by her career, but spent most of her off-hours avoiding a violent ex-husband. All this baggage aside, we hit it off right away and began dating exclusively.

Three weeks in, Maria called me and told me she was "late." I gave the only response I could. "Don't worry about it. I'll push the dinner reservations up to eight o'clock. Not a problem." She began crying and within seconds, I felt sick. We weren't going to dinner at all. We were going to have a baby. God, I thought, I'm going to have a baby with a woman I hardly know. I was terrified!

Maria and I talked for weeks, but there was really nothing to talk about. Accident or no accident, the baby was on its way. I broke up my home and moved in with her.

To make a very long story short, it didn't take long for me to realize that Maria was psychotic and we could barely stand to be around each other. I slept on the couch and spent all of the time I could away from the house.

Then I fell in love! Cameron Alexander was born at an even eight pounds, with light hair and blue eyes. For three days, it was a happy time. But Maria decided to breastfeed, so the doctors wouldn't prescribe meds for her mental turmoil.

Still, I chose to stay and take responsibility for my actions. I needed to insure there would be no regrets later on. Don, I tried harder with this woman than anyone else I've ever been with. It was a futile attempt. She's a bona fide fruitcake!

After lots of accusations, several domestic disputes and one conversation with the police, I moved out. I set up temporary camp at a friend's home, sent weekly support checks and even visited with Cameron for three consecutive weeks. The first road sign to hell popped up when I dropped Cameron off and Maria questioned, "Where did the bruises on his legs come from?" I felt sick. The real cruelty had begun.

Since last seeing Cameron, my attorney has advised me to lay low and let Maria's rage enter into a calmer state. Though it pains me not to see my boy, there doesn't seem to be a choice. I understand this is a long-term issue, so maybe it's the best strategy. I'm not so sure. When did the world actually decide that fathers are of less value than mothers?

So my dilemma is this: I haven't seen Cameron in eight months. So do I step into a ring, knowing I can never win, for the sake of saying that I tried? Understanding that there's no chance for an amicable resolution, do I pull on a baby until he snaps in half? Knowing I'm at the mercy of a woman who will go to any means to keep me from him, can

I live with the fact that I may never be allowed Cameron's friendship – never mind maintaining the hope of being his father?

Well, buddy, although I thank God for flight delays, my plane was just called to board so I've got to cut you off here. I'm sure you'll be relieved. It was good spending time with you in Atlanta. It really has been too long. I look forward to hearing from you.

Take care,
Dewey

P.S. One last question: I'll love Cameron every day of my life, but does it really count if he never knows it?

There was no phone number, so I sent an honest reply to the return address. Basically, I told him:

I can't believe it's been seven years since we last spoke and only you could manage to find this path to travel down. There is only ONE option. How 'bout you dig your head out of your backside, do the right thing and think about your kid before yourself? You're probably just suffering from the proverbial mid-life crisis, Johnny Appleseed. Do whatever you must to stay in your son's life. He only has one dad.

As I recall, I closed with, "Let's not wait so long before we hear from each other again." But I never heard from the jackass again. I saw his dad a year or so later and learned that Dewey "did not appreciate the advice." I remember thinking, *Too damn bad*. From then on, our friendship had become estranged.

~ ~ ~ ~ ~ ~ ~ ~ ~ ~ ~ ~

I sat on the deck for a long while with the letter in my lap, thinking about Dewey. I also thought about how I didn't make peace with my father before he passed and how it had haunted me ever since. *It was Dewey's fault we parted ways*, I told myself. But when you got right down to it, it didn't matter who owned the blame. No matter how difficult it was going to be to face him, I decided not to give Dewey the same guilty gift my father had given me. It was time to make peace. *Forgiveness has to be more important than pride*, I thought, and told Bella so.

"That's a great idea," she said, "I bet it'll be like you two never parted ways."

"I doubt that," I said.

"Wanna bet?"

"A dozen clam cakes at Flo's," I said and we shook on it.

After keeping my uneventful appointment with Dr. Rice, one phone call to Dewey's cousin confirmed that he now lived just outside of Chicago. I jumped back on the Internet to earn us a few more frequent flyer miles.

I took one look at the puzzle on the dining room table and snickered. *Looks like you're going to have to wait.* I grabbed Bella's hand, and we were off and running again.

~ ~ ~ ~ ~ ~ ~ ~ ~ ~ ~

When we got to Dewey's front door, I was surprised to find the lack of grandeur I'd imagined. My childhood friend hadn't made the money I'd expected him to. I was also surprised to feel as nervous as I was. I suppose I could have blamed the queasiness on the cancer that grew inside me, but I knew better. Wobbly knees weren't a symptom of my illness. I rang the doorbell, looked at my wife and took a deep breath. We waited.

The door slowly opened and the old friend I'd expected to be standing there was nowhere in sight. Instead, an old decrepit fellow appeared in the threshold, hunched over and in obvious pain. I searched his face and gasped. *It's Dewey.* He was still heavy, but this time it wasn't from food. He was swollen; sick and swollen – especially his bottom lip. *Oh, God,* I thought and felt a sudden pang of guilt for missing out on his obvious struggles.

"Yes?" he asked. "What can I…" He paused and studied my face. "Don?" he asked, and his eyes immediately showed signs of disgust.

I was taken aback and skipped a breath or two. As I stood there, frozen, Bella stepped forward and extended her hand. "Hi, Dewey. It's Bella." She glanced over at me. "Don and I traveled a long way to come see you."

He nodded at her, but turned his gaze back to me. His face remained stoic, though I knew he was anything but happy with our unannounced visit. After an awkward moment standing in his threshold, he took a step back and turned sideways. "Alright, come in," he said.

I'd be lying to say it was easy to step into that house. *This was a big mistake*, I thought, and brushed past him as he closed the door behind us. This wasn't going to be easy and I could feel it. Any wrongs that occurred between us were not yet forgiven – or forgotten.

Taking the lead, Dewey escorted us into his humble living room. There, seated on the sofa, was a young man who Dewey reluctantly introduced. "This is Cameron, my son," he said.

I nodded, thinking, *Dewey did the right thing, after all*. "Nice to meet you," Bella and I said in unison. We shook hands with the young man, as we joined him on the couch.

There was an awkward pause, when Dewey told his son, "This is Don DiMarco and his wife, Bella." He shrugged, adding, "We were friends…once."

A sharp pain shot through my upper abdomen, but I never let on. Again, I wasn't convinced it was from the cancer. Bella grabbed my hand and squeezed it. We both knew that she'd just lost a dozen clam cakes.

Cameron politely excused himself. He obviously did not want to witness any of this. As he walked away, I envied him. Don took a seat in his worn recliner and I wondered whether the ridiculous distance between us was too great to overcome.

After an obligatory offer of food and drink – which Bella and I both declined – Dewey cut right to the chase. "Why are you here, Don?" he asked.

I didn't know what to expect by coming here, but it wasn't this. I swallowed hard. Although Bella didn't say anything, she gave my hand another squeeze – clearly trying to transfer some of her strength over to me. "To make peace," I said. "Dewey, listen. I've come to say I'm sorry for..."

"Peace?" he interrupted, with a snicker. "Why now?"

"Because it's been too long," I told him, my tone growing in volume. *It was your damned fault we went our separate ways*, I yelled in my mind. As he shook his head, I still chose logic and added, "Because you and I have been friends since we were kids and life's too short to hold grudges." My body tensed with equal amounts of anxiety and a growing anger.

He shook his head again. "There was a time when I needed you, Don, but you..."

"But I didn't tell you what you wanted to hear," I interrupted. "Right?" I shook my head. "You were looking for an easy out and I wouldn't give it to you, right?"

He stared at me hard, with hate in his eyes. If it had been decades earlier, we would have been throwing punches right there and then – and we both knew it.

I turned to Bella and half-shrugged. "I tried," I said and started to get up. "Let's go home."

Bella nodded and began to push herself up from the couch.

The look in Dewey's eyes instantly changed. "Wait a minute!" he said, his voice rising an octave. "You're right." He stared at me again, collecting his thoughts.

"If you leave now, we'll never see each other again," he said. As Bella and I sunk back into the couch, he slowly extended his hand. "I'm sorry, too."

I took his hand in mine and shook it hard. Every bad feeling that I'd just experienced was instantly replaced by a sense of gratitude for having finally made the trip. "Okay then," I said.

"Okay then," he repeated, offering his first smile.

While Bella squeezed my hand again – trying to reclaim her clam cakes – I used my other hand to point to his lip. "What the hell happened?" I asked.

He half-chuckled and rolled his eyes. "I got on the morphine and wanted to see how powerful it was, so I started chewing on my lip and couldn't feel a thing." He shrugged. "I guess I should have stopped long before I did."

His slurring dialect was tough to understand, but I was all ears. "Yeah, you probably should've," I kidded him. "But why the morphine?"

"Let me get you a cold drink," he said. "This may take a while."

We all carry our own cross, I thought.

~ ~ ~ ~ ~ ~ ~ ~ ~ ~ ~ ~

Upon his return, Dewey handed us our drinks and began to explain, "A while back, life seemed too good to be true...and it was." He shook his head. "It was July. I was in the company warehouse, horsing around with a few of the guys when I tripped over a box. As I went down, I braced my fall against a wooden shelf that held some cleaning supplies. I fell hard, but my left hand prevented me from going to the floor. If I hadn't braced myself, I would have landed head first. I kept thinking how lucky I was – idiot! Right away, my hand and wrist began to swell and it was painful. *Damn*, I thought, *I've got a sprained wrist*. I actually had to remove my watch because of the swelling.

"Two weeks to the day of the initial sprain, I awoke to find my left hand so swollen that it didn't even look human. The pain was incredible. I mean, I honestly can't even explain the pain, except to say that I felt like my skin was on fire. I couldn't bear my own wedding ring. The only way to get it off would have been to cut it, and that wasn't an option. I woke Maureen, my new wife, and showed her. She couldn't believe it. We both thought I must have broken a bone in my hand. I had never gone to the doctor for the sprain. I mean…it was only a sprain. Now, I was thinking I probably should have gone because something wasn't right. The pain was mind numbing. I couldn't think of anything else. It just took over everything – my body, my mind.

"I called my doctor's office and was told he couldn't see me until October, three months away. I wasn't surprised. This guy was good, but he was affiliated with a pool of doctors that had sold out to the HMOs. The minimum wait to see him was usually a month. I explained to the receptionist about my hand and she told me to go to a walk-in clinic that picked up the overflow of people like me who needed a doctor and couldn't get an appointment.

"To make a really long story short, after months of visits with my primary doctor, who referred me to one specialist after another, I was diagnosed with Reflex

Sympathetic Dystrophy, or RSD, a very rare disease which prevents a person from healing properly. Basically, the brain continues to send messages to the body that a certain area needs to be healed when it doesn't." Dewey mentioned the technical terms, but I had a hard time following him.

Most of it didn't make sense to me – the brain wave patterns, nerve dysfunction, and things like that. I had no idea what to say.

"Some say that the pain's worst than having cancer," he added.

Out of the corner of my eye, I saw Bella flinch. I never moved an inch. "Is that right?" I managed.

He nodded. "I can't even explain the constant pain," he said. "It's agonizing…and it's changed my life."

I reached over to hug Dewey but stopped. I didn't want to cause my old friend any more pain.

"It's okay," he said. "The morphine pump they put in my back has been working well."

We hugged.

After a moment, Dewey chuckled, cynically.

"What is it?" I asked.

"Who would have guessed that all this pain – even my death – would be caused by three brutal letters?"

"RSD?" I asked.

"No. HMO."

I nodded. *You're not alone*, I thought, *we're all dying*. But I never told him about the blood in my stool, the random vomiting, the sharp abdominal pains that often bent me in half and the debilitating fatigue. And from the look I shot Bella, she wasn't going to tell him, either.

As we waited for Maureen to come home, Dewey asked, "By the way, when did you get so serious?"

"Huh?"

He chuckled. "The Don DiMarco I remember had everyone in stitches. That's always been your gift." His eyes drifted off to a kinder time. "I always swore I'd see you on The Tonight Show making the whole country laugh."

Bella nodded. "I agree," she said.

"You never know," I told them both. "It ain't over yet."

~ ~ ~ ~ ~ ~ ~ ~ ~ ~ ~ ~

We ate a nice meal, the five of us, before bidding our farewell. I was still missing Riley and the kids from the Charlotte trip.

At the door, I shook his hand one last time. "Dewey, again, I'm sorry for…"

"Knock it off," he interrupted. "It's already forgotten. I was stupid." He shook his head. "There were so many times I wanted to call you but didn't." He grinned. "But we're here now, right?"

"Right!"

"Well, it doesn't look like we have another fifteen years," Dewey said. "What do you say we get together same time next year? I'll even head out your way next time."

"Sounds great," I told him and never once considered telling him I was the one who probably wasn't going to be around. "Let's do it, buddy," I said, concealing the fact I was ready to collapse from exhaustion.

He turned to Bella. "Will you make sure for me?" he asked.

She kissed him on the cheek. "I will," she promised.

Chapter 9

I missed the puzzle and if we were going to finish it, we needed to get moving. As I worked, Madison and Pudge looked on and listened to my history lesson. "The first puzzle was made in the mid-seventeen hundreds by a London engraver and mapmaker," I explained. "He mounted one of his maps on a sheet of wood and cut around the borders of the countries using a sharp saw."

Madison looked as though she understood. Pudge was already lost.

"Puzzles were designed to teach British children geography. Toward the end of the century, drawings were glued on the front of the wood, while a pencil traced where the cuts should be made on the back. Cardboard puzzles came next, like a giant cookie-cutter that made complicated patterns."

She nodded.

"But the wooden puzzles stayed more popular than the cheap cardboard puzzles. By the early nineteen hundreds, many were pictures of scenery, trains and ships. Before long, puzzles became harder and adults began doing them as much as the kids. They were even used as advertisement and given away with toothbrushes." I looked up. Madison was still with me. Pudge was in Never Land. "During the Great Depression when no one had any money, puzzles bought a whole lot of entertainment for a small price. It could be done by one person or a group, and would occupy hours. And they could be recycled. They could be broken apart and put back together by someone else."

"But why do you like to do them so much, Poppa?" Madison asked.

"Because they're more fun than watching TV." I gave her a wink. "And if they're addictive, they're as harmless as stealing one of your grandma's cookies."

She giggled and nearly woke Pudge from his daydream.

As we talked about everything and nothing at all, Pudge eventually returned to the present and said, "I wanna be like my friend, Brian Andrade. He's not afraid of nothin'!"

"I doubt that's true, Pudge," I told him. "Besides, you know there's nobody else like you, so why would you want to be like anyone else?"

"Because we're supposed to try out for the play at school and…"

"And?" I abandoned the puzzle and looked him in the eye.

"And part of me wants to do it, but part of me's too scared."

"Everyone's afraid of something."

"You're not," he blurted and said it with such conviction that I almost believed him.

"Are you kidding? I've been afraid of things my whole life. Everyone is. The question is whether or not you can be brave enough to stand up to your fears." I looked at them both. "Don't ever let any of your decisions be driven by fear." My mind quickly flashed pictures of Vietnam and facing my estranged friend, Dewey, and I nodded with conviction.

"What are you afraid of?" he asked, challenging me.

I didn't hesitate and went down the only path I've ever traveled with the kids – honesty. "I always wanted to try stand-up comedy, but never had the guts," I admitted and thought for a moment, remembering my wise mother's words: "Encourage someone and they'll be grateful. Inspire them and they'll never forget." It wasn't on the honey do list, but I figured, *what the hell?* I peered into Pudge's innocent eyes. "I'll tell you what – why don't you and I make a deal. If I can get on stage and try stand up comedy, then you can try out for the play. What do you say? Is it a deal?"

"It's a deal."

As I wondered what I'd just gotten myself into, we shook on it. "Sometimes, you have to stand up, Pudge. Courage is one of the few things you can fake in life and get away with. Even if you don't feel brave, just act like you do and the rest of the world won't know the difference."

They both nodded. "And that's not all," Pudge said.

I awaited an explanation.

Madison jumped in, saying, "And leave more than what you take, right, Poppa?"

"That's right," I said. "See…you've both been listening."

~ ~ ~ ~ ~ ~ ~ ~ ~ ~ ~ ~

The bet haunted me right away and I told Bella about it. She laughed so hard I thought she was going to blow a gasket. "You really are pulling out all the stops, aren't you?"

I smiled, thinking, *Public speaking is feared more than death. If I can overcome that, then cancer should be no big deal.* "I figure it's time to overcome something I've feared my whole life. No regrets, remember?"

"I know," she said, "no regrets." She hugged me and I watched as a mischievous grin forced its way into the corners of her mouth. "But this one's not on the list, either," she teased, "and you only have one item checked off so far."

I thought about the little voice inside my head – or heart – that was constantly telling me to *hurry up with the list*, but I decided to ignore it. "I know," I told Bella, "but this may be bigger than anything on that list."

Grinning, she gave me another hug. "Relax, funny man. I know. I'm just teasing you."

~ ~ ~ ~ ~ ~ ~ ~ ~ ~ ~ ~

The next day, I was sitting on the toilet – going another round with the constipation – when Bella barged in with the telephone in one hand and a slip of paper in the other. "You're on Wednesday night," she announced, "open mic." She smiled at me. "I'm on the phone right now with John, the booker at Stitches Comedy Cafe."

"What?" I asked in the loudest whisper I could.

"Yep, he'll be there," she said to John and walked out of the bathroom to leave me alone with my panic. For the first time in a long time, I had a chance of depositing something into the porcelain bowl.

~ ~ ~ ~ ~ ~ ~ ~ ~ ~ ~ ~

The moments leading up to Wednesday night lasted an eternity. I wrote some jokes, rehearsed them, then wrote more and rehearsed them, too. I had to scrap my fat jokes about myself because they no longer applied. I memorized and paced, memorized and paced. A few times, I even dry-heaved, imagining a crowd of strangers staring at me like I was stupid – and not being all that far from the truth. That was the thing; the more I tried to visualize myself succeeding on stage, the more I could see an embarrassing failure awaiting me.

Though they begged, I pleaded just as hard with Riley and Michael to miss my first performance. They reluctantly agreed, as long as they could "sit in the front row for the second show."

~ ~ ~ ~ ~ ~ ~ ~ ~ ~ ~ ~

Bella drove, while I pretended to study the cheat sheet of jokes on my lap. It was unseasonably warm out, but not nearly warm enough to produce the giant sweat rings that grew under my armpits. A few miles up the road, my forehead began dripping onto the page of jokes, smearing a few of the unproven punch lines.

"Relax," she said, "You know the material inside and out. You're going to do great."

I understood what she was saying, but she had no idea of the powerful storm raging inside me. My heart was pounding so hard I couldn't hear myself think, never mind read. My breathing felt short and labored, and I was drenched in sweat.

She looked over at me and smiled. "We've arrived."

~ ~ ~ ~ ~ ~ ~ ~ ~ ~ ~ ~

Though it didn't make me feel as good as I'd hoped, the place was almost empty. It made sense. It was an open mic on a Wednesday night, promising a handful of amateurs and even fewer laughs. Bella and I searched out John, the booker. He was seated at the bar with a checklist in hand. "You're going on fourth," he told me and looked up from his clipboard. "Relax. You'll be fine."

I have no idea who the three were who went before me, or how they did but I'll never forget the moment the host grabbed the mic and announced, "Now let's give a round of applause for another first-timer, Don DiMarco."

Bella rubbed my back for luck, two-dozen people began to clap and a bolt of terror struck my heart. *You went to 'Nam*, I told myself and willed my legs to move toward the stage. *You can do this!* With a racing heart and a cotton mouth, I climbed the three giant stairs that led to the stage, grabbed the microphone from the stand, wiped my arm across my forehead and faced the crowd. A bright obnoxious light blinded me and I couldn't see a thing. It was the most beautiful light in the world. I took a deep breath and couldn't believe when the first few words came out of my mouth. "Believe it or not, I actually learned about the birds and the bees from watching two dogs go at it," I said. "I was no more than eight, sitting in the backseat of my father's Cadillac, second-hand smoking a pack of Pall

Malls when two dogs, locked together, hobbled out in front of our car – the male stuck in the backside of the female. My dad looked into the rear-view mirror and smiled. 'The ol' boy ran out of gas,' he said. 'She's just towing him home.'

No one laughed. My pulse quickened even more. *Come on, folks*, I thought, *I'm seconds away from a stroke up here.*

I gave a fake chuckle. "I swear my childhood was like the deleted scenes from the movie, *Deliverance*." In a business where some type of reaction is absolutely necessary to press on, silence killed quicker than colon cancer. I swore I could hear crickets in the back of the room. I kept going, trying not to rush off the stage. "Life's all about choices, isn't it? I recently had to make a difficult choice – get rid of the cigarettes, or kick the heroin. Quitting smoking isn't easy. I had no choice, though. It was slowing me down on my paper route."

Some guy in the back laughed. I wondered if it was from another joke he'd heard.

"They had to fit me with a nicotine vest, 500 milligrams coursing through my body."

Silence.

As if I were trying to defend my dignity in a dunce cap, I told a few more bad jokes and actually finished with, "Goodnight, folks. You've been great," thinking, *I guess that's what happens when you memorize everything.*

Dripping sweat, I walked off the stage and straight into Bella's open arms. I totally bombed and couldn't have been happier for it. *I did it!* I'd faced the monster, and though it wasn't pretty, I'd survived. When we broke the embrace, I looked up to find her crying. "That bad?" I asked.

She shook her head, but said nothing.

I grabbed her hand. "What is it, hon?"

"I'm just proud of you, is all," she said, but we'd been together too long to pull off even the kindest fib. They were tears of sorrow. Even though there were still moments when I forgot I was dying, the truth of it lived with Bella every minute of the day.

"Oh, babe," I said and held her hands tight.

"Tough crowd tonight," I heard John say behind me, interrupting our moment. "Want to try it again next week?"

Without even thinking, I nodded. "Sure. Why not."

Bella discreetly wiped her eyes and shook her head. "Great. Another week of torture," she teased.

I kissed her, and thought, *Fear can be so damned exhilarating!*

~ ~ ~ ~ ~ ~ ~ ~ ~ ~ ~ ~

The following week, Riley and Michael hurried into the joint for a table up front. I walked in smiling, took one look around and felt like vomiting. *Oh God*, I thought. *This isn't last week. Now it's real.* There were a hundred people in the audience. I'd be lying if I didn't admit that I wanted to walk out of the place and apologize to my family on the long ride home. *But Pudge will be unbearable to face*, I knew, *and he's going to face at least this many people for his play. Granted, it'll be an easier crowd than this, but he's only five.* When I did the math, it seemed like a fair deal. My own words came back to bite me:

"All you have to do sometimes is stand up. Courage is one of the few things you can fake in life and get away with. Even if you don't feel brave, just act like you do and the rest of the world won't know the difference." I took a deep breath and joined my family at the table up front.

Bella took my sweaty hand in hers and tried to soothe me. "You're gonna be great tonight," she promised.

I looked at Riley and Michael. They were nodding in agreement. I felt like crawling out of my skin.

It was the same torment while waiting. It was the same blinding light once I'd coaxed my legs onto the stage. I even told a few of the same jokes that had bombed, adding, "Have you ever wondered at what point in people's lives they decide to give up on dental hygiene?"

A hush ran over the crowd. They were with me, waiting for the payoff.

"Seriously," I said, "on what day do you wake up and say, 'You know what, I'm never brushing my teeth again – ever!'

Two people chuckled – I think.

"Well, let me tell you. For me, that day's today."

The same people laughed.

"My Nana, God rest her soul, suffered from this lazy affliction. Before she passed on, we gave her the nickname Summer Tooth." Again, I tried to time the pause. "Some 'er green, some 'er black and some 'er missing." I shrugged. "It was so bad that pudding became a challenge."

The two drunkest people in the place laughed before I was escorted back to my table by my family's applause. The rest of the audience remained quiet.

Bella stood to kiss me, Riley's eyes were swollen from crying, and Michael shook my hand. "That took real guts," he said.

I felt like I was in shock. From the moment we'd arrived, I just wanted to get up there, deliver my lines and get off. The laughs didn't matter all that much – which was a good thing. If I'd learned anything from my recent cooking class, the real value was in the effort – not the outcome. *But why do I have to suffer each time I go up?* I wondered. *Why can't I just remember that it's not so bad getting up there?*

One of the other comedians came over to the table. "Don't sweat it. Tough crowd tonight," he said.

"That's what they told me last week," I replied, still dazed from the experience.

He laughed. "Now that's funny," he said.

"How long you been at this?" I asked.

"About a year."

"So when does it get comfortable?"

He looked at me and grinned.

"You know…at what point does the fear leave you?" I clarified.

He laughed again. "As far as I know, it never goes away. But that's the reason we get up there and do it, right? To feel alive."

His name was Smokin' Joe Holden. I asked him to join us at the table and he did. We were the two oldest guys in the place, so we hit it off right away. He explained, "My daughter was going to have a baby and

I was going to be a grandfather at forty-one years old. I thought – my life is half over. If I don't do it now, I'll never do it. I was working two jobs that weren't making me happy. I eventually talked to a friend. 'What do you want?' he asked. 'To be a stand up comic,' I told him. 'Then do it. Do what makes you happy. If you get paid for it, even better.' Today, if only for my twenty minute set, I'm living my dream by making people forget their problems."

"That's great," I said.

"So why are you putting yourself through all this?" he asked.

Everyone at the table tensed. I quickly broke the tension. "Very similar reasons, my friend."

He nodded once, but as he excused himself he leaned into my ear. "I do a set every Sunday over at the Gazebo Room. Why don't you join me? It's a good audience. Most of the comics I know try out all their new material there." He handed me his business card. "Give me a call, if you're interested."

"I will. Thanks."

Riley held my hand all the way to the parking garage. "You just wait til I tell Pudge what his Poppa did tonight!"

A giant lump formed in the base of my throat. *I can't believe that I actually considered escaping*, I thought.

~ ~ ~ ~ ~ ~ ~ ~ ~ ~ ~ ~

Over the next few weeks, Joe brought me to a few different clubs. One was a bachelor party where no one listened to a single joke. At a different club, I asked to do a ten-minute set. The booker laughed. "What do you want to do, cut your own album tonight?" he asked. I got the standard four minutes.

The vast majority of my stuff bombed, but I was more interested in facing the fear and overcoming it. To me, the lonely stage was the perfect place for me to grow as a human being.

I suppose I started to show some real signs of pain and fatigue when Riley expressed her concerns. "Maybe you should slow down a bit and take better care of yourself, Dad?"

"I can't, sweetie," I told her. "For the first time in my life, I'm living."

~ ~ ~ ~ ~ ~ ~ ~ ~ ~ ~ ~

Right around that time, as a gesture of kindness from a few talented comedians, I was invited to the big dance. It was a charity fundraiser, with eleven other comics, a few of them national headliners.

A crowd of three hundred and fifty had gathered in the large, smoke-filled room, while I stood trembling at the bar awaiting my turn to take the stage and make the audience squeal with laughter. Smokin' Joe was the host of the night and opened up with a hilarious fifteen-minute set. He poked fun at everything from his strong New York accent to his first prostate exam. "And have you heard about this new Viagra for women?" He shook his head and twisted up his face. "Not for my ol' lady. That's like lighting a single match stick to a block of ice."

With each laugh, the crowd loosened up. My heart pounded out of my chest and my shirt was already drenched in rings of sweat. Bella kept looking at me, smiling.

Steph Collura went on next and she was non-stop funny. From her weight problem to her daily difficulties with marriage, she reminded the audience of how important it was to laugh at themselves.

As if I were watching the night from a distant window, everything felt surreal. I kept scanning the crowd. *There are three hundred and fifty people here*, I thought. *And you're afraid to speak in public. What are you – insane?*

Bella threw me a thumbs-up and mouthed the words, "I love you." Riley and Michael were beaming with pride.

Tony G., the Italian Don Rickles, took the stage next and from the moment he grabbed the mic, no one was safe. He rolled over the crowd like a thunderstorm. By the time anyone knew what had hit them, the after effects were nothing but laughter and people holding their sides in pain. He was a real pro.

Oh God, I kept repeating in my head and honestly thought I was going to pass out.

Christian Shaw took the stage, pointing out that he was the only black man in the joint. Everyone laughed. Reminiscent of a young Chris Rock, Shaw's style of comedy was smooth one minute and physical the next.

Jay "Dunny" Donovan grabbed the mic. This thirteen-year veteran of stand up had commuted from Boston and had the accent to prove it. A regular at Nick's Comedy Stop, he'd also honed his craft at different clubs in New York. In the end, he finished with an impression of an inebriated SpongeBob Square Pants and left the stage to a roaring applause.

"And let's welcome our newcomer for the night, Don DiMarco," Smokin' Joe announced.

I don't know how I did it, but I forced my legs up the stairs to the stage and grabbed the microphone. It's hard to explain, but at that moment I felt like I'd been doing stand-up comedy for years. "I broke down on the way over here," I said and paused.

The enormous crowd waited.

"My car's fine. It's just that the song *Wind Beneath My Wings* came on the radio and I couldn't take it. I had to pull over to the side of the road and have myself a good cry."

In the rear of the audience, like an angel sent from heaven, some lady burst out laughing. Unfortunately, her laughter was anything but contagious. Although I tried to will myself to enjoy the set, by the second joke, I was already babbling like a drunken auctioneer. "This stand-up...comedy thing...is all new to me," I stuttered, "I'll try anything, I guess. I raised hamsters...for a while. To be honest, they're tough to herd. And...they kind of freak me out." I paused, wiping the sweat that poured from my brow. "Did you know that the harder you squeeze their bellies, the more their eyes bulge?"

A few guys standing at the bar began laughing. I quickly looked over. They were talking amongst themselves. I soldiered on.

"My kids – no matter how much I tried to get rid of them, they always followed the car home. Seriously, though, being a parent isn't easy, is it? I remember when my son, Robby, was at that young age where he could be very inconsiderate of other people. One night, we were enjoying a picnic at a rest area just off the highway when he decided to devour a bag of cheese puffs all by himself. It was dark, he was tired and with the orange powder completely covering his fingers, he mistook his thumb for a cheese puff. One chomp later, he let out a howl that had two dozen sweaty men running out of the woods." I shook my head. "I swear that boy has no respect for the privacy of others."

There was awkward laughter – people trying to be kind.

"And the little bugger had a bad habit of picking his nose. 'Stop eating sweets,' I'd tell him, 'you're going to rot out your teeth.'" I offered another head shake. "Tastes like candy, but *it's snot*." I counted three full seconds. "Poor kid. It wasn't his fault he was so slow. When he was young, he was drinking from the toilet when he split his head open and suffered some pretty serious brain damage. It was so bad we had to have a plate put in his head. The wife and I couldn't afford metal, so the doctors went with a paper plate." I shrugged. "I don't think it worked the same. Every time we went swimming, the plate got wet and Robby started talking with a lisp."

There was less laughter.

"He was the first boy in his high school's history to play field hockey. His junior year, the season was going great until some of the guys on the football team confused his plaid skirt for a license to abuse him." I shook my head again and put on a sad face. "That's all I have to say about that."

After another impregnated pause, I said, "Thankfully, his college years proved less violent. He was playing badminton on a full scholarship. Plagued with injuries all season, he was in a real heated match when he lost the shuttlecock in the sun. All of a sudden – SMACK – it hit him right between the eyes! He was out cold, out of a scholarship and his dreams of playing professionally were gone forever."

I paused to take a sip of water and listened as private conversations began to pop up at different tables. I quickly looked at my watch. *One minute to go…thank God!*

"Recently, for my fiftieth birthday, Robby rented me a stripper dressed in a Western getup. I'll never forget that night. I felt so embarrassed. Robby said he wished he could have afforded a female stripper, but money was tight."

I scanned the crowd. Most everyone – except my family – had given up on me. They were smiling, laughing and enjoying my set, as though they didn't realize I was bombing terribly. With a grin, I winked at them.

"Before I get kicked out of here, let me share a story that might help some of you folks. Last year, I was out doing some Christmas shoplifting when a junkie wielding a knife assaulted me. For anybody who's ever been mugged, you know what a terrifying experience that can be."

The same guys at the bar laughed, their backs now turned to me. *Your timing's off, fellas*, I joked with myself.

"I suppose I was lucky, though. It was a butter knife." I shook my head one last time. "He must have carved for three solid minutes before he broke the skin."

As I started to place the microphone back into the stand, my family's table erupted with applause. A few of the tables around them followed suit. I paused and put it back to my mouth. "Thank you," I told them, though I doubt anyone but Bella, Riley and Michael would have known what I meant. I looked over to see them wiping tears. I wished they were tears from laughing so hard, but I knew better. I rushed over to them.

Ed Glavin wrapped up the night. From the time he appeared, his comical presence hypnotized the crowd with everything from impressions to props. He also quelled the ignorance of a heckler like a lion tamer at the circus. "Can you buy men's clothes where you got that shirt?" he asked, but the man never answered. And the punk never opened his mouth again. I wish I could have enjoyed it, but my head was still spinning.

Glavin got off the stage and walked right over to our table. He pointed to me. "You've got big ones," he told me.

"Thanks," I told him. "It means more than you know."

"No problem. I'll see you at the next show."

"Not likely," I said. "Tonight's my last night. I'm retiring early."

He shrugged. "Well, for whatever it's worth, you gave it a real shot, and that takes big ones!"

I thanked him again and got up from the table to walk away from the shortest, craziest life I'd ever known. As we walked to the car, I pictured Dewey's swollen face and laughed to myself. *So much for the To-night Show*, I thought, but I didn't take three more steps before I decided, *But it really doesn't matter. It's all about the experiences in life…not the successes.*

~ ~ ~ ~ ~ ~ ~ ~ ~ ~ ~ ~

A few anxious nights later, I sat in a packed auditorium and watched my courageous grandson deliver his lines like a pro.

When the cast took their final bow, Pudge looked me straight in the eye and smiled. There was no need to say anything. The tears in my eyes were filled with pride. We both understood what it had taken. Through all the doubts, past all the nerves – he'd stood up, too.

Chapter 10

The first red and orange leaves began to appear and an early autumn was upon us. Fall had always been my favorite season, but this year it arrived as a brutal reminder of the few moments I had left. Cancer symptoms aside, I was chomping at the bit to get back to the honey do list, and I told Bella so.

My appointment with Dr. Rice was spent playing hit or miss with new medications – a cocktail of pills – to combat constipation, fatigue and nausea, along with all the side effects of the pills themselves. It was a cruel juggling act, but I was grateful she was right there to help me keep the balls in the air for a little while longer.

After taking the grandkids to watch my beloved Red Sox get obliterated by the Baltimore Orioles, I returned to my masterpiece. I had to laugh. Like a shoe-making elf, Bella was pushing my next dream hard. A handful of brochures had magically appeared on the puzzle table, along with a Post-it note: "I'm coming with you this time." With a smile, I began skimming through them. They were for dude ranches located in Arizona. *A childhood fantasy of being a cowboy, an adulthood of loving the music and the idea of sleeping under a sky that never ended – all encouraged by my love of Louis L'Amour books,* I thought. *It can now come true.* As I read the pamphlets, I wondered what I'd look like in cowboy boots and a real Stetson hat.

The first ad read, "Experience the Old West! This historic ranch, founded in the early nineteen hundreds, is one of today's premier guest ranch resorts. The beautiful window to our western past will build memories for a lifetime."

The second was equally appealing. "Guest ranches, or dude ranches as they are more commonly known, have been around since the late eighteen hundreds, offering a glimpse into the past and a haven for relaxation. Welcome to one of Arizona's most authentic ranches."

The last, however, was the keeper. "Guest ranches in Arizona are a glimpse into the past, but with all the modern amenities. These might include a day trip to the Grand Canyon, fishing on the Colorado River, visiting a local ghost town, or getting your kicks on Route 66. Our charming, informal ranch gives you a feeling of the Old West. Whether you are busy all the time or just want to take it a little easier, your time here will be a vacation free of crowds, lines and stress. We guarantee you will know everyone within hours."

The brochures were nice, but it was time to live the experiences rather than read about them – as I had my whole life. "Isn't it going to be too hot this time of year in Arizona?" I joked with her.

"But it's a dry heat," Bella countered.

"An oven is a dry heat, too…right?"

She laughed. "I can't wait!"

"Me, too!" I admitted. I checked the dates. The timing was spot on, so I booked it – a small casita with a real Mexican queen-sized bed, a fireplace and a private porch.

On the night before we left, Michael and Riley came by with a new pair of cowboy boots they'd bought for me. "We figured that you'd want to pick out your own hat," Michael said.

Once again, Riley did her best to hide her grief. This time, I let her cry into my shoulder for as long as she needed. "It's okay, babe," I told her and she let it all out.

A half hour later, I tried on the boots. They were painfully tight. "They're perfect," I lied. "Thank you."

~ ~ ~ ~ ~ ~ ~ ~ ~ ~ ~ ~

Bella and I arrived at the ranch to find a beautiful view of the mountains from all sides. Nestled amongst tall pines, juniper and mesquite, it was an inviting respite. I fell in love with the place right away. It was hot, but not nearly as uncomfortable as I thought it might be.

"Howdy, folks. Good to meet ya," Gloria said and welcomed us with a pair of strong, open arms.

We were escorted to our personal hacienda, decorated with a Southwestern flare. I placed the bags on the bed and whistled. The thick-walled adobe dwelling was an Old West postcard of charm. The room itself was just what the doctor ordered – a getaway of seclusion and solace.

Gloria caught our reaction and laughed. "How 'bout I give y'all my two-dollar tour?"

With a nod, I followed Bella out into the desert sun.

We visited the ranch's general store and met Louise. "I actually came here as a guest a few years back and loved it so much I decided to move down here and work," she said.

"Good for you," I told her.

In the tack room just outside the stables, Gloria introduced us to one of the ranch's three wranglers. "This is Alden Marques," she said. "We call him Al."

The man was a true cowboy. He dressed the part and looked as tough as rawhide. When he spoke, though, it was easy to pick up on his softer side. "Pleased to meet you both," he said in little more than a whisper and shook our hands.

I couldn't help but pick up on his melancholy disposition.

As we walked out, Gloria whispered, "As much as he fusses after the animals on the cattle drives, that sweet man wouldn't hurt a horse fly."

Bella and I exchanged a glance. She smiled.

We toured the sprawling grounds where horseshoe pits, a swimming pool and a hot tub were desolate of life. "The workers live on site," Gloria said, "and since we'll be treating you like family, I hope you'll see fit to do the same?"

"Absolutely," Bella replied.

The main lodge was separated from the kitchen and dining room by a small stone courtyard. As we stepped in, I could tell the lodge was the main focus of the dude ranch. Decorated in western décor, the giant Mohave building was where everyone gathered to talk about his or her day. A huge fireplace, surrounded by comfortable couches and chairs, created a relaxing atmosphere. There was even a stack of classic western movies on hand.

The cozy courtyard, built for outdoor dining and evening entertainment, led us into the dining room. "This is where everyone meets for breakfast at the crack of dawn, dinner at high noon, and supper when the day's chores are through – except on days when our cook, Mrs. Gomes, grills outside."

A sweet looking grandmother, dressed in a red and white checkerboard smock, was marinating some type of beef in the kitchen. As we passed by, she waved.

"There's also Paul and Lisa who live on the ranch with their daughter, Mykala. Paul does a little bit of everything, but mostly leads trail rides and works with the horses. And Lisa helps me with booking reservations, serving meals, dishwashing and some of the housekeeping. Mykala's six and she's pretty much all the inspiration we need around here. Wherever the action is, that's where you'll spot her – especially on the horseback rides."

"You've got quite a family down here," I said.

"Sure do. Y'all just wait 'til you meet Dusty. He's a real hoot. Besides making sure the ranch runs smoothly, he also does most of the singing and campfire story telling. You're gonna love him."

A border collie ran up to Bella and stood by her side, waiting to be petted. "This is Molly," Gloria said. "She tags along on all the trail rides with our yellow Lab, Bailey." She bent to rub the friendly dog's neck. "She's very playful. She'll chase a stick all day long, if you're throwing it. And she loves to swim."

"Where's Bailey?" I asked.

"Probably napping in the shade somewhere." She looked at me and winked. "Bailey's a little older and wiser than Molly here." Gloria looked up from the dog and scanned the ranch. "Except for Pumpkin, our goat, you've met just about everyone."

"What about the horses?" Bella asked.

Gloria placed her hand on my wife's shoulder. "Trust me, over the next few days you'll get to know them better than any of us."

I picked up a stick and threw it for Molly to fetch. Gloria shook her head and laughed.

~ ~ ~ ~ ~ ~ ~ ~ ~ ~ ~ ~

Below the pines, there were thousands of acres of open desert landscaped with towering saguaro cactus and desert flora. There were beautiful mountains and desert vegetation everywhere – miles of Joshua trees, ocatillos, barrel cactus and other cacti. There were no subdivisions, city skylines, or the noise and distractions that came with them.

After taking in the most gorgeous sunset I'd ever seen, we joined the other guests for our first taste of Mrs. Gomes's cooking. It wasn't the beans and pork I'd expected. Served buffet style, Mrs. Gomes put out a feast of split pea soup and vegetable-filled egg rolls, with dipping sauces. Carved roast prime rib of beef in a horseradish marinade was complemented by a steamed green bean and carrot medley. For dessert, a pastry table was set up under one of the trees. It was so good that I ate as much as I thought I could handle.

After dinner, Dusty broke out his guitar and harmonica, ready to kick up his heels and tell stories. As darkness set in, he built a marshmallow-roasting campfire and sang a few songs we knew – and many more we'd never heard. I was hypnotized by the fire and hoped it wasn't a sign of where I was heading.

Between songs, Dusty explained, "In the late eighteen hundreds, young men eager for a day's pay would join on as wranglers to drive cattle herds. They lived on the trail, sleeping and eating with the cattle. That's how they got the name cowboys."

Everyone nodded. I pulled Bella closer to me.

"And as you'll see later this week, the stories of the cowboy out on the range are tales of rugged adventure."

I gave my wife a squeeze. The dancing fire made her face look even more beautiful.

"Night," Mrs. Gomes said to everyone and excused herself at an unusually early hour.

As we enjoyed some relaxing fireside conversation with our new friends, Dusty sang two more songs before he put away his guitar. I wondered why – until we sat in silence for a few moments with nothing but the stars. I can only describe it as spiritual. Here we were – sitting with a couple dozen people we'd only just met – staring up into a twinkling sky, and I felt an incredibly close bond with each one of them. No one said a word. The peace and quiet of the beautiful night was bringing each of us back to a time that was more innocent and kind. The night brought a nip to the air, but the crackle of the fire fought it back just enough. With Bella snuggled safely in my arms, it was miraculous.

Suddenly, I was overcome with a feeling of despair. It was as if someone had thrown a wet blanket of angst and sorrow over me, completely covering me in darkness. My mind spiraled downward faster than I could control it. *I'll be gone soon. Bella will be alone. What about the kids? How can it be over for me? Dear God, how…* With every good cell left in me, I fought to push the negativity out of my head and heart. As this ruthless battle raged inside of me, Bella glanced up at me and smiled. I smiled back – and even added a wink. And as she turned back toward the fire, my mantra began. *Concentrate on the present. Just enjoy what you have left… what you have right here, right now…*

~ ~ ~ ~ ~ ~ ~ ~ ~ ~ ~ ~

The next morning, we awoke with the sun and prepared to venture out on our first trail ride. Stacks of flapjacks, bowls of steaming oatmeal with cinnamon and fresh blueberry muffins were waiting in the dining room, and I realized why Mrs. Gomes had excused herself so early.

As if she were our mom, she packed bags of beef jerky and trail mix. I felt like a kid again, heading out into the wild unknown.

Before we made it past the lodge, my new boots were killing my feet. I had to hurry back to the room and change them. "Don't you dare say anything," I told Bella.

She laughed and held up the camera. "It's not me who's going to tell."

"Just take the pictures from the waist up," I said and swallowed another pain pill.

She promised.

~ ~ ~ ~ ~ ~ ~ ~ ~ ~ ~

We got to choose, so Bella and I joined Al and Mykala in the slower group. "It'll be a slow walking ride," he promised, as we followed him down to the stables.

He looked at Bella and then at the horses. "Scout will be perfect for you," he said and led a black and white Pinto with one brown eye and one blue eye out of his stable to be saddled. Bella approached the horse and stroked his mane. They hit it off right away.

Atop a Palomino named Lucky, who had crooked hindquarters, Al looked at me with his sad eyes. "Maybe Diablo for you?" he suggested and watched my face cringe. He grinned. "I'm playing. We'll get you on Jumbo. He's an old gentleman."

"Great. Thank you."

Jumbo was a snowflake Appaloosa, weighing every bit of two thousand pounds, with a hind end the size of a billboard. I swallowed hard when I saw him.

~ ~ ~ ~ ~ ~ ~ ~ ~ ~ ~

While most of the other couples headed off for a challenging mountain ride with Paul and the dogs, Al and Mykala took Bella and me – along with two other couples: Tony and Liz, and Mark and Lynn – out on a nice easy ride. As soon as we left the corral, Lucky took the lead and was much too selfish to give it up. I quickly took notice. Al turned back and shrugged. "They're like kids," he said, "And Lucky'll turn on any one of them, if they try to take his spot."

Right from the start, Jumbo liked to stop a lot and eat, depositing just as much from the rear. Though part of me envied him, I jerked on the reins to get the gentle monster to move. Al turned back again. "Like I said, these horses are like little kids. Each horse has its own personality, its own character. They get excited, impatient…and they also try to figure out who's in control."

I pulled hard on the reins, but Jumbo just kept munching.

"Believe it or not, there's such a thing as being too gentle," Al added, "You gotta let that ol' butt biter know who's ridin' who."

So I did. I pulled as hard as my aching muscles would allow and felt the horse move under me and start clodding up the steep trail.

"That's it," Al said. "That's tellin' him."

After enjoying a long silence, Bella called out to Al. "Why are all the horses male?" she asked.

He never hesitated with his answer. "'Cause the mares can be tough…moody, if you know what I mean." He grinned. "…especially that special time of the month."

Everyone laughed.

There was nothing to see but beautiful desert scenery surrounded by three majestic mountain ranges. It felt like we were back in the untamed days of the Old West. There was a tremendous variety of desert vegetation and rock formations. Al stopped us a few times to take in the sights and smells of the open desert. "We have a few thousand acres available to us, but for today we won't venture out too far."

I kept trying to find a comfortable position in the saddle and was pleased that Jumbo didn't fuss. The old-timer turned out to be just as accommodating as Al.

We spent the morning riding out to some sandy washes. On the way, Al pointed out the local vegetation and wildlife. With the exception of two jackrabbits, one coiled snake and a family of circling vultures, the Arizona desert was barren of life. Bella kept looking up, concerned.

"They must have spotted you from the time we left," I teased her.

Al chuckled. "Not likely," he said, "but they're definitely hoping for something to lay down and die."

I had to laugh. In light of my worsening condition, Bella didn't think it was all that funny – but I did.

After washing down Mrs. Gomes's bagged lunch with a full canteen of water, we headed back to the ranch. "Before this desert sun gives those vultures what they're looking for," Al said.

No one argued – not even Mykala.

Amongst the ruggedly beautiful, wide-open land, the slow scenic ride through the Saguaro cactus challenged the cowboy in all of us. My legs ached something awful. I could hardly stand, never mind sit anymore. As we rode back, though, I became more concerned about what might be eating at Al.

~ ~ ~ ~ ~ ~ ~ ~ ~ ~ ~ ~

Two hours after we'd made it back to camp, Paul and his entourage came hooting back onto the ranch. They were covered in dirt and smiling. I looked at Bella. "That's us tomorrow," I said.

"If I can get my muscles to climb back on Scout."

We ate real mesquite barbecue on long tables with checkerboard cloths. There were ribs and chicken, pork and beans, four-alarm chili and homemade corn bread. Though I knew my stomach would toss and turn, causing me half a night of lost sleep, my taste buds won out, and I exercised my dinner muscle for a solid twenty minutes. While we ate, Paul and Al gave an impromptu class on how to groom and saddle horses, and also covered roping on a dummy cow. I snuck Molly and Bailey a few ribs.

"Don't get caught," Bella whispered.

"Why? They're not supposed to eat goat?" I quietly asked.

She looked at me, curiously.

"Well, I haven't seen Pumpkin all day, have you?"

She slapped my arm.

After chewing three antacids, I took in a game of horseshoes but decided to sit out the line dancing. I'm glad I did. Watching my beautiful wife spinning and laughing made my excruciating pains more bearable.

It was getting late when another friendly couple, Tommy and Chrissy, invited Bella and me to a poker tournament in the lodge. "Thank you, but I think we'll have to pass tonight," Bella said. Instead, we got into our swimsuits and claimed the hot tub to ease some of the saddle sores we were already feeling. Like wrinkled prunes, we held each other and soaked. I'd never seen so many stars twinkling within reach. Without ambient light, heaven looked even closer than the poker tournament.

~ ~ ~ ~ ~ ~ ~ ~ ~ ~ ~ ~

On Sunday morning, on bended knees, instead of pleading for a cure or more time, I gave thanks for all the goodness in my life. It's the strangest thing, but I felt so much better, so much closer to God by saying thank you instead of begging please.

We were served a light buffet breakfast so Mrs. Gomes could attend church. As I drank a mug of strong coffee, I scanned the mountains and sighed. *It's only been three days, but it already feels like home.*

~ ~ ~ ~ ~ ~ ~ ~ ~ ~ ~ ~

While others headed down to the stables, Bella stopped me. "I don't think my body can do it again today," she said. "If you want to go on without me, I'll…"

"Nonsense," I said, "I'm sure we'll find something else to do. Besides, the cattle drive's in two days." I thought about Dr. Rice's wise words and shrugged. "There's nothing wrong with saving our energy." I never admitted it, but I couldn't have been happier. My entire body throbbed.

As we walked back to our hacienda, I caught Bella's mischievous smile. *She knows my pain*, I decided, *and she's taking one for the team.*

Within the hour, my resourceful wife had us heading out to an old ghost town named Oatman. Even though we bounced around in the wagon, I was excited to be on the impromptu field trip.

Oatman was named in honor of Olive Oatman, a young girl kidnapped by Mojave Indians and later rescued in 1857 near the town. It served as a railway passage for two years before the tent camp evolved into a gold-mining center. In 1915, two miners struck ten million dollars in gold. By the following year, the town's population grew to more than three thousand.

Good fortune went as quickly as it came though. In 1921, a massive fire claimed the smaller shacks in town. Three years later, United Eastern Mines shut down for good. From then on, Oatman struggled to survive by tending to travelers on U.S. Route 66.

As Bella and I walked the old western town, two burros roamed the very streets where gunfights were staged on weekends. The weather was exactly as Bella had predicted – delightful, with low humidity.

We visited the Oatman Hotel. Built in 1902, it was a run-down, two-story adobe structure that had once hosted miners, movie stars and politicians. It was Clark Gable and Carol Lombard's honeymoon spot in 1939; the major attraction that still kept the hotel doors opened. "Mr. Gable returned here many times to play poker with some of the locals and enjoy the tranquility of the desert," the guide explained.

All along the wooden walks that lined the town, vendors sold handmade leather goods, Indian jewelry and knives. Bella did her usual browsing and bought a handbag for Riley before we stepped into the Mission Inn for lunch and a sweating pitcher of ice-cold lemonade.

Before we boarded the wagon heading back to the ranch, I posed in Michael and Riley's boots for a couple of full-length photos. "I can't believe you carried those all the way out here," Bella said and snapped a few more pictures.

~ ~ ~ ~ ~ ~ ~ ~ ~ ~ ~ ~

The night before the big cattle drive, Mrs. Gomes prepared a feast fit for royalty; a buffet of fried catfish, chicken fried steak, crispy ranch chicken with cranberry sauce and all the fixings. For dessert, she outdid herself with homemade cookies, warm breads and apple pie. I told Bella, "You'd better watch out. I think I'm falling in love with that woman."

Bella shoved another cookie into her mouth and laughed. "I think I am, too."

~ ~ ~ ~ ~ ~ ~ ~ ~ ~ ~ ~

No one stayed behind. Ranch hands, guests and every horse at the ranch headed out for the two-day drive. Though I worried about my physical limitations, I was confident that my cowboy spirit was going to generate enough adrenaline to get me through.

We set out at a nice easy pace, but I could tell by the way Paul and Al were riding in circles that the pace was about to pick up. It did. With both wranglers at the lead of the caravan and Mrs. Gomes's covered chuck wagon bringing up the rear, all the rest of us had to do was stay in the middle and keep up. It proved to be a grueling task, and I doubled up on the pain meds just as soon as we stopped for a drink of water.

We traveled through beautiful mountain meadows and rugged pine forests for hours without seeing another human being. Though it felt like a thousand miles, we only traveled ten the first day. The herd of cattle that had been grazing in a giant mountain pasture was patiently waiting to be shipped back to the ranch's empty corrals for branding, vaccinating and sorting. While we set up camp, Paul and Al rode out with Dusty to search for a few wanderers that had strayed from the herd. Tony, Mark and Tommy joined their flank. I was happy to stay behind and help pitch the tents.

Though we ate under the same desert sky that night, it felt different; more real. I imagined the hard men who had gone before us, driving cattle, and I realized that my childhood dream had come true. Bella was helping Mrs. Gomes dish out some biscuits and gravy, along with some beef and barley soup, when I stepped up behind her and kissed the nape of her neck.

She startled and looked back. "What was that for?" she asked with a smile.

"For continuing to make my dreams come true."

Mrs. Gomes wiped her hands on her apron and grinned. "I don't suppose my biscuits might fetch the same affection?" she asked.

I planted a big one on her cheek.

She laughed, heartily. "Y'all come and get it!" she called out.

~ ~ ~ ~ ~ ~ ~ ~ ~ ~ ~ ~ ~

The campfire burned brightly, and Dusty's stories and music were more spirited than ever. *I just hope my snoring doesn't bother any of them*, I thought. Sleep, I'd found, was the best remedy for dizzy spells and nausea.

~ ~ ~ ~ ~ ~ ~ ~ ~ ~ ~

The next morning, the aroma of bacon and eggs woke me. I gently shoved Bella. "Let's go, Annie Oakley," I told her. "We got work to do."

Everyone was gathered around the chuck wagon, talking and laughing about the day's work ahead.

"How'd you sleep last night, Don?" Mrs. Gomes asked, as she spooned some grits into my plate.

I was going to answer when Dusty said, "Like a bear."

Everyone laughed.

"I'd say it was more like three bears," Lisa added.

"I snored, huh?" I asked, thinking, *With the medication I'm on, it's a wonder I even woke up.*

"Is that what you call it?" Dusty asked. "I've been to chain saw competitions that weren't that loud."

Everyone laughed, Mykala and Bella the loudest – everyone but Al. He was sitting alone under one of the pines.

When I figured they'd given me all the ribbing I deserved, I excused myself from Bella and Mykala, and joined my lonesome friend. "What's got you so happy?" I teased him before sliding down the pine tree beside him.

He looked up and smiled. It was only out of courtesy.

"Your horse up and leave you?" I joked.

His face turned painful and I cringed. I'd said the wrong thing. "I'm sorry, Al. I didn't mean to…"

"Close," he said. "It's my girl that's left me."

For a moment, I didn't know what to say. The man was heartbroken over a recent breakup and here I was sitting with both feet in my mouth.

He shrugged. "Time's going to heal it, though… right?"

I sat for a minute with him in silence. "Time will grind down the edges, so it doesn't hurt so much," I finally answered, "and when enough time passes, the pain will feel so dull that you won't even notice it anymore." I didn't know whether I should, but I placed my hand on his shoulder.

He never flinched. "I don't know how to put the pieces of my life back together," he said.

This one I knew. "Just start with one piece at a time. When the time's right, you'll see the whole picture."

He took my words to heart and nodded. "Thanks, Don," he said, extending his hand. "I'm mighty obliged."

I almost laughed, thinking, *It's me who should be thanking you for the small opportunity to make a difference in this world.* "Don't mention it, my friend," I said, and then gestured toward the chuck wagon. "That Gloria's a real looker…and even a blind man could see she's got eyes for you."

He tried to fight it, but he blushed.

"You might want to rope her in before one of the other cowboys gets to her."

He watched her for a while and shrugged. "So you reckon she's got eyes for me, huh?"

"Yup. I sure do."

~ ~ ~ ~ ~ ~ ~ ~ ~ ~ ~ ~

I was terribly sore, but it was a good sore. Ignoring my body's complaints, I helped to round up the cattle. As I worked, I took in the beautiful scenery before me. Bella laughed with Lisa and our new friends, making me feel my love for her right down to my brittle bones. Al was hollering at some of the stubborn cattle, while Gloria stared at him. Mrs. Gomes sat with Mykala and watched her family with worried eyes. Paul was galloping up and down the meadow, scaring the strays back into the herd. When they were all together, Dusty sat high in the saddle of his surefooted horse. "Okay. Let's move 'em!" he yelled.

And we did. In the warm Arizona sunshine, past the tall aspens and beyond the mountain breezes, we moved them through the wooded rolling hills toward home.

Somewhere along the trail, I gave a whole new meaning to riding high in the saddle. I was actually standing up in the stirrups because I couldn't sit anymore.

Twelve hours and fifty blisters later, we drove every head of cattle into their barbed wire pens. I'd never felt so tired, or such a sense of accomplishment in my life. I rode over to Bella and grabbed her hand.

"You okay?" she asked.

"Honestly...never better," I answered.

~ ~ ~ ~ ~ ~ ~ ~ ~ ~ ~ ~

The following morning, after we'd packed to go home, Bella and I made our rounds to say good-bye. "Thank you for your hospitality," we told each of them.

The answer was always the same. "It was our pleasure," they said and meant it.

Mrs. Gomes boxed one of her apple pies for us to take home. "We'd love to have you again," she said. "Happy trails."

I hugged her tight.

Dusty caught us out in the yard. "Keep your eyes peeled for varmints. I'm told there are lots of 'em back in the city."

I laughed enough to hurt my aching body.

As we strolled through the ranch for the last time, I told Bella, "I can see why Louise left everything to come live here." And then I pictured Madison and Pudge. I missed them badly. I patted Molly and Bailey and headed for the shuttle bus.

On the ride back to the airport, Bella said, "I loved the people, the food, the horses – everything." She turned to me. "What was your favorite part?"

"Besides sharing it all with you, probably the breakfast with Al on the cattle drive." As much as the trip was a dream come true, I felt real magic by being there for someone who needed me.

The answer surprised her but she didn't question it. "I'll never forget it," she said, her eyes drifting back to our recent past.

"Me, either," I said, hoping that my memories were going to last more than a lifetime.

As we boarded the plane for home, I thought about crossing another dream off of my honey do list and felt torn. *Only three to go*, and therein lay the bittersweet dilemma – *the more I get done, the less I have to do*, I realized. It was the doing – not the already been done – that was becoming much more precious to me.

Chapter 11

After all of the travel, it had been a tough couple of weeks. I was feeling more fatigued than ever and the pain medication wasn't working nearly as well. I called Dr. Rice and got an appointment for that afternoon. Along with a detailed description of my symptoms, I filled her in on Bella and my recent adventures.

"Wow, it all sounds so exciting! What's been your favorite so far?"

I didn't even have to think. "Meeting new people and being able to lend a hand whenever I can; finding forgiveness and taking risks I would have never taken…" Her grin stopped me in mid-sentence. "What?" I asked.

"That's great," she said, still wearing her grin. "But I was referring to the places you've visited."

I chuckled. "Oh…right!" I thought for a second and shrugged. "Truth is…it doesn't really matter where you go. It's about the memories you make while you're there."

After increasing my pain medication dosage, she explained, "Your recent tests show that your red blood cell count is very low," so she also prescribed an iron supplement for anemia. "How's your family?" she asked.

"They're great," I told her. "I have a trip to the zoo planned with my grandchildren tomorrow afternoon." I shrugged. "But I promise to take it easy."

"Mr. DiMarco, you take it any way you can get it."

~ ~ ~ ~ ~ ~ ~ ~ ~ ~ ~ ~

The zoo was only three towns over, but we'd planned the trip for weeks. Reputed to be one of the finest small zoos in the United States, the ninety-two acres were surrounded by paths and ball fields, monuments and memorials.

From the moment we arrived, I felt like sliding into a coma from the pain and nausea. Even with the increased dosage, I knew the entire day was going to be a test of endurance. I gritted my teeth and grabbed both Madison and Pudge's hands. "Let's go have some fun," I told them.

We walked through the gift store where overpriced stuffed animals nearly twisted Pudge's neck off his shoulders from gawking. After passing the Wildlife Center and Café, we came to our first exhibit. It was an enormous underwater tank where two river otters swam and played. They were mischievous and fun to watch, so we stood and watched for what seemed like forever. The beaver and harbor seal exhibits were next. The beavers looked to be in the same ill mood as me. The seals did nothing but swim in circles. "This stinks," Pudge complained.

We marched on.

The black bears had a wonderful habitat with a waterfall, pool, trees and lots of rocks. I told Pudge, "Look up!" One of the bears was in a tree, looking down at us. Just then, another came right up to the glass and stood on his hind legs, trying to sniff through the corners. Madison was thrilled and squealed in delight. I smiled, but didn't have the energy to drum up the enthusiasm I knew she was looking for. We stood a while longer, watching a third bear pace in front of a heavy steel door. "Looks like he's waiting to be fed," I told the kids.

At the north end of the zoo, two female Asian elephants promised to amaze us with their tricks. Both broke their promise. One stood under a wooden platform, using it as shade and to occasionally scratch her enormous back. The other faced a concrete wall, as if she'd been put in time out, and refused to turn around. Even with all the toys lying around their yard, they were definitely not in the mood to play. I didn't blame them.

"Why won't they do tricks?" Pudge asked.

"Probably because they've been doing tricks their whole lives and are tired now," I answered.

Both kids looked up at me, but didn't question the explanation. I was glad.

The Environment Center was advertised as the zoo's crowning jewel. There were ten exhibits in all; mountain stream, kettle hole pond, a vernal pool, tidal salt marsh and barrier beach – all teeming with wildlife. The concept was intended to teach children about the important role that clean water plays in the eco-system, but it smelled like sulfur and stunk bad enough for me to step outside and wait by the shorebird exhibit.

The bald eagle and coyote exhibits sat side-by-side creating the chance to view the New England forest. Though we tried for a long time, we couldn't find the eagle. Madison finally concluded, "He's not there." The coyote, however, was lying out in plain sight, snoozing the day away in his rock den.

Both the cougar and bobcat, two species of feline predators, paced like inmates serving out a life sentence. I was thinking, *The bobcat is surprisingly small* when Pudge said, "It looks like she's smiling at me, Poppa."

"That's because she's hungry," I said and thought that Madison might wet herself from laughing so hard.

As the autumn sun beat down and punished me, we crossed a red covered bridge onto a traditional New England farm. With its barn, barnyard and two pastures, this was where the real fun began. They had three horses, a few milking cows, two goats, a sow and her young – all of it designed to be interactive. As the kids petted their new friends, I fed change into an old crank vending machine for two handfuls of feeding pellets.

The pony rides were short but sweet – *thank God* – while the Choo Choo was a nice break from the walking. It was no more than a tractor dressed like a train. For two bucks a ride, I talked the kids into going twice, and would have paid for rides all afternoon if they'd let me.

The brook walk looped around the waterfowl pond where hundreds of ducks and noisy trumpeter swans begged for food. There were park benches on both sides to take a rest and admire the scenery. I didn't want the kids to know how nauseous and fatigued I felt from the increase in medication, so we spent as much time as we could there. It was a good thing Madison reminded me to bring bread. We fed the squawking birds for a half hour.

The red fox and raccoon exhibits were a chance to visit our nocturnal neighbors up close and personal. "A lot of these guys hide right in the neighborhood and come out at night to eat our trash," I told them.

"I wish I was a raccoon," Pudge said.

"I bet you do," I said and ruffled his hair.

Madison laughed again.

The North American bison and white-tailed deer finished off the death march. For a breed of animals known for roaming and grazing, even romping, every one of them was at a standstill.

"You guys ready to call it quits?" I finally asked.

"Okay," they agreed. I'd never heard a sweeter word in my life.

~ ~ ~ ~ ~ ~ ~ ~ ~ ~ ~ ~

While we waited for Riley to pick them up, we worked on the puzzle. I was completely drained and my head was banging, but I still told stories in hopes it would take my mind off the agony. "I once made a puzzle of King Tut's chair. Once the chair was finished, the rest of the puzzle was all purple. Other mind-bogglers were those that had all their pieces cut the same. On one, I'd gotten all the way to the last piece when I discovered that it wouldn't fit. I had to take it apart in sections until I found my mistake."

"Yikes," said Madison.

"And then there was the *Lucky Lady*. With a white background filled with clover and ladybugs, it was almost impossible to make any headway on it. I finally turned it over and did it from the back." My head felt like it was going to explode.

Once they left for the night, I took two big, white pills and eased into bed.

~ ~ ~ ~ ~ ~ ~ ~ ~ ~ ~ ~

As I nodded off, for whatever reason I remembered my grandfather used to tell the scariest bedtime stories. "When I was just a boy," he'd say, "I went to a dance out in the woods of Maine where we lived. A man, strange to our parts, walked in and approached Claire Nemo, my next-door neighbor, and asked her to dance. She accepted. Halfway through their waltz, he noticed a crucifix hanging around her neck. He let out a terrible scream, yanked it from her and ran out of the hall. On his way out, he placed his hand on the wall. The imprint of his hand is still imbedded in that plaster today. From that day on, everyone swore that pretty Claire Nemo had danced with the devil."

Compared to his tales about being buried alive, this story added nothing to my nightmares. "In the old days," he'd say, "some of the corpses that had been exhumed were discovered to have fingernail marks clawed into the coffin's interior lid. Asleep in their deep temporary comas, these poor souls weren't dead at all when they were committed to the ground."

I remembered being terrified by his pre-wake stories; the barbaric days when medicine was primitive, embalming fluid was yet to be concocted and families held wakes in their parlors. I recalled being scared to death over the tales and that I also enjoyed listening to each spooky word. For years, I imagined the same horrid fate for myself. The chills of it always woke me, panting and covered in sweat.

This time was different, though. When I opened my eyes, it was so pitch black I had to question whether I was alive or dead. And if it was death I now experienced, that sick sense of being alone left no mistake: *I'm in hell.* The sadistic silence, unforgiving and eager to punish, forced my breathing to quicken, while terror struck my racing heart. *I'm still alive!*

Fragmented memories raced back, but the puzzle was too complex. Fear had brutally awakened the senses and the fight or flight push of adrenaline rushed through my veins. I was too restricted, too confined to move an inch. Amid the thousand spiraling thoughts, I made a mental note to run through the checklist. My extremities tingled from the lack of circulation, and as if it had been placed under a rock, my head throbbed. My throat was parched like a cracked desert. I screamed at the top of my lungs, but heard only a demented whisper return. Tears began to well, old stinging tears. I was suffocating in a bank of stale air that was emptying fast, while six feet of earth covered me. The weight of the world was literally resting upon my constricted chest. As if that weren't horrid enough, reality hit – I was sharing the burden with those who had long decomposed. My childhood nightmare had come true. *I've been buried alive!*

Those few on Earth above me; those who might have even cared enough to unearth me weren't ever going to search. They had already mourned the loss of my life, experienced closure with my soul and were now longing to move on from the memory of my face.

Left alone to panic in the bowels of the earth, I quickly reached the realization, *No matter how loud I scream, there's no way someone will ever hear me. And even if they do, there'll never be enough time to dig me out.*

It was cold, very cold, and the dampness seeped into my bones. Small parasites would soon feed on my flesh. Breathing had become more difficult, reality too unbearable. I prayed hard, but the despair was so consuming that I doubted my words would be heard. There wasn't any response.

I often wondered what I would do if I only had minutes left to live. *Will I feel sorry for myself that it's over? Will I embrace the opportunity to pass over? Or will I simply rejoice in the miracle of life I'd been given to experience? What's the last thing I'll feel?*

In the tight quarters, I felt nothing but the cold and shivered. "Make it quick," I muttered through the sniffles.

"Make what quick?" answered a mysterious voice.

My body convulsed, but the casket's lid stopped me from completely jumping out of my skin. I was surprised my heart hadn't given out yet. "Please God... NO!" I screamed.

The disembodied voice returned. "Open your eyes," it demanded. This time, the tone was more firm.

I dreaded the sight of the demon and clenched my eyelids tight.

"Come on, Don," the voice said, more gently. "It's time to wake up."

My mind took off at a sprint. It sounded like Bella, or more precisely, someone who was trying to sound like her. I held my breath.

When I breathed again, I smelled the scent of Ivory soap and dryer sheets. And then someone kissed me. Gently and with love, someone kissed my forehead. I took another deep breath, drummed up all the courage left in my body and forced open my eyes. *It's Bella!* As reality registered, I shook my head. "I just dreamed that I'd been buried alive."

Bella grabbed my face, stared into my eyes and kissed me again. "Not on my watch," she whispered.

While the sweat dried, I thought about my grandfather – and wanted to be remembered, but not in the same way. *He'd certainly made a lasting impression, though.*

~ ~ ~ ~ ~ ~ ~ ~ ~ ~ ~ ~

Two days went by before the kids came over again. This time, I had more strength. I took the wooden treasure box out of the closet and showed it to them again. I needed to know they wouldn't forget it. "Every man finds a treasure in his life," I reminded them, "and you two are mine."

Since they were old enough to understand, I'd explained that my most valuable possession in the whole world was kept inside the secret box and that they could have it once I was gone. As a result, a trust had been forged between us – them, for not opening the treasure box with the secret inside; me, for protecting it until the day it was theirs.

We puttered around all day until the newspaper was delivered.

After fantasizing about seeing my own name in print, I realized that every once in a while, a simple story had the power to move people's hearts. I felt blessed for such a rare opportunity and shared it with my attentive grandchildren.

~ THE DAILY TELEGRAM ~

A Benefit for Isaac
by Max Jacobson

At six months old, Isaac Brault was diagnosed with a very rare disease called mitochondrial disease with pyruvate dehydrogenises deficiency. With only a few hundred cases known worldwide, currently there is no cure for the degenerative neuromuscular disease that affects multiple systems in the body such as the heart, lungs, kidneys, vision, hearing, muscles and digestive system.

As a result of this disease, Isaac has suffered profound hearing loss, low energy, poor growth and very low muscle tone. He has difficulty holding up his head and sitting up.

"When he was a baby, Isaac's muscles were so cramped that he couldn't even straighten out his arm," says his mother, Theresa (Delaney) Brault, a 1991 graduate of B.M.C. Durfee High School. "The acids in his body had reached deadly levels before the doctors diagnosed his disease correctly."

"Tragically, some kids are dying early because similar diseases go undiagnosed," she says. "There are grieving parents out there who believe their children have died of SIDS (Sudden Infant Death Syndrome), but these babies actually suffered from a metabolic disorder. These kids look normal and only start showing symptoms at six to nine months of age. If Isaac had not been diagnosed early, he would have been one of those terrible statistics."

Brault, an audiologist by trade, is very interested in bringing awareness to her son's little-known disease. "Isaac is such a miracle kid," she says. "He takes experimental, or research (not FDA approved) drugs called DCA that are only administered in a couple of hospitals around the world. Isaac receives his at the Children's Hospital in Boston and the medication is definitely helping."

Essentially, Isaac's body cannot break down sugar and carbohydrates on its own. His medication helps to regulate his metabolism by breaking down those carbohydrates and sugars that would otherwise become toxins, poisoning his organs. In the end, the medication is also the only thing that gives him the energy he needs to get through each day.

Although he is nearly two years old, Isaac's muscles are so weak that he can only roll over. "We're hiring a therapist to come in and teach him how to crawl," says Mom.

"Isaac's deaf and we're not sure if he'll walk or talk, or even what his life span might be, but we do know how incredibly blessed we are for our family and friends – people who share both our tragedies and triumphs."

Isaac's grandmother, June Delaney, of Earl Street, says, "When Isaac was first born, he cried for nine hours a day. At first, the doctors thought it was acid reflux. Many tests were conducted and they quickly discovered he had a hearing problem. The doctors then thought it was Cerebral Palsy. Isaac wasn't putting on any weight. And then they diagnosed his illness correctly."

Although Isaac has problems holding up his head, requires a feeding tube and is confined to a wheelchair, he doesn't let his disease get him down. He's a very happy boy who is always smiling. According to those who adore him, he enjoys spending time with his family and especially playing with his three year-old sister.

Isaac and his family don't take much for granted. Without question, the young boy is surrounded by the love and care that he needs. But much more is required, according to his family. Isaac needs financial assistance to help fund the medications and therapy that keep him smiling.

To help fund Isaac's medical needs, the Brault Family is inviting anyone who'd like to help make a difference in Isaac's life to attend an upcoming benefit dinner. A buffet of home-cooked delights will be served, while a DJ will spin a list of dance favorites. An autographed photo of Boston Red Sox player Trot Nixon, a signed Boston Bruins hockey puck, autographed books, as well as other special prizes will be raffled off to help earn money.

Isaac's benefit dinner will be held on Saturday at the Liberal Club, located at 20 Star Street, Fall River, MA at noon. Tickets are $12 each and are available at the door. Donations are also accepted and appreciated (a tax ID # is available for larger donations).

"We're hosting the benefit to help fund Isaac's experimental medicine, the vitamins which help him retain his energy and to help set up his home as more handicap accessible," says June Delaney, "things that would make for a better life for my grandson."

Isaac's family says they are grateful for all the support and compassion shown them.

I finished the article and thought, *Wow! We really don't have to look too far to see someone who has it worse.* I looked up at the kids. "So, what are we gonna do about it?" I asked. "What are we going to do for Sir Isaac?"

"Help!" Madison answered and ran off to find the materials she needed to make the boy a card.

With Bella's nod, we sent all we could, or at least enough money to get Isaac by for a month.

On the morning we mailed the card, I asked the kids, "How does it make you feel to help someone who needs it?"

"Really good," Pudge said. Madison agreed.

"Remember guys, the most important thing in this world is to make sure you're there for other people when they need you." I winked at each of them. "Because someday, it might be you asking for the help. And when you put others before yourself, you might even forget about your own problems for a while." Remembering my time at the Arizona dude ranch, I knew for a fact this was true.

"So, leave more than what you take...right, Poppa?" Madison asked.

"You've got it, kid!"

Chapter 12

A few long weeks of recuperation made me itch for the road. Bella and I always talked about buying an RV and traveling the country when I retired. The plan changed a little. The pretty leaves had long since fallen and the trees were now stripped to bare, bony limbs. Autumn was quickly turning into winter and the weather was starting to become foul. With the clock ticking faster than ever and Dr. Rice's enthusiastic blessing, we decided to avoid the first snowfall and rent a motor home to travel the entire eastern seaboard all the way to the Florida Keys. The idea was to experience the open road and meet some real, flag-waving Americans along the way.

~ ~ ~ ~ ~ ~ ~ ~ ~ ~ ~ ~

We spent an entire afternoon looking at used RVs and listening to the empty promises of an annoying salesman. Even though he pled, there was no way we could afford one of the massive forty-two foot diesel pushers, so we finally agreed on a thirty-six foot Winnebago. It was cream colored with splashes of green and brown covering both sides. With thirteen thousand miles on her, this non-smoking unit still smelled new and included every amenity you could imagine. In the galley – wood-style vinyl flooring, laminate counters, refrigerator, a three-burner range with oven, microwave, and a dinette booth that Bella thought was "darling." There was a stained carpet in the lounge, with a TV, VCR and manual shades. Up front, there were leather captain's chairs. A private bath with a shower was located toward the rear and a nineteen-inch television sat in the bedroom. Outside, a patio awning, satellite dish and cheesy external shower completed the package.

By the time we made our decision, I felt so sick and aggravated I was actually looking forward to haggling the price.

"For this beauty, you're looking at eighteen hundred dollars a week, with five thousand down as a security deposit," the salesman started.

"Eighteen hundred?" I said. "For a used RV?" Bella walked away.

"Well, it's pre-owned," he said.

"So it's used, then?"

"Sir, this baby has a Triton V10 310 hp under the hood and a one-hundred-twenty-gallon tank to get you and the Missus wherever you need to go."

"Which means we'll get eight miles to the gallon." I glared at him. "I'm not sure you're saving us any money with that pitch."

"List price for this unit right now is seventy-four thousand nine hundred."

"But I'm not looking to buy it, am I?"

He pulled at his collar. I was starting to get to him. "How many weeks do you need it for?"

"Four, maybe five."

"Let me go talk to my manager and see what we can do."

"I appreciate that." As he headed for the showroom door, I called out after him. "Make sure you let him know that the carpet's stained."

He looked back at me for an extended moment, nodded once and disappeared into the building.

I looked over at Bella. She was still shaking her head. "We're almost there," I told her, pleased that I still had some real fight left in me.

My new friend reappeared five minutes later with their final offer. "Fifteen hundred dollars a week, with three thousand down."

I called Bella over. "We have a deal," I said and thought, *We would have been just as happy in the thirty-footer, but what the hell.*

We signed some papers, cut a check and were off on our next adventure.

~ ~ ~ ~ ~ ~ ~ ~ ~ ~ ~ ~

I'd placed a few more pieces into the puzzle when I looked up to find Bella standing in the doorway. "Ready?" she asked.

I nodded and put in another piece. "Looks like we'll have to abandon the puzzle again for a while."

"Not really. There's another puzzle we can work on together." She showed me two shoeboxes overflowing with family photos and a couple of empty scrapbooks.

I smiled, thinking, *It's gonna be a great trip.* I carried the last of the luggage into the RV, along with a stack of paperbacks, hard covers and some audio books, and a full bag of rattling pill bottles.

The route had been mapped out days in advance: Massachusetts, Rhode Island and Connecticut by back roads. New York by way of the George Washington Bridge, down the New Jersey Turnpike, with a stop in Atlantic City. A leisurely pace through the Pennsylvania countryside and then we'd coast into Maryland. Washington D.C. was another stop and then Virginia where my old Army buddy, Cal Anderson, waited to put us up for a night. The plan included hopping from one diner to the next all the way down to the Florida Keys.

Bella made one last call to make sure Riley had all of our contact information. We kissed for luck and were on our way.

~ ~ ~ ~ ~ ~ ~ ~ ~ ~ ~

We made good time through Massachusetts and the postage stamp state known as Rhode Island. Our first stop in Connecticut was at a travel plaza, which was also known as a truck stop in my day. Though they welcomed RVs in a designated quiet zone away from the big rigs, I was more interested in the stainless steel diner located in the rear of the massive lot. This one had recessed lighting, lots of neon signage and a railroad-car-like roof. The bright red porcelain exterior and cream-colored lettering made me feel like a kid again.

As we walked through the front door, I spotted a plaque on the wall and pointed it out to Bella. Titled "The Ten Commandments," it started out with "Thou shalt not worship golden arches" and ended with "Thou shalt not hang out and order nothing but coffee."

We laughed, grabbed two stools at the counter and skimmed through a pair of sticky menus. "I don't see any chicken parm," she teased.

With the exception of Flo's Clam Shack, I ate chicken parm whenever we went out. Bella was always trying to get me to try something new but I wouldn't. Clam cakes, chicken parm, or anything on the menu at a greasy spoon was what I loved. For whatever reason, it didn't matter what I ate at a diner; mushroom and cheddar omelets with pancakes swimming in butter and syrup; bacon cheeseburgers and fries with a coffee malt – either one finished off with a healthy slice of apple pie. And I had to have my apple pie. If the grandkids were around, I ate my veggies. But when they weren't, I loved my junk food – even though Bella always gave me a hard time about it. I closed the menu and blurted, "I really do love these places."

An old man sitting beside me nodded. "Me, too," he said, thinking I was talking to him. He extended his wrinkled hand. "Name's Ed."

I shook it. "Nice to meet you, Ed. I'm Don." I leaned back so he could catch Bella's smile. "And this is my bride, Bella."

"Nice to meet you both. So you like diners, do you?"

I nodded. Lorna, the counter waitress, took our order and walked away. Without being asked, the old man began a history lesson. "The word diner is short for dining car," he said, "a kind of railroad car. That's where they got their style."

"I didn't know that," I fibbed, trying to make him feel good.

"Yep. Since diners became a part of the American landscape more than one hundred years ago, these old lunch wagons have touched millions of people."

I nodded.

"After fast food places started to get popular in the 60s, diners tried to separate themselves from that image. A revival began in the late 70s and three diner builders started making them again in the old style. They called it a retro look – folks like us wanting to go back to the values of yesterday. Since then, diners have become popular places where people from all walks of life can share a home cooked meal and some friendly conversation."

I nodded again, waiting for him to continue. But he didn't. As abruptly as he'd begun, he was finished. The rest of the time was spent on comfortable small talk like the weather and baseball and devouring a couple of blue-plate specials – mine, more bland than I'd ever ordered.

~ ~ ~ ~ ~ ~ ~ ~ ~ ~ ~ ~

Whenever we were parked, Bella and I worked on the scrapbooks. I finally understood the value of photographs.

When we were moving, she prodded me, "Tell me a story." The funny thing is – although she'd heard them all a dozen times before, she never tired of my ramblings. As much as I loved telling them, she enjoyed watching me flail my hands around while I searched my memory and shared each vivid detail.

A few stories later, we were in New Jersey. We'd landed at another roadside restaurant where men and women of the road gathered for the taste of coffee and pie. There were lines of rigs parked out front, some drivers sleeping in the cabs. The lettering on the doors and lights in the grills were as unique as their owners. Theirs was a separate culture. I liked these people. I'd met hundreds of them at McKaskies and always considered them honest, hard-working folks. The stories of their lives were all unique, each offering a lesson from which we could all learn.

This diner had a barrel-shaped roof outside, with a long row of swiveling stools bolted to the floor inside. It was narrow; heavy with stainless steel inside and out. One look around revealed that it served unpretentious meals at reasonable prices. Best yet, it served breakfast at any hour of the day.

I grabbed for a menu when Bella whacked my arm and pointed at the menu. "It's for sale," she said.

"What's for sale?"

"This diner."

And then I saw it. The ad was on a separate sheet of paper floating inside the menu:

> Built in 1949, Mom's Diner was set up on Route 1 in Avenel, New Jersey and has operated here since. But we are ready to retire! Mom's can accommodate nineteen stools at the counter, with ten booths for a total capacity of fifty-nine seats. The diner was remodeled seven years ago. Some of the renovations included replacement of the original

stools and booths. As part of the sale, we
are also including cabinets, pantry display case, juice machine, soda machine,
coffee machine, the original refrigerator,
and all fluorescent light fixtures. Only
$36,000 in "as is, where is" condition!
See the cook if you're interested.

I looked up to find an old man slinging hash. He
was whistling a happy tune. Considering the place was
over fifty years old, it was in remarkable condition. *If
only we could*, I thought, and suddenly realized the future was no longer mine. Though I should have lived
my entire life in the present, the future was the last
place for me now. It was painful.

Bella must have watched the excitement drain out
of my face. When I looked back at her, she was hiding
behind her menu, sniffling. I didn't say anything.

A brunette with the nametag, Jeanne, approached.
"What'll it be, folks?" she asked.

I looked at my wife. "Let me guess," I said, "a
poached egg and dry, wheat toast for me, right?"

She turned to the waitress and rolled her eyes.
"Don't mind him," she said. "I'll have a blueberry muf-
fin, grilled, and the big kid over there will have a mushroom and cheddar omelet, with a short stack of blueberry pancakes on the side."

Smiling, the woman scratched the order into her
pad and left us.

"Now that's freedom," I teased Bella.

She grinned. "You've been good. Besides, the pancakes have blueberries in them."

I laughed.

~ ~ ~ ~ ~ ~ ~ ~ ~ ~ ~ ~

Heading southwest, we didn't stop again until we passed a battered road sign reading, Atlantic City.

As we sauntered down the boardwalk, we were awed by the mix of glitz and filth, and were easily lured into one of the gaudy casinos. Both of us decided to try our hand at roulette. She played twenty-one red and stayed with it. I chose thirty-three black. Within a half-hour, my frustrated wife was broke, while I was seven hundred dollars richer. My number had come up four times. As a rookie mistake – or more likely, beginner's luck – I never cleared my chips from the table each time I'd won. The dealer chuckled at my naïve grin and Bella's jealous pout. I tipped him well.

Excited to discover this new world, I lost the next few spins and cashed out. Fortunately for Bella, I was more than willing to share my winnings.

Dressed for the stinging winter wind, we walked hand-in-hand into the afternoon sun. Not fifty feet down the boardwalk, we happened across the strangest sight. A young woman with no arms or legs was lying face down on a hospital gurney, playing an electronic keyboard with her tongue – the notes to "Somewhere over the Rainbow" ringing out over and over again. While her people sat nearby and watched, hoards of compassionate strangers dropped crisp bills into the five-gallon bucket set before her. *It's like fishing in a stocked pond*, I thought and to Bella's surprise, I dropped a fifty-dollar bill into the bucket. Bella looked at me. I shrugged. "That had to be the worst exploitation of a handicapped person I've ever seen."

She nodded. "But that's only because we haven't seen what the government's done to her."

"It's amazing how lucky we are," I said and turned up the collar on my jacket.

~ ~ ~ ~ ~ ~ ~ ~ ~ ~ ~ ~

Nearly an hour after the sun had set, we crossed the Potomac River into the Lover's State of Virginia. I stopped to get directions to any place that provided water and electric hookups; a place where we could dump out, fuel up and spend the night.

Just outside the campground, I filled the rig and handed the attendant a hundred dollar bill.

He shook his head. "Your money's counterfeit," he said.

Our winnings from the casino were actually funny money. Bella's face grew nervous.

The man grinned. "But it's green," he said and took it.

It didn't take a half hour to find our spot and hook up. All night, Bella babbled like a schoolgirl, while my eyes grew heavy. The medication was doing a job on my attention span. No matter how exhausted I felt though, it was good to get caught up on each other's lives.

~ ~ ~ ~ ~ ~ ~ ~ ~ ~ ~ ~

After breakfast, we were off to the capital. It was dawn when we walked the length of the Vietnam Wall. I wasn't sure how this would make me feel, but I was glad we made the trip. Some people took tracings. Others cried on bended knees, leaving behind letters that visitors could read. Besides these emotional letters, I took note of the dog tags, medals, cans of beer and cigarettes left behind at the base of the wall; gifts from living Vietnam veterans to their departed brothers. I'd healed more than I thought and was happy for it. It was humbling, but as we turned to leave Bella pointed out a dozen Asian tourists hanging all over the Vietnam Monument, taking pictures. She shot me a mischievous grin.

The Washington Monument was too much of a hike in my condition, the Lincoln Monument at the reflecting pools was something to see in person, but 1600 Pennsylvania Avenue wasn't nearly as interesting as the reenactment of Lincoln's assasination at Ford's Theater. The National Archives building, home of the Declaration of Independence, was our next stop. The single piece of yellowed parchment was protected by armed guards and rested under several inches of bullet proof glass. It was reputed that if anyone attempted to break the glass in order to steal or desecrate the document, the vault in which it was housed would automatically drop several stories beneath the ground. I stopped and made a funny face at one of the guards. The man laughed at me. "This isn't Buckingham Palace," Bella reminded me before we were off to Arlington Cemetery.

It was pouring rain, a freezing rain, when we barely steered the giant RV through the gates. On our right, we watched as five uniformed men on horseback and a rider-less horse pulled a caisson behind them. The flag-draped casket was all I needed, to know that this was a military funeral procession. We followed a good distance behind.

"Get out of here with that RV!" someone yelled at me through the cracked window.

I rolled it down. "Excuse me?"

The disgusted groundskeeper shook his head. "Privately owned vehicles aren't allowed on the grounds. Turn it around and park it at Fort Meade through the same gate you entered."

"Oh, we're sorry," I said. "We didn't know."

The man shook his head again and stormed off.

No sooner did we park, the rain slowed to a cold drizzle.

Our first stop was at JFK's gravesite. Even in the heavy mist, the eternal flame flickered in the gray sky. While Bella went hunting for John Kennedy's brother, I read several of the famous president's speeches and inspirational quotes carved into the surrounding granite walls. Within minutes, my scout wife returned and reported, "Bobby Kennedy's up on the hill around back. It's only marked by a plain white cross."

I shrugged. "I wonder what Audie Murphy's stone looks like."

For a solid half hour, we searched the beautiful, sprawling grounds but couldn't find the most decorated war hero in American history. Finally, with the reluctant help of our groundskeeper friend, we located it. Amongst a sea of enormous and expensive headstones, Murphey's small slab of granite listed the awards and medals he'd earned. The list started at the top of the tiny stone and ran all the way into the ground. I whistled in admiration. Looking at the huge stones that surrounded him, it was clear that while some people tried to purchase eternal honor, others actually earned it.

After paying tribute to the members of the space shuttle who'd died in a tragic explosion, we visited the Tomb of the Unknown Soldier. Though there were several people milling about, I was hypnotized by the rigid soldiers who guarded the sacred tomb in the horrendous weather.

Cold was one thing, wet was another, but when put together things got miserable real fast. As we left, Bella and I shared the same pride. Even with its faults and imperfections, D.C. – the soul of America – could make the numbest American feel alive. The patriotism, the brass bands, and the stars and stripes all caused their share of goose bumps – sometimes even ordering human hairs to snap to attention.

~ ~ ~ ~ ~ ~ ~ ~ ~ ~ ~ ~

Not five miles from the Iwo Jima Monument, Cal Anderson was waiting for us. He'd insisted we stay with him at least one night. Though Bella wasn't keen on the idea, she finally agreed.

After an exchange of hugs, Cal eyed me up and down. "Don't you look like the walking dead," he barked. It was a phrase we used back in '68 for guys who didn't look like they were going to make it.

I laughed and patted his big round belly. "I appreciate that, Slim."

We were just starting a good joust about our aging appearances when Cal's wife, Karen – the very girl he'd worried himself over all those years ago – asked, "How 'bout we take you two out to our favorite rib place?"

Bella's eyes lit up. She never passed on ribs.

~ ~ ~ ~ ~ ~ ~ ~ ~ ~ ~ ~

As we ate, Cal never shut up. "I remember 'Nam like it was yesterday," he said. "And what a thrill it was. Sometimes, I actually wish I could go back and relive it!"

Bella and I exchanged a quick glance. Cal was telling a different version from the one we'd recently relived. *How strange to have once been close to someone,* I thought, *and now…I don't even know who this person is.*

As we left the restaurant, Cal approached the hostess. "Could I please check your lost and found box?" he asked. "The last time I was in here, I forgot my sunglasses."

His wife shook her head and walked out. Cal had obviously run this same scam a time or two before.

After rustling through the box, he finally nodded and chose a pair.

"Aren't those ladies glasses?" the hostess asked.

"I hope not," Cal said, smirking, "'cause they cost me a small fortune."

~ ~ ~ ~ ~ ~ ~ ~ ~ ~ ~ ~

On the way back to their place, Cal and I sat in the front seat of the car, while Bella and Karen talked in the back. Cal spoke softly, so his wife wouldn't hear. "You been following the problems overseas?" he asked.

I nodded, but it was the last topic in the world I wanted to discuss. He obviously didn't feel the same.

"What bullshit," Cal said. "We should go in there and kill 'em all!"

Oh boy, I thought, *I hope this doesn't come up at the house. Bella will be beside herself.*

But of course, it did. We weren't past the threshold when Cal and Bella squared off. "So you think we should kill 'em all, huh?" she asked.

With a grin, he nodded. "Sure do. And then let God sort it out."

"Now that's intelligent," she said, glaring at him. "You're a true humanitarian," she added. With the most subtle nod, Karen agreed.

As I cringed, Cal's face started to turn crimson. He turned to me. "Is she always like this?" he asked, trying to retain some pride through humor.

I saved him. "Only when we're staying at a friend's house," I joked and then steered the rest of the conversation back into the past where it was much safer. Cal was a tough, hardheaded vet, but he had no idea how much conviction my wife held for human life.

The rest of the night, she and I exchanged a few grins. Once, Karen even joined us. To keep the peace, we turned in early. Bella was so fired up she tossed and turned, trying to get to sleep. I sat on the toilet, fighting two of my fiercest enemies – nausea and constipation. After the second round, I pushed something out. Wiping the cold sweat from my brow, I cleaned myself and stood to flush when I noticed that my pencil stools were now chalky white. *Oh, that can't be good*, I thought, and quietly slid into bed.

~ ~ ~ ~ ~ ~ ~ ~ ~ ~ ~ ~

Early the next morning, we left and headed south through Virginia. Bella was still tired, so she took a nap in the back of the RV. I spotted another silver bullet on the side of the road and pulled in. It was almost lunch. *I'll bring her back a grilled cheese sandwich and a cup of tea*, I thought and locked up the rig. I couldn't wait to sample their apple pie and talk to some more grass-root folks.

As I hurried out of the cold and bellied up to the bar, I sat alongside a middle-aged man. We exchanged nods. "Name's George Cournoyer," he said and extended his hand. He had gray hair with a moustache and beard to match. He actually looked like the country music star, Kenny Rogers – except on a scarecrow's frame, and without a whole lot of sleep.

I shook his hand. "Good to meet you. I'm Don."

He looked out of the diner window toward the RV and then back at me.

"Me and the wife are down from Massachusetts, doing a little sightseeing," I explained.

He coughed once and nodded. "Nice country up there in New England." He wore faded jeans and matching jacket, and old scuffed cowboy boots that were once brown. A John Deere ball cap pushed back on his head; the curled visor was stained with oil and grease. That, and the red plaid shirt, told me he was a trucker.

I agreed and ordered the cheeseburger special. "Sure is," I told him. "But I figured I'd like to see a little more of the country before it's too late."

"Folks are always running to something...or from something," he said. With a fresh pack of cigarettes in front of him, George coughed hard again. "I've been up and down these roads for years. Believe me, there ain't nothing to see that you can't catch at home."

"You're probably right," I said. "I just felt I'd regret it if we didn't get out and see it all. You know what they say – life is what happens while you're planning for the future."

He turned and gazed at me for a moment. His tanned face was weathered and cracked, but his eyes were a deep crystal blue, almost haunting. "It never ceases to amaze me how folks will go to the ends of the Earth to find what's right in front of them the whole time," he said and placed some money on the counter to cover his bill.

As the waitress delivered my lunch, I sat dumbfounded.

He stood and said, "Friend, the only road worth traveling is the one that leads you home, 'cause that's where your family and friends are. It's the only place any of us really belongs." He patted my back. "Good luck to ya," he said and headed out into the sun.

As if a giant light had just illuminated my entire existence, I suddenly realized, *I've always lived the way I wanted, surrounded by the people I love.* I called the waitress over. "Can I get a grilled cheese and cup of tea to go?" I asked, filled with more urgency than I'd ever felt toward finishing my honey do list.

She wrote it in her pad.

"And can I also get the burger wrapped?"

With the food in hand, I hurried back to the RV with my head in a spin. My mind wanted to finish the list, but my mind wasn't driving anymore. My heart and soul were in charge now, and I thought, *Maybe that's the way it should have been from the start?* I woke Bella. "What do you say we go home?" I asked her. "I really want to see Riley, Michael and the kids."

She wiped her eyes and sat up to kiss me. "I was hoping you'd say that."

As I pointed the RV north, I told her, "We made it all the way to Virginia, so I'm still crossing it off the list!"

She just smiled.

Only two dreams to go, I thought and let my mind wander to a place where I could hear my grandchildren's laughter.

Chapter 13

After spending my last magical holidays with Madison and Pudge, and every second of their school vacation with them, I decided they needed a break from me, and that I needed to return to the doctor's office for a much-needed tune up.

While killing time in the waiting room, I pondered my dream of working as a newspaper reporter. Truth is, if it weren't for the responsibilities to my family, I would have changed jobs every two years. I wondered whether it was time to check off another dream from the refrigerator list. *But there's so little time left*, I pondered, *and I'm not gonna spend it unless I can write something that'll have a real impact...* And then it hit me. *I know exactly what I'll write!*

The nurse approached the waiting room with my thick chart. "Mr. DiMarco, the doctor is ready for you," she said with a smile.

Slowly I stood and made my way toward her. "But am I ready for her?" I asked, teasing her. "That's the question."

Dr. Rice was in her usual cheerful mood, and after my honey do list update, she got right down to business. "Tell me about your pain levels."

"It's gotten real bad," I admitted. "And although I don't even want to imagine how bad it's going to get, I'm even more petrified it's gonna slow me down before

Bella and I..." I stopped. She understood our goals. There was still a lot to do with little time to do it in.

"Alternative treatments may help you cope with the pain," she said and took a seat to explain. "Some patients in advanced stages of the disease try to avoid the side effects of pain medications by using alternative treatments such as acupressure, acupuncture, deep breathing, and even music therapy. Soothing music has been proven to calm the body." Smiling at my confused reaction, she clarified, "We need to keep you on the pain meds, and unfortunately the dosages and the side effects that go with them will also increase, but there's nothing wrong with practicing some deep breathing exercises along with scheduling weekly massages. It's all about maintaining the highest comfort level you can and every little bit of this extra effort will help."

Before I finished my nod, she left the room to retrieve some pamphlets on the benefits of deep breathing and massage. Upon her return, she concluded, "When the pain is bad, you need to ride the wave. It's not the best surfing in the world, but it will eventually subside. Remember that." She patted my shoulder. "Slow, deep breathing and soothing music will definitely help."

"Okay," I said. "I'll try it."

"Great, and we'll need to take some blood before you leave. We need to stay on top of your counts."

~ ~ ~ ~ ~ ~ ~ ~ ~ ~ ~ ~

With the help of Riley's contacts, I got my one and only shot as a freelancer, or stringer, for the local paper.

I spent ten times the effort on that one piece than other reporters would have ever bothered. But it was a one-shot deal for me. I needed to get it right – for several reasons. Even Bella pretended to complain about all the time I spent on the computer.

I turned it in and the editor called two days later. "Not a terrible piece for your first," she said. "I had to make the usual changes though."

"Okay, thanks," I said, pretty sure that I'd just received a backhanded compliment.

There was a pause. "Listen, if you're looking to learn the business, I have plenty of work I need to assign," she offered.

"Thanks," I told her, "I'll have to check my schedule to see what I can fit in." It was the best way I knew of avoiding the cancer talk.

"Fair enough. Just let me know," she said and hung up.

~ ~ ~ ~ ~ ~ ~ ~ ~ ~ ~ ~

It was a random Tuesday morning when I picked up the *Daily Telegram* and flipped through it. My spirit soared. My piece was buried on page seven. Its placement didn't matter to me. I bought ten copies and raced home to Bella. She cried when she read it.

The following night, Madison and Pudge came over, and I pulled out the newspaper. I was so happy for the opportunity to share the article I'd written about their mom.

~ THE DAILY TELEGRAM ~

Riley DiMarco-Resonina:
Riding for a Good Cause
by Don DiMarco, Correspondent

The t-shirt read: Will of Iron, Legs of Steel and Heart of Gold. Riley DiMarco-Resonina's words, however, proved that beneath the catchy logo there is even more...much more.

On March 8th, the compassionate Somerset resident will participate in a very special and powerful event. She will take four days out of her life to join an army of three thousand six hundred bicycle riders. Together, they will travel from Boston to New York, three hundred grueling miles, to help fight in the battle against AIDS. For now, her first challenge is to train for each trying mile.

Riley admits, "Obviously, I'm training for a good cause. I felt it was time for me to do something big – something that would challenge me as much as AIDS challenges thousands." As an advocate for disabled children and a mother of two little ones, since May, Riley has taken every free moment to prepare for the long journey. "I've worked with free weights and Nautilus equipment, but the real training has been riding twenty-five to fifty miles every other day," she says. Before meeting that first challenge head on, there is another obstacle that looms over her like a dark cloud. Before ever reaching the starting line, she must raise fifteen hundred dollars. The second challenge begins.

"We're riding to raise money for the AIDS-related services of the Fenway Community Health Center," explains Riley, "and together, we hope to raise more than three million dollars for individuals with AIDS and important AIDS prevention programs in Boston." Raising her eyebrows, she confesses, "It's not easy...the word AIDS leaves a negative misconception in many minds. The truth is that AIDS is no longer a gay disease. Today, the deadly disease afflicts more heterosexual teenagers and infants than ever before."

Tragically, AIDS has accounted for over three hundred thousand American deaths in the last fifteen years. That's five times the number of Americans that died in the Vietnam War. Fortunately, with people like Riley DiMarco-Resonina, the Fenway Community Health Center can make a difference. According to her, "Recently, a home for babies with AIDS burned down. The Fenway Center stepped in and donated thousands to rebuild."

In the meantime, with the help of her husband, Michael, Riley physically prepares for the final challenge – The Boston-New York AIDS Ride2. For four days, she will volunteer to tax her body, while sleeping under the stars at night. On the first day, she must ride one hundred miles. The second day, a mere fifty, but all hills. Then, she'll be halfway home. Ironically, her only hope is that people will pledge their support and turn her own determination and efforts into victory.

A motto used by the riders was taken from Dr. Martin Luther King Jr: "The ultimate measure of a person is not where they stand in moments of comfort and convenience, but where they stand at times of challenge and controversy." Riley DiMarco-Resonina has chosen to use her twelve-speed bicycle to stand up against a challenging and controversial disease. All tax-deductible pledges should be sent directly to:

Fenway Community Health Center
Attn: Ride Pledge Office
100 Massachusetts Avenue
Boston, Ma. 02115

Please use Riley DiMarco-Resonina's rider number, #6511B, when making your contribution. Riley will do the rest.

~ ~ ~ ~ ~ ~ ~ ~ ~ ~ ~ ~

I searched the kids' faces. They were sincerely impressed. "So because your mom turned out to be such a wonderful person, my life has been a great success, understand?"

They nodded.

"Now isn't that the best gift you could ever give your mom and dad?" I asked.

They nodded again.

"I'm glad you agree."

~ ~ ~ ~ ~ ~ ~ ~ ~ ~ ~ ~

Bella cut out the article and framed it. That night, Riley and Michael insisted on taking us out to celebrate. Even with the increasing pains in my abdomen and kidneys, I couldn't refuse. We ended up at a local Japanese Steak House that Bella and I had never been to. *What the hell?* I thought and tried two bites of sushi – the cooked kind. "Only seals should eat the raw stuff," I told them.

~ ~ ~ ~ ~ ~ ~ ~ ~ ~ ~ ~

The following morning, the pain was so intense I finally surrendered and scheduled a masseuse to come to the house.

I felt awkward, but Bella swore, "You're going to love it. Believe me."

I couldn't have been five minutes into my first massage before I was drooling like a baby. I'd never felt so relaxed. Christine, the masseuse, worked the knots out of my neck, the steel out of my back and for a while, I almost believed she might dig the cancer out of my poisoned organs. No such luck. Instead, she turned my arms and legs into rubber bands, and if only for a few moments, removed the weight I carried in my mind. It was a wonderful gift and I wondered, *Why did I wait until the end of my life to enjoy this?*

Before she left, I scheduled weekly massages with her.

~ ~ ~ ~ ~ ~ ~ ~ ~ ~ ~

That afternoon, a check for thirty-five dollars arrived in the mail, signed by Tracy Kippenberger, publisher of the *Daily Telegram.* It was the only check I'd ever earned that I had no intention of cashing. *Pulitzer prize-winning journalism or not, I gave it my best shot and at least played the game*, I decided – before folding up the check, placing it in my shoebox and crossing off another item from the honey do list.

Bella approached me and grabbed my hand. "I love you," she whispered.

I kissed her hand.

She stared out the kitchen window and sighed. "This snow is really starting to get old," she complained and shook her head.

Instantly, I had an epiphany. On a whim, I told her, "I have a surprise for you."

"What is it?" she asked, her eyes sparkling.

"It wouldn't be a surprise if I told you, would it?" I asked.

As my mind drifted off, I let the love of my family wash over me. *Good or bad, life is best when it's shared*, I thought, *whether it's first-hand experiences or second-hand stories.*

Bella, on the other hand, squirmed with curiosity.

~ ~ ~ ~ ~ ~ ~ ~ ~ ~ ~ ~

Before I knew it, Bella and I were back in Dr. Rice's office for my blood work follow-up. Just as soon as Dr. Rice entered the room, I knew she had more bad news.

"What is it?" Bella asked, beating me to the punch.

The kind doctor shook her head. "The cancer has metastasized outside of the liver and spread to the lymph nodes. And…" She paused, looking deep into my eyes. "…it's moving fast now."

"And before it's over, it'll be everywhere, right?" My rhetorical question made my wife squirm even more.

Dr. Rice half-nodded. "It could reach your bones and lungs." She shook her head. "You need to…"

"Pick up the pace," I said. "I got it."

She never argued the point.

Chapter 14

Trying to make up for the time that would be lost, I worked on the puzzle until we absolutely had to leave for the airport. It was a good thing we kept the luggage out. Two of the bags weren't even unpacked from the last trip.

I was feeling worse but kept it to myself. Like termites through an old house, I could actually feel the cancer spreading, poisoning one organ after the next. No matter, with the selflessness Bella had shown by spending her honeymoon healing my soul in Vietnam, it was going to take more than cancer to stop us. *If our recent trips have taught me anything, it's so important to get away and make memories with the people you love — cancer be damned!*

~ ~ ~ ~ ~ ~ ~ ~ ~ ~ ~ ~

I'd jumped on the net and did the research. Barbados meant "the bearded-ones," named after the island's fig trees, which had a beard-like appearance. According to the pictures, it was paradise on earth. *And it's about time*, I thought.

With Riley's help, I was able to make the plans, pack the bags and keep my secret.

Right up until the time we pulled into the airport's icy parking lot, Bella was relentless. "Okay," she said, "I know we're going on a trip. But where?"

"Will you stop," I laughed. "I packed your mittens and scarf. You'll know soon enough."

We checked in at Gate 11, Flight #7438, destination, Barbados.

"Oh Don," she squeaked and nearly crushed my disappearing body with a bear hug.

~ ~ ~ ~ ~ ~ ~ ~ ~ ~ ~ ~

On the plane, I reported my findings to Bella. "Barbados was founded by a tribe of cone heads, overtaken by a tribe of cannibals who probably ate them, conquered by the Spanish, and later colonized by the English. I figured it was perfect for you!"

She laughed. "I bet it is."

The flight was rough, but as we circled a rugged strip of land, I looked out the small window and saw miles of white sand beaches. I nudged Bella and pointed. "Welcome to Barbados," I whispered. All along the shore, large stretches of white sand were broken by beautiful coral formations. We placed our trays back into their upright positions, fastened our seat belts and smiled. Anywhere that land met ocean, a little piece of heaven could be found.

~ ~ ~ ~ ~ ~ ~ ~ ~ ~ ~ ~

The airport was under heavy renovations, so we had to exit the plane on the tarmac and make our way through a maze of scaffolding to the terminal. The heat was almost as oppressive and punishing as Vietnam. I pulled at my collar and looked over at Bella. She was huffing and puffing too. "Hey, it beats the snow," she said with a grin.

Customs consisted of two people who looked very unhappy with their jobs. With no air conditioning, I didn't blame them. After a couple of bad looks, our papers were stamped. "Thank you," I said to the girl. If I didn't know better, I would have sworn she snarled at me. *You'd fit in well at the Department of Motor Vehicles*, I thought and tipped a local boy to drag our luggage out to the curb.

~ ~ ~ ~ ~ ~ ~ ~ ~ ~ ~ ~

The cab driver drove us from the airport to the parish of St. Michael located between Bridgetown and Speightstown.

The hotel sat right on the beach but didn't look like much from the outside. Once we crossed the threshold though, I quickly realized why I'd paid as much as I did. It was gorgeous, maybe even the paradise they showed in the pictures.

There were three crystal blue pools that layered one atop the other, dumping into a final lagoon by way of a giant rock waterfall. "Gorgeous," Bella sighed and hugged me from behind.

We unpacked and spent the first day adapting to our new surroundings. It's funny how my memories of this play out in fragments – a late breakfast that I found repulsive because the cheese was sweating and the warm pints of milk showed a grinning goat on the back of the cartons; entire families of Brits and Australians on holiday by the pool; trays of strawberry and banana daiquiris. I can still picture the young con art-ist trying to peddle his fake jewelry on the beach and me shooing him away from Bella, as if he were an RV salesman. We ran into the cleaning lady three times. From her broken English, I learned that her name was Rosa and she worked three jobs. I can still see my beau-tiful wife lying on a white lawn chair under a palm tree, reading a book and laughing. Everyone smelled like coconut and everyone was smiling. Lunch was buffet style with hot dogs and barbecue chicken. Though I hid it from Bella, I couldn't eat. I'd been sick to my stomach since we landed and it wasn't just from mo-tion sickness. Forgive the graphic detail, but my stool was starting to show increasing traces of blood again each time I managed to go. And, there were moments when I felt like I'd swallowed a handful of broken glass. I tried breathing through it each time. *One, one-thou-sand…two, one-thousand…three, one-thousand…*

Bella asked, "Are you feeling sick?"

"Not too bad," I lied. I didn't need Bella's futile worrying to slow us down. Bottom line – I was dying and nothing was going to stop that. From here on, as my friend Billy Hutchins would say, *We need to drive this thing until the wheels come off and we head into victo-ry lane – out of gas, all banged up, and the doors torn right off it.*

~ ~ ~ ~ ~ ~ ~ ~ ~ ~ ~ ~

At dusk that first night, I was invited to play cricket on the beach with some of the young natives who'd gotten off work from the hotels. "Come on, Mon!" a skinny man with long dreadlocks yelled at me, extending a flat paddle in my direction.

I couldn't resist and got up from my beach chair. As I slowly made my way down the beach, I warned them, "I used to play baseball when I was a kid."

I swung and missed three times. They all laughed and kept on laughing. I looked up to find Bella taking pictures and laughing right along with them. The sun was just going down. It was beautiful. I suppose they took my age into account and gave me a few extra swings. I took a couple deep breaths and by the fifth swing, I connected and looped one into the ocean. "Yoohoo!" my wife cheered and the men took turns congratulating me. For such poor people, they seemed so happy. They were friendly and relaxed, and from the looks of it, not overly burdened with the worries of most. I watched as the sun shimmered on the horizon, throwing off colors I'd never seen before. Having been born in paradise, my new friends had been blessed and obviously knew it.

"Time to eat," Bella called out. I looked up to find her waving me to her. My body tingled and I wondered, *Lord, what did I ever do to deserve such a woman?* I still loved my wife as passionately as the rainy day we'd met.

~ ~ ~ ~ ~ ~ ~ ~ ~ ~ ~

The hotel's restaurant was an open veranda glowing in candlelight, illuminating the smiles of those who dined under its giant thatched roof. Dinner was formal, by reservation only, and though I still felt exhausted and terribly ill, I didn't want to miss anything. The beat of the calypso band and the certain disappointment in my wife's face made me bite my tongue and endure with a smile. From the length of Bella's smile, it was well worth the discomfort.

I awoke earlier than Bella and stepped out onto the small balcony that overlooked the beach. In the growing light, I read one of the hotel's many tour advertisements:

> Barbados was born from sugar and rum in the days when pirates roamed the sea. With a history rich in folklore, there are stately plantations of Jacobean and Georgian architecture set amid the chattel houses. Trace the roots of a proud and determined people, a nation that has risen above its past. Barbados has many natural phenomena: underground caves of waterfalls and lakes, ocean tide pools, flower forests, mangrove swamps and many indigenous species such as the Barbados green monkey. The Caribbean is also full of people who are larger than life. Allow them to touch you with their colorful stories, endless energy, and love of life. Tour the island and…

Bella stirred from her sleep. I went to her.

~ ~ ~ ~ ~ ~ ~ ~ ~ ~ ~ ~

On our first morning walk, we came across an older man raking seaweed on the beach. "Good morning," I called out to him.

"Good morning to you," he said with a smile, "and a glorious afternoon and evening, too."

"We hope."

"Name's David," he said, "if you need anything, please feel free to call on me, yes?"

I stopped. "Actually, my wife and I are interested in touring your beautiful island, but don't want to do it from the windows of a bus."

He leaned on his rake and looked at me, but said nothing.

"We'd like to get a native's perspective of the island and…"

"I see," he said and thought for a moment. "I have a friend, Philip, who knows every road and back, but…" He looked embarrassed to go on.

"Yes?"

"He charges one hundred fifty U.S. dollars for the day."

"That's reasonable enough," I said. "When can he take us?"

"I can arrange it so that you leave tomorrow morning, yes?"

"That would be great. It'll give us a full day."

~ ~ ~ ~ ~ ~ ~ ~ ~ ~ ~ ~

As promised, at first light, Philip waited for us at the hotel's front gate. He opened the Toyota's rear door for

Bella and greeted me with an extended hand. "Good morning, sir," he said.

I was pleased to discover that his English was better than mine. "Good morning," I said, "but please don't call me sir. I'm Don and that pretty lady right there is Bella."

Both he and Bella smiled. He nodded. "Okay then, Don and Bella," he replied, "let's go tour the island." One handshake later, we were heading away from the luxury we'd known for two days toward poverty unlike anything I'd ever seen.

As we drove, I prompted Philip to describe his world. Without hesitation, he explained, "The first settlement in Barbados was Holetown, originally named Jamestown after King James the First of England. It acquired the name Holetown because of the off loading and cleaning of ships in the very small channel located near the town. Speightstown, however, was the first major port and commercial center of Barbados. Neglected over the years, I'm happy to say it's since been revived. There are excellent hotels and restaurants in the area, as well as a new art gallery."

As he spoke, Bella and I pointed out the shacks with no windows, tin roofs and naked children running around barefoot.

Philip's first stop was at the Baobab Tree in St. Michael. "Out of little seeds, great things can grow," he said and opened the door for Bella to get out and take a closer look.

The tree was enormous. "It's also known as the Monkey-bread tree," he explained. "It would take

fifteen adults joining with outstretched arms to sur-
round its circumference."

I whistled and bent to read the inscription on the
wooden plaque:

> Baobab Tree (Adansonia digitata) One
> of the two mature trees in Barbados. This
> remarkable tree of girth 44.5 ft (13.6m)
> is believed to have been brought from
> Guinea, Africa around 1738 making it
> over two hundred fifty years old. Its jug-
> shaped trunk is ideally suited for storing
> water, an ideal adaptation in the dry sa-
> vannah regions of its native Africa.

Without another word, Philip allowed us the time
we needed to take in the experience. Bella leaned into
my ear. "Make sure you thank David when we return
to the hotel. Philip's a fabulous guide," she whispered.

"He is," I said. "And I will."

Our second stop was at St. James Parish Church
in Holetown. Philip cleared his throat. "Built in 1847,
St. James Parish Church is among the four oldest sur-
viving churches in Barbados. In the southern porch of
the church, a bell with the inscription, 'God bless King
William, 1696,' can be found. It pre-dates the American Liberty Bell by fifty-four years."

My wide-eyed wife and I toured the place. There
were ancient mural tablets, stained glass windows and a
dilapidated cemetery at the rear of the chapel.

~ ~ ~ ~ ~ ~ ~ ~ ~ ~ ~ ~

As we pulled up the long drive to St. Nicholas Abbey, the well-preserved mansion showed off its curved Dutch gables and chimney stacks. "This place was built in 1660," Philip said. "The rubble walls are made of boulders held together with a mixture of egg white and coral dust. There was no cement available when it was built." While he hovered around the car outside, Bella and I purchased two tickets and took the tour.

Past the deplorable slave's quarters, we were led into an old horse stable where we sat in metal chairs and watched a 1930s film on sugar plantation life. Meant to attract tourists, it had the opposite effect for Bella. She was appalled. As we walked back to the mansion, the tour guide said, "The history of our slaves is quite interesting."

Bella grabbed my arm and stopped me. "Can we please leave?"

I nodded and looked back once at the old sugar plantation's slave quarters. It was unimaginable how civilized people could treat others not so long ago.

Philip smiled when he saw us marching back to the car. "I'm not surprised you did not want to stay," he said and threw open Bella's door.

Back on the road, he explained, "With the need to harvest sugar to make rum, it was the Dutch who first supplied the forced labor from West Africa. The slaves came from Sierra Leone, Guinea, Ghana, the Ivory Coast, Nigeria and Cameroon, though many of them did not survive the journey. For those thousands who did reach their destination, they found their plantation owners to be cruel and without mercy. To meet the labor demands – kidnapping, as well as welcoming convicted criminals onto its shores, were two other popular means of obtaining servants."

Bella stared out her window in silence until Philip brought the car to a sudden halt and leaned over the front seat. "Wait till you meet this character," he said.

We got out and watched as a grown man scurried up a palm tree with a machete clenched in his teeth. With one swipe, he cut down two coconuts and slid down the tree to greet us. With one coconut bouncing in his left hand, he spun it in a circle, whacking at it three or four times with his machete. He then gave it one final cut, threw a straw into the small hole and handed it to Bella.

She accepted the gift. While the man worked on mine, Philip whispered, "He'll be wanting a dollar for each, you know."

I handed the man his money and put the straw in my mouth. The coconut water was cool and refreshing, tasting a little like melon with a hint of nut – and it didn't set my stomach on fire as I'd feared.

Once we'd finished our drinks, with the speed and agility of a marksman he sliced the coconut in two, exposing the soft white meat inside.

Philip watched our faces and laughed.

~ ~ ~ ~ ~ ~ ~ ~ ~ ~ ~ ~

As we drove north, our friendly tour guide said, "As you'll soon see, the sandstone cliffs rise hundreds of feet above the sea where Barbados meets the Atlantic Ocean. The waves are so bad on the northern coast that swimming is forbidden."

He wasn't kidding. While Bella and I spent a half hour taking pictures, the raging Atlantic beat on the coral formations below, creating an unforgettable display of untamed power.

We'd ventured south when Philip began pointing out the monkeys in the trees. "Watch out for these thieves. If you're not careful, they'll take everything from you."

We laughed.

"Funny, huh? I'll show you." After a hundred more yards, he pulled over.

The area was thick with poverty, but I'd learned to trust Philip and stepped out of the car. There was a young man standing off the side of the narrow, dirt road. He had a small monkey perched upon his head. Philip waved the man over and handed me a stalk of sugar cane. "Pretend you're eating this," he whispered.

I did. Sure enough, the monkey flew off his owner's head, bounced toward me and stripped the sugar cane out of my hands before I knew what had happened. While Philip grabbed his side in laughter, the monkey climbed back on top of his owner's head and enjoyed his snack. "Thieves, I told you," Philip said and laughed some more.

I tipped the man with the monkey for allowing Bella to take pictures of his friend sitting on top of my head. Philip checked his watch. "We should get to Harrison's Cave."

~ ~ ~ ~ ~ ~ ~ ~ ~ ~ ~ ~

While waiting in line to buy tickets, a large man with a British accent began making obnoxious remarks. Before long, it looked like he might get violent with another tourist, who had been offended. My reaction was to shield my wife when I realized, *She'll be on her own soon.* The reality of it stung worse than ever.

Starting at the Visitor's Center and gift shop, we were driven in electrically-powered trams down into a deep, dark hole. The mouth of the cave was narrow and the floors were slick. As the walls closed in, I saw they were perspiring. "This is as close to hell as I ever want to go," I whispered and slid closer to Bella.

"Stop it," she said and slapped my arm.

"Harrison's Cave is a unique phenomenon of nature," the tour guide said over the intercom. "Please take note of the amazing stalactites hanging from the roof of the cave and stalagmites that emerge from the ground." A room within the cave opened up and glistened like diamonds in water. "The stalactites and stalagmites were formed over thousands of years. In some places, the stalactites have reached down to the stalagmites, forming the spectacular white pillars you see."

It was breathtaking. Bella took her pictures and we continued down. The caves were beautiful, but they did lack one thing – natural light. *Even the prettiest things cannot be appreciated without light,* I thought.

At the lowest level in the cave, we were invited to leave the tram and walk alongside a waterfall that plunged into a deep emerald pool below. It was remarkable, but at the same time – between the crippling nausea and growing claustrophobia – I couldn't wait to leave.

Bella looked at me. "I'm ready to go, too," she whispered.

~ ~ ~ ~ ~ ~ ~ ~ ~ ~ ~ ~

Our final stop with Philip was at The Emancipation Statue. As we pulled up, I wasn't surprised he'd saved it for last.

The statue symbolized the breaking of the chains of slavery at Emancipation. "Although slavery was abolished in 1834," Philip explained, "it was followed by a four-year apprenticeship where free men continued to work a forty-five-hour week without pay in exchange for living in the tiny huts provided by the plantation owners."

I shook my head alongside my wife's.

"Freedom from slavery was celebrated in 1838 at the end of the apprentice period, with over seventy thousand Barbadians of African origin taking to the streets with the Barbados folk song." He pointed to the plaque on the statue:

> Lick an Lock-up Done Wid, Hurray
> fuh Jin-Jin (Queen Victoria).
> De Queen come from England to set we
> free
> Now Lick an Lock-up Done Wid, Hur-
> ray fuh Jin-Jin

"Many Barbadians refer to the statue as Bussa, the name of a slave who helped inspire a revolt against slavery in 1816."

On the way back to the hotel, Philip concluded his history lesson. "Barbados remained a British colony until internal autonomy was granted in 1961. The island gained full independence in 1966, but still maintains ties to the Britain monarch through a Governor General."

I paid Philip his one hundred fifty dollars, plus a hefty tip and could not thank him enough.

He nodded his gratitude. "They say knowledge is power, my friend. The more people who know about suffering, the less chance it will happen again...yes?"

"Yes," Bella said and we wished him well.

~ ~ ~ ~ ~ ~ ~ ~ ~ ~ ~ ~

The rest of the week was spent in a painful haze, but I survived it by concentrating on my wife's contagious smile.

Water sports included kite surfing, parasailing, kayaking, scuba diving and renting a WaveRunner. I considered taking out the Jet Ski, but told Bella, "One bad fall and I'm done." She agreed.

The island music was a mix of calypso and reggae. There were plenty of outdoor bands and clubs to dance the night away. Though I chose to pass on the limbo contests, we did dance a few of the slower numbers.

Every morning, I spoke with Rosa, our cleaning lady. I could only make out three or four words each time, but it was enough to learn about her life. "After here, two jobs more," she said, "for college, my daughter." As she shared her dreams with me, a mother's pride illuminated her dark, tired eyes.

Souvenir shopping quickly became Bella's favorite part of the trip and she purchased a pair of seashell earrings right away. The narrow streets and crazy taxi drivers made it a daring adventure. We stopped at a cigar factory and watched the natives turn giant dried leaves into tightly rolled cigars. I bought two; one for me – which I had no intention of ever smoking – and the other for Michael. The local artisan's shops specialized in handcrafted sculptures and paintings, most with loud, bright colors, themes of the sea, or their ancestors working the sugar fields. Bella bought a small watercolor for Riley and rum cakes for everyone else.

~ ~ ~ ~ ~ ~ ~ ~ ~ ~ ~ ~

On the final day of our belated honeymoon, we ordered room service in the morning. At six o'clock, there was a knock at the door. Bella got up and answered it. There was no one there. The wait staff had confused the room numbers. The folks across the way were getting served. She looked at the alarm clock. We still had another hour of sleep before breakfast. As I stirred, she said, "You get the door next time."

I nodded and closed my eyes. One wink later, a knock struck our door again. For a second or two, I couldn't move my legs. I was paralyzed. Panic rushed through my aching body and I quietly begged, *Please, God, not here. Not now.* Finally, something gave and I was able to swing my swollen feet onto the floor. It took a minute, but I met room service in the blinding light of the cracked door. Looking back at Bella, I'd never been so grateful for the use of my legs. I signed for the meal and tipped the boy what anyone would – given that they'd just experienced a miracle.

After I showered, I left the bathroom to find Bella waiting for me – her fist clenched and extended. I opened my hand to receive the surprise and she placed a seashell earring into it. I looked up to find her wearing the other one. "What's this for?" I asked.

"Do you know what day this is?" she asked.

My mind raced. *It's not our anniversary or either of our birthdays.* I shrugged.

"Today is exactly twelve months and one day from Dr. Rice's prognosis."

"And I'm still here," I said, my eyes immediately starting to water.

"Yes, you are," she confirmed, her eyes filling too.

"Then miracles *do* happen."

She hurried into my arms.

~ ~ ~ ~ ~ ~ ~ ~ ~ ~ ~ ~

Though Bella was reluctant because of my poor health, I insisted we go on a snorkeling trip to celebrate. We boarded the giant catamaran to the spiritual beats of reggae. The captain was Australian, the two crewmembers were island natives, and the other six couples were celebrating their marriage vows as well.

As we sailed out to one of two coral reefs, I watched as one of the crewmembers – a Raja man with long dreadlocks – dove off the bow of the boat and swam to shore. Within minutes, he returned with a bag of fish that looked like sardines. "I wonder what those are for?" I asked Bella.

She shrugged and put on her snorkeling gear.

I slipped on my life vest and inflated it until I looked like the Michelin Man. Bella laughed but I wasn't taking any chances. I could only swim as far as my arms would take me. Treading water had never been my strong suit. As I fumbled with my fins, the same Raja guy took off at a full sprint from the back of the boat and dove into the water without a mask or snorkel. I waited for him to come back up, but he didn't. I looked to both sides. He still wasn't there. Seconds later, his head popped up like a fishing bobber and he was smiling. "Come on, peoples," he said. "You'll want to see this."

Following Bella, I eased into the warm water like the old man I'd never imagined I'd become and floated for a few seconds until I knew I wasn't going to sink. I placed the snorkel into my mouth and lay on my belly, submerging my mask.

It was a foreign world; a beautiful world filled with schools of colorful fish flying high above coral mountain ranges. I took a couple deep breaths when I saw him. Our Raja friend was sitting on the ocean floor, waving one of the sardines in front of him. It took a few seconds before an enormous sea turtle hovered over him for the snack. My mouth must have been hung open because I gagged on water and had to clear it from the snorkel.

Raja man brought the ancient sea turtle so close to Bella and me that we were able to touch it. I felt so relaxed and happy, floating weightlessly and holding hands with my lifelong love.

After exploring the second reef, we managed to get back on the boat, exhausted but thrilled. "Incredible," I said to Bella.

She kissed my salty cheek. "Thank you. I've waited my whole life for that swim. It was even more amazing than I'd imagined."

"Sorry it took so long," I said.

"Nonsense," she countered. "We did it and that's all that counts."

I nodded and took her into my arms.

On the trip home, we were served plates of flying fish and native brown rice. Suspended in thick nets just above the water, Bella and I drank rum punch from plastic cups, cuddled and witnessed the most spectacular sunset I've ever seen – maybe even better than the Arizona desert. "Perfect," Bella kept saying. "Just perfect…"

~ ~ ~ ~ ~ ~ ~ ~ ~ ~ ~ ~

On the morning we packed to leave, I caught David on the beach, raking the seaweed the tide had delivered the night before. "How are you, my friend?" I asked.

He leaned on his rake and smiled. "I hear people talking sometimes about the old man cleaning the beach, but look at this…" He waved his hand, gesturing to everything that surrounded him. "I work all day in paradise. There is no bad job here in Barbados."

I nodded. *The people of Barbados make their own choices now*, I thought, and then wondered if that were true. *Rosa is a free woman, but she enslaves herself to three jobs to liberate her daughter from poverty.* "How much does it cost to go to college here?" I asked David.

He searched my face for the reason I was asking, but he never asked. "Around one thousand U.S. dollars a year."

I thanked him for everything and then left to help Bella fit the souvenirs into our overstuffed luggage.

~ ~ ~ ~ ~ ~ ~ ~ ~ ~ ~ ~

As we checked out, I stole one last glimpse of paradise. Each face was bronze and beaming with happiness, their bodies sculpted in muscle. The friendly sun warmed the hearts of the coldest men and it was infectious. Like the people, the sturdy palm trees bent to the soothing ocean breezes, while every color of the spectrum created a botanical feast. Standing on a beach of powdered sugar, the rush of the gentle waves matched each breath and a simple peace overtook me. The sun's warm fingers caressed my tingling skin and the salty taste of the Caribbean quenched my thirst for fun. I watched as the cherry-red sun sat on the horizon, promising another magical day. And though it was time to go, I had to smile. I didn't need to own any of it, nor ever visit again. On the darkest, coldest, most painful nights, I could simply close my eyes, search the blessing of a memory and return to Barbados once again. I turned to find Bella standing at my side and wrapped my arm around her shoulder. "I really am sorry I never took you here sooner."

"Enough of that. We came when we were supposed to."

"Do you have the envelope?" I asked.

She handed it to me. "This is a good thing you're doing, you know."

I shrugged. "Better late than never, I guess."

I handed the desk clerk the envelope and carefully explained, "I need it to be hand-delivered to Rosa, the cleaning lady who works in the mornings. Do you know the one I'm talking about?"

She smiled. "We only have one Rosa. I'll make sure she gets it."

I returned her smile, confident that Rosa would receive our gift. What the desk clerk didn't realize was that the envelope contained one thousand dollars and a short note reading, *Rosa – please use this money to free up some of your time to spend with your family. Thank you for everything. The service was wonderful – Don and Bella DiMarco.*

Chapter 15

By spring, Bella's second set of brochures had unexpectedly appeared. It was the information needed to live my last dream and complete the honey-do list. It read:

> Cape Cod Deep Sea Fishing – Fish in the heart of New England's largest natural habitats. Beginner and experienced anglers alike will enjoy the deep sea fishing aboard one of our climate-controlled boats. Catch codfish, pollock, haddock, mackerel, wolffish, flounder, and even the occasional striped bass and bluefish. From a four-hour excursion to an overnight marathon trip one hundred miles offshore, we offer a wide variety of deep sea fishing venues. We've been fishing these waters for over forty-five years, so we know where to get you hooked in. Whether you are a beginner or an old pro, come and experience deep sea fishing excitement at its best! Each trip is limited to the first fifty people so don't wait.

I had just breathed my way through a barrage of pain – *one, one-thousand...two, one-thousand...three, one-thousand* – when I closed my heavy eyelids and let myself drift away…

~ ~ ~ ~ ~ ~ ~ ~ ~ ~ ~ ~

Being prone to seasickness, I popped two motion sickness pills and three pain pills an hour before the boat left the dock.

On board, I was a sponge, listening to every detail of instruction and advice that the captain and crew offered. I definitely did not want the big one to get away. I asked more questions than anyone. "Can we bring home whatever we catch?"

Randy, the first mate, nodded. "You can bring all your fish home, as long as they're legal size. We'll even clean them for you."

"But I don't have a fishing license."

"No license needed to go saltwater fishing," he explained.

While the captain allowed the boat to drift from one spot to another until he found the best fishing ground, I took a seat along the railing and prepared my rented gear. We anchored and began bottom fishing using whole clams for bait. At first, the fish didn't bite.

"Patience," Randy said with a smirk, reading my frustrated face.

Things changed in a hurry. My first catch was a codfish. It took me almost ten minutes to land the thirty-pounder and it was at least four feet long.

"It's a baby," Randy said, as he ran over to help me take it off the hook.

"Baby?"

He nodded. "These guys get real big. The annual catch of cod amounts to tens of thousands of tons every year."

Baby or no baby, I couldn't wipe the smile off my face.

We caught pollock next. It ran in schools, measured no more than three feet and weighed an average of ten pounds. But oh what a fight!

Haddock ran in deeper waters. Out of the fifty people onboard, only one guy landed one. It was three feet long and all of thirty pounds.

As the sun rested on the horizon, a large school of mackerel found their way onto our lines. Maybe ten pounds, a foot long each, we took hit after hit. As I landed my fourth, Randy talked about bluefish. "They're voracious creatures," he said, "feeding on squid and schools of small fish. They're reported to feed until their bellies are full, regurgitate, and feed again as long as there's food. They've even been known to attack swimmers. Bluefish are exciting to land though, and they're real tasty if you eat them when they're fresh." No one caught a bluefish, though.

As I took joy in ravaging the school of mackerel, a guy sitting next to me landed a rare wolffish. It had large jaws and sharp teeth. Randy was careful unhooking it. "These critters have a bad habit of attacking people in the water and when they're caught they're just as dangerous," he warned. The demon fish was five feet long and must have weighed more than fifty pounds. It bucked and fought for its life for a long time on the deck. I understood its desperation.

While other anglers had luck catching a few flounder, no one saw fin or gill of any sculpin, sea robin, or spiny dogfish.

And then it happened – the big battle I'd been dreaming of my whole life; I felt something grab my bait and the line ran under the boat, bending my pole in half. Randy rushed over, but I waved him off. I let the fish run for a spell, gradually tightening the drag on my reel.

"It's a big one!" Randy yelled and everyone stopped what they were doing to watch.

I reeled. He fought. I reeled. He fought. A good twenty minutes went by and my hands began to throb. I was sweating, but I still waved Randy off. "I want this one alone," I told him. Two jerks and one quick reel later, the monster leaped out of the water. It was a striped bass and easily seventy pounds. I worked him a few minutes more before placing all six feet of him into Randy's extended net. Some of the folks on the boat applauded. Randy helped me take the whopper off the hook and I struggled to hold it in mid-air for a few precious moments. Its body convulsed for the water. My arm throbbed from its weight. And then to everyone's surprise, I dangled it over the side of the boat and let it go. Splash!

"Are you crazy?" Randy squealed, looking over the rails for the disappearing fish.

I smiled. "What can I say? It was his lucky day."

As we headed back to port, Randy cleaned and filleted my fish for a generous tip, but he still refused to speak to me. He didn't understand. My dream had come true. My list was complete…

~ ~ ~ ~ ~ ~ ~ ~ ~ ~ ~ ~

I emerged from my daydream and shuddered. I looked down at the brochure and caught the caption at the bottom: "Adult trips only. No children allowed." A slap of reality struck me hard. *The hourglass is running out,* I thought. *We're only given so many moments and once they're spent, they're spent.* Making the most of each one became so much more important when there were only a few left. *And besides,* I thought, *I'm too damned tired to go fishing!*

I got up from my chair, went to the refrigerator and put a huge check mark through the entire list. *Enough,* I thought. *It's time to get to the important stuff.* Terminal illness had a brutal way of rearranging priorities.

I picked up the phone and called Riley's house. Madison answered. "Wanna go on a picnic?" I asked her.

"Yahooooo!" She dropped the phone and screamed her joy all the way down the hall. I listened as she and Pudge celebrated, their telephone dangling from the kitchen wall.

I palmed a handful of pain pills and washed them down with a gulp of water. I then called Bella at work and told her that we'd be by to pick her up in an hour. As I gathered my car keys and wallet, I thought about calling Riley and inviting her along, but figured it would only make her feel bad when she couldn't go. She was working a lot and couldn't spend much time with me. I could hear the guilt in her voice each time she said, "Sorry, Dad."

"That's the funny thing about kids," I told her. "You've got to feed them."

With whatever energy I had left, I spent as much time as I could with Madison and Pudge – scheduled around the daily cat naps that helped me retain my strength. I was almost to the car when my neighbor, Beatrice Goran, caught me in the driveway.

I didn't care much for the spinster Goran. She was the type of person who spent so much time dying that she never actually lived. But she'd been our next-door neighbor for decades, so I gave her the respect due anyone. I listened to the "mind vampire" lecture on the words "integrity" and "truth." It didn't take long for me to realize I'd volunteered to listen to the foolish babble of someone who didn't grasp either. All the while, I thought, *If I cared any less, I'd be sleeping.*

As she went on, I fought to hold back the yawn, but it was a losing battle. The hum of Ms. Goran's nasal monotone was a fierce enemy and I quickly discovered that my will was no match.

I seriously don't have time for this, I thought.

"But I told Mr. Feeney, years ago," she said, "that Melissa was a hussy..."

I hid the yawn behind my hand and looked away. The catty woman was the cure-all for insomnia. Appearing interested became my greatest challenge, but every few seconds my mind wandered and I drifted off. *I wonder how the Red Sox are doing in spring training?*

"But of course, no one listens to me," she went on.

Shoot, I thought, *I forgot to drop off the movies at the video store. That's all we need, more late fees. I should own that store by now.*

"So what do you think of my new hair style?"

Hideous was the first thing that came to mind, but I smiled. "I think it looks great. It really frames the features of your face." I couldn't help it. I drifted off again, my eyes still staring straight into hers. *Was I supposed to get milk or bread this afternoon?* I couldn't remember. *To hell with it. I'll get both.*

Several minutes were lost to oblivion when Ms. Goran called out, "Donald?" brutally dragging me back into the present.

"Yeah?"

"I just asked what you thought of all this?"

I shook my head. "You know…I'm standing here…thinking…what a predicament."

An eternal moment later, the vicious hen nodded and grinned. "I know. I know exactly what you're saying."

I went for broke. "I guess what really matters is what you think, right?"

She kept nodding and a look of satisfaction crept into her beady eyes.

Though I was starting to feel like an RV salesman myself, I was relieved with my clever save. She wasn't about to let me go, though. Without mercy, she forged on and covered topics of conversation that couldn't have been less interesting. "And I heard that Gus and Jodi might be splitting up…"

I tried hard to stay with her. Just to stay sharp, I shook my head, occasionally smiling and replying to each comment with something silently sarcastic in my mind. Before long, my internal defenses took over and my mind mercifully whisked me away. *I need to call Dewey. It's been over a month since we've talked.*

After several minutes of ignoring Ms. Goran to her face, I emerged from my fog. Without thinking, I blurted, "Yeah, right!"

She immediately ceased her ramble. "Excuse me?" Her face contorted.

I could almost smell the embalming fluid boiling in her veins. I couldn't believe I'd just slipped and spoke aloud. "Oh, I'm sorry. I was just thinking about something else."

"Well then, I'm sorry to be boring you," she said, auditioning her sympathy face for me.

You have no idea, I thought. "No, not at all." I then put on the biggest smile, hoping to end our painful dialogue. Actually, it was so much more than hope. It was a prayer.

"Well, okay then. I can see you're busy," she muttered, and with a snooty nod my prayers were answered. The deadly conversationalist moped away.

Thank God people can't read minds, I thought. *Ms. Goran's "truth" would take on a whole new meaning.* I suppose she did serve a purpose though. She reminded me of the people I did want to spend my time with. I rushed off to pick up three of my favorites.

~ ~ ~ ~ ~ ~ ~ ~ ~ ~ ~

Once Bella and I grabbed the kids, she promised them a trip to Newport, Rhode Island, to see the mansions. On the ride there, Madison squirmed in her seat. "Tell us a story, Poppa," she said. "Tell us a story about when you were a kid."

I looked in the rearview and smiled. "My brother Joseph and I got into our fair share of fights growing up. He was the tough guy but I could hold my own. We boxed in our bedroom and wrestled in the mud, but being the bigger brother, he always enjoyed it more than me."

They each laughed.

"I was eleven years old when some bullies jumped me and beat me up. And the worse part was they scratched up my new bike – The Blue Devil. When my father got home from work, he asked me what had happened to the bike. I told him and he yelled at me, telling me never to let anyone pick on me, and that I needed to stand up for myself.

"Although I was still afraid of those kids, I figured my dad was right and I couldn't let it happen again."

Peering into the rear-view mirror, I shrugged. "And then, one day Ronnie Forrester – the worst one of them all – began chasing me home from my paper route. I was scared to death. Ronnie was a big kid who was a little 'touched in the head.' I told Joseph about it. I think he was afraid too, but he was also very angry.

"That next week, Joseph rode along with me on my paper route. For the first time in a long time, I felt relaxed. And that's when Ronnie showed up at the railroad tracks and stopped us. As he walked up to us, he kicked my bike and smiled at me. I was so mad – but really scared too. Ronnie stared right at me and told me it was a mistake to bring my brother for protection; that he was going to still get me.

"Joseph's face was bright red and he started really yelling at Ronnie, telling him to stop picking on me.

"Ronnie got right in Joseph's face and said he was going to beat us both up.

"I couldn't believe it, but Joseph just smiled. That's when Ronnie's face turned red and he started screaming, telling us to finish the paper route and then meet him at Lincoln Park under the old roller coaster in an hour. He said he was gonna kick both our butts. He started to turn around when he stopped and warned us not to be late or else he'd get us both alone.

"Even though I was angry that Ronnie had kicked my bike, I was so scared. I remember with each paper I delivered, that fear kept getting bigger and bigger until I was in a full panic."

Madison and Pudge were sitting on the edge of the back seat, their mouths half-opened.

"When we arrived at Lincoln Park, there was a circle of bikes and scooters waiting for us. The whole neighborhood was there. I jumped off my bike and followed Joseph into the crowd. That's when I knew – with all the kids watching, there was no way I was gonna back down. While my best friend, Dewey, patted me on the back and the neighborhood cheered Joseph and me on, I felt like I was gonna throw up.

"What a nightmare! Ronnie was waiting and he looked real mad. Joseph walked right up to him and that's when the crowd began to yell, 'Fight…fight… fight…' It didn't look good.

"While Ronnie and Joseph started calling each other names, my knees began to shake and my shirt was already soaked in sweat. My heart pounded in my chest and I started to feel real dizzy. That's when Ronnie said he knew us DiMarco boys wouldn't fight; that he knew we were chickens.

"Right then, Joseph jumped on Ronnie like a jungle cat. And without thinking, I followed my brother in. Before I knew it, they were both on the ground and Joseph was pinned under Ronnie. The good news is that Ronnie was looking straight up at me, while Joseph had the bully's arms pinned behind him. I didn't know how it happened, but I could see Ronnie had no way to protect himself. That's when Joseph began yelling at me to pound him. And I did. I started pounding away.

"While Ronnie screamed bloody murder, I punched his face. He cried and I punched his face. He bled and I kept punching. 'No one kicks my bike!' I screamed, and with each one of my punches, my fear of him became smaller and smaller."

The kids were still wide-eyed, but now they were grinning.

"Eventually, I got off. And when Ronnie rolled over, I saw Joseph smiling. I reached out my hand. My big brother grabbed it and jumped to his feet. The crowd went nuts – clapping and hooting and hollering. No one expected to see the bully get beaten."

I paused for affect. "As we walked away, I felt so proud – first, because I really believed my brother was a hero; and more importantly, because I'd faced my worse fear and was able to walk away with my head held high."

"Wow, Poppa!" Pudge said. "That's a great story!"

I nodded. "And the best part of it is – no one ever touched my bike again."

Madison and Pudge were grinning when I noticed Bella staring at me with that disappointed look I despise.

"What?" I asked.

"Nice story to be telling these kids."

I looked back in the rearview mirror. Their young faces were beaming with pride. I felt stupid. *Bella's right,* I thought. *Even if I am running out of time, they're still too young for some of my tales. It's inappropriate.* "Sorry," I whispered, realizing I wasn't through making mistakes.

Bella laughed and grabbed my hand. "You big goon," she teased.

~ ~ ~ ~ ~ ~ ~ ~ ~ ~ ~ ~

We spent the morning on Bellevue Avenue checking out The Marble House, The Breakers and Rose Cliff. The kids were too young to appreciate them.

We ate our lunch at the Brick Alley Pub – a table of fried, cheese-covered appetizers for Bella and the kids, a bland salad for me. I ate two bites of lettuce and thought I was going to puke up my pancreas. As we finished our lunch, I spotted a baby – maybe a year old – looking at me from the safety of her mother's shoulder. I made funny eyes at her and she started to laugh. Her mother snapped back around and looked at me.

"Your baby's beautiful," I told her, hoping to put her at ease in this scary day and age.

She smiled and turned to the little girl, "Say thank you, Paula."

The baby placed her hand to her chin and signed "thank you" to me.

I was taken aback.

The woman chuckled, explaining, "I work with babies and small children, teaching them sign language. Kids actually pick it up quicker than verbal skills." She looked at her daughter and winked. "The downside is she's too lazy to talk now." She then told Paula, "Tell this man what you think of the Red Sox?"

The little girl pumped her arms into the air in a show of victory.

"What about the Yankees?"

The little girl puckered her lips and let out the loudest raspberry.

Bella and I laughed. Only in New England!

It was a beautiful day. Children played tag and old people fed pigeons. Madison and Pudge, however, wanted to hit the cobblestone streets where we took in the arcade and a candy shop. Pudge nearly crashed through the front door.

By dusk, we lay on a blanket at Brenton Point. With my head in Bella's lap, I watched as grown men skillfully maneuvered large, expensive kites on the gale ocean winds. As if I'd forfeited my remaining energy to the sun, I felt exhausted. It was a good tired, though, and I thought, *What a shame this day has to end.*

As I slid the key into the ignition, I looked in the rearview mirror and saw Madison smiling at me. "Thanks, Poppa," she said. "It was the best day ever!"

My heart melted away the sharp pains in my torso. "My pleasure, sweetheart. Now let's go home and add a few pieces to that puzzle."

~ ~ ~ ~ ~ ~ ~ ~ ~ ~ ~ ~

For a few weeks after, we stayed close to home and did just that. I doubled up on the massages, practiced more deep breathing, and when I wasn't drooling from a medication-induced coma, we worked hard on the puzzle. There was great comfort in the familiarity of home and family. I told the kids, "When I was not much older than you, I remember some of the puzzles had a different picture on each side, so we had to figure out which side of the piece went to the puzzle we were working on. When we got one side done, we'd tear it apart and work the other side. That's what got me hooked on jigsaw puzzles."

I couldn't have been more pleased. The closer the kids and I got to finishing, the more we could see the big picture. We'd gotten so much accomplished that we were almost done. It was sadly amazing how fast the time had flown by. It scared me beyond explanation.

~ ~ ~ ~ ~ ~ ~ ~ ~ ~ ~ ~

I still had some good days, but when they were bad, they were really bad. In fact, for our first wedding anniversary, I couldn't get out of bed. Believe me, I tried, but it was no use. I was in too much pain and beyond exhausted. "I'm so sorry," I told Bella. "I was hoping to take you dancing."

"Will you stop," she said and fed me vanilla pudding so that the medicine wouldn't completely eat away whatever remained of my stomach lining. "We're together and that's all that matters to me," she added. "There'll be time to dance."

"You better believe it," I promised.

Chapter 16

Something came over me – an unexpected surge of will power – and I suddenly felt compelled to volunteer some of the time I had left with people who were even worse off than me. By giving something back and lending a helping hand, I knew I would enrich my life and maybe even make a difference in someone else's. Although I'd never needed her permission for anything, this was different. There were so few moments left. I asked Bella what she thought.

"I think it's a terrible idea," she said, her smile threatening to crack her face in half.

"Good," I said. "I thought you would."

I researched the Make a Wish Foundation and was humbled by their incredible mission. Since 1980 – after a little boy realized his heartfelt wish to become a police officer – the foundation had enriched the lives of thousands of children who suffered from life-threatening medical conditions. Through its wish-granting work, it offered miraculous experiences to children and their families, eventually blossoming into a worldwide phenomenon. A network of more than twenty-five thousand volunteers – serving as wish granters, fundraisers, and special event assistants – enabled the foundation to serve children with terminal illnesses.

I was most interested in participating in the wish experience. Thanks to hardworking volunteers helping to "share the power of a wish," more than one hundred twenty-seven thousand children had experienced moments of hope, strength and joy.

There were four types of wishes: wishes to go somewhere, to meet someone, to be someone or to have something.

Some had gone to Top Gun School, Disney World and the Super Bowl, while others had even gone swimming with dolphins. I got choked up when I read that one of the children spent her wish on a shopping spree for homeless children. Another seven-year-old little boy lived in a neighborhood where most kids couldn't afford ice cream. His dream was spent dressed as the ice cream man, driving around, ringing a bell and handing out free cones.

There were children who'd requested and met movie stars, famous musicians and professional athletes. There were others – if only for a few precious moments – who became princesses, pro wrestlers and commercial actors. One young boy asked to be a worker in a pickle factory. He got his wish and performed every job they had. Aspiring maternity ward nurses, lighthouse keepers and even superheroes realized their dreams.

My refrigerator list paled in comparison to the miracles this foundation had performed. *I just have to get involved in this*, I decided.

I placed a call and a pleasant woman on the other end named Nancy explained what it took to get involved. She said, "We should have something in two months and…"

"Time is a rare commodity right now," I politely interrupted and briefly explained my situation.

"Then how about The Tomorrow Fund?" Nancy asked. "You could donate money to help support terminally-ill children and their families."

I took down the information. "That's great, but I'd like to do more than send money."

"There's another organization called the Chemo Angels. They send cards and gifts to those undergoing treatment for cancer. Believe me, they're a real ray of sunshine to those who deserve to be pampered."

"They correspond with cancer patients?"

"They sure do. In fact, many Chemo Angel volunteers are also people who have been affected by cancer in some way. Each one of them has a desire to brighten the lives of cancer patients."

"That's great and I plan to look into it, but I was thinking about giving my time…maybe something more up close and personal."

Nancy thought for a minute. "How about volunteering at a children's hospital?"

"Yes." It was the answer I'd been looking for. "Yes, that's it! Thank you, Nancy."

~ ~ ~ ~ ~ ~ ~ ~ ~ ~ ~ ~

The state's premier pediatric facility was designed in collaboration with doctors, nurses and other health care professionals, as well as parents and children. Earning worldwide recognition for its family-centered environment and expert staff, it also had the area's only pediatric oncology program. They provided diagnosis and treatment to kids, ranging in age from newborn to eighteen years old.

Comprehensive treatment was provided for infants, children and adolescents with cancer and blood disorders. Special expertise and programs existed for children with leukemia, brain tumors, lymphoma, hemophilia and sickle cell disease.

Volunteers had to submit an application with references, provide an updated immunization record, agree to a tuberculosis test, complete an orientation to hospital policies and procedures, and commit to a minimum of four hours each week for at least four months. I wasn't sure about the last requirement, but decided, *if I don't meet it, I'm not real worried about being sued.*

It was a cold morning when I arrived for my orientation. Though I expected to be joined by others, it was just me and Carissa Kennedy, my bubbly guide. "On behalf of volunteer services, welcome," she said, with a brilliant smile. "We appreciate the time you're taking from your personal life. I hope you gain as much from the experience as the patients do."

"I have no doubt."

"Our volunteers are a talented group of people who make a huge difference in the kids' lives and there are lots of opportunities to make that difference. You could greet visitors and patients, be a liaison for patients and families, or even assist in the emergency room. Some volunteers like to deliver flowers and mail."

"I was hoping to do something more directly with the kids."

"We have many volunteers who visit with patients or hold the hand of a chronically ill child. Some read to the kids and others assist those with disabilities."

"I'll take it," I said.

Carissa looked at me. "Which one?" she asked.

"All of the above."

~ ~ ~ ~ ~ ~ ~ ~ ~ ~ ~ ~

It was a child-friendly atmosphere, including a life-sized playhouse. We were at the end of a corridor when I spotted a plaque on the wall. It read "Everybody can be great because anybody can serve. You don't have to have a college degree to serve. You don't have to make your subject and your verb agree to serve. You only need a heart full of grace. A soul generated by love." – Martin Luther King, Jr.

"I like that."

"Me, too," she said, "but my favorite quote is, 'We cannot always return an act of kindness to the person who bestowed it, but we can pay back the debt by helping others.'"

"Nice."

As we marched up one corridor and down the next, Carissa filled me in on my rights as a volunteer. "Just so you know, you have certain rights when you're giving your time here." She began counting on her fingers. "The hospital promises you a clear volunteer assignment, fulfilling work, training, informed involvement, supervision, respect, your time put to best use, safe and healthy working conditions and recognition of your service."

"Wow, good for you. That's a lot to remember," I teased.

She giggled.

"Recognition?" I asked. "Are people really concerned with that when they volunteer?"

She shrugged. "Nobody that I've met yet."

~ ~ ~ ~ ~ ~ ~ ~ ~ ~ ~ ~

Upon completing my week of training and orientation, I started spending time with the kids. At first, I read to two of the older ones – sixteen and seventeen, respectively – who were near their end. Both were sedated and submerged in hospital-induced comas. After each page I finished, I looked up for a reaction. There was none. Through my own ungodly suffering, I kept right on reading, hoping that on some level my presence brought them some comfort.

I went whenever I could physically make it, which wasn't nearly as often as I would have liked. For the first time since being diagnosed with this evil and greedy disease, my will was no longer as strong as the bad cells that multiplied inside me.

It's difficult to explain the symptoms. I'd suffered from the flu a few times in my life; times when body aches, cold sweats, fever and chills made me want to lay down right where I was and curl up into the fetal position. With cancer, this would have been a good day. Cell by dying cell, my body was shutting down.

Two weeks had passed before I was introduced to some of the younger children by the nursing staff I'd grown to care for. These honest little people asked me some of the strangest questions. "Why is your nose so big?" one small lad inquired.

"It was a gift from my father."

"Do you like candy canes better than candy corn?"

"I've never met a candy I couldn't get along with."

"Why are you really here?"

Even though I knew the answer, this was a tough one. "To make you smile," I said, but the truth was a bit more selfish than that. Deep down, I knew I was there to face my paralyzing fear of death and to make peace with it. It seemed reasonable enough. These children had just come from heaven and were already returning home. *Who could be closer to God than that?*

Each time I stepped into the hospital, I nourished my soul, all the while wondering why I hadn't been walking through that same door for years. And each day was different.

I met a ten-year-old girl suffering from an inoperable brain tumor who wore a rainbow-colored clown's wig given to her by one of the Shriners. "If people are going to stare, then let's give them something to look at," she told me.

I'd never felt so much pride in the strength of another person's spirit.

The very next day, I passed a small boy who was crying. "Please, Mommy," he begged, "don't let me die."

I felt my knees start to give and caught myself.

Nurse Pynaker came out of the room and looked at me. "He's not ready," she whispered.

"I guess not. I'm fifty-seven and I'm not even ready."

"Age doesn't matter," she said, "The soul knows when it's time."

~ ~ ~ ~ ~ ~ ~ ~ ~ ~ ~ ~ ~

It was a random Thursday morning when I stepped into a little girl's radiant smile. She was sitting at the end of the day room, playing with a doll. When she saw me, her big blue eyes lit up. I could feel my heart melt. The shading on her scalp told me she'd once had dark hair. The paleness of her skin told me her life was fading too. I approached and extended my hand. "I'm Don," I said. "And what's your name, beautiful?"

"Sophia," she said and put down her doll to shake my hand. We sat for a few moments when she turned to me. "I have cancer," she said.

"Me, too."

"Mine is called lymphoma."

I nodded.

"Are you scared?" she asked.

I hesitated, unsure of how I should answer; whether or not I should be honest. But she saved me by putting her hand in mine.

"There's nothing to be afraid of," she promised. Her eyes were penetrating and wise beyond their years. "We're not alone, ever…none of us." She had a sense of her own power and shared it selflessly.

I had no choice but to believe and fall in love with my new friend, Sophia.

~ ~ ~ ~ ~ ~ ~ ~ ~ ~ ~ ~

As knowledge is power, I conducted my usual research and discovered that Sophia was fighting a vicious monster. Lymphoma – sometimes referred to as blood cancer – was either categorized as Hodgkins or non-Hodgkins. In Sophia's case, the cancer cells were most prominent in her marrow before spilling over into her blood where it quickly spread to the lymph nodes. Though non-Hodgkins lymphoma was the sixth most common cancer in the United States, at Sophia's age, she'd had a one in one hundred thousand chance of getting it. And she'd hit the lottery. *What luck.*

After a few visits, Sophia confided in me. "The only thing that bothers me is that I've lost my hair," she said, the sorrow in her voice apparent. "It used to be curly, you know."

I nodded, feeling a pang of guilt. I'd never received chemo or radiation treatments, so my brown locks were still intact. I made my decision right then and there. *I haven't been bald since serving in Vietnam, so it might even feel good*, I figured.

~ ~ ~ ~ ~ ~ ~ ~ ~ ~ ~

Just as I finished the job and unplugged the clippers, Bella and Riley stepped into the bathroom. Riley shook her head. "You really are a beautiful man, Dad," she said, her eyes misting over.

I shook my head. "I'm not sure about that, but I do have a beautiful daughter."

Bella stepped up, rubbed my head a few times and then kissed it.

"And a beautiful wife," I added.

~ ~ ~ ~ ~ ~ ~ ~ ~ ~ ~

The following day, Sophia watched me walk into the day room, but didn't say a word. I approached her and smiled. "You didn't know it was me?" I asked.

She nodded. "I'd recognize you anywhere," she squealed, her eyes sparkling. "But what did you do?"

I winked. "It's only hair, right? Who needs it?"

She jumped into my arms for a hug.

"Looks like we'll both save money on shampoo," I told her, trying not to cry.

~ ~ ~ ~ ~ ~ ~ ~ ~ ~ ~ ~

While still at the mercy of my own death sentence, for some of the finest days of my life, I visited with Sophia whenever I could. Most of the time, we didn't talk. We just held hands. Though I hoped I was helping her, I knew better. The healing power of her touch was unlike anything I'd ever experienced.

I contacted my lady friend at the Make a Wish Foundation and told her Sophia's story. I had no idea I'd called too late.

~ ~ ~ ~ ~ ~ ~ ~ ~ ~ ~ ~

It was a Wednesday evening, just past dusk, and though I didn't realize it, Sophia and I were about to speak for the very last time.

"If you had one wish that could come true, what would it be?" she asked.

The hair on my arms stood erect. I'd just contacted Make a Wish for her and I never did believe in coincidences. I thought for a second and said, "On the day I stand before God…that He'll smile at me," I answered. "What if you had one wish that could come true, what would it be?" I reciprocated.

She looked into my eyes and without hesitation said, "That your wish will come true."

I almost chuckled until I saw she was serious. We sat there holding hands for a long time – or at least a long time for us.

Finally, she asked, "Do you doubt that God will smile at you?"

"I've done some things in my life I'm not proud of," I admitted.

"But God forgives everything, right?"

"I guess that depends on which path you take in life."

She shrugged. "But how can there be a wrong path…as long as you're trying to get home to Him?"

I looked at her, but had no answer. *Such wisdom for a little girl…*

She yawned twice and I summoned the nurse to help her back to her room.

"Sweet dreams," she told me, as I left for the night.

"Sweet dreams, beautiful. I'll see you tomorrow," I said and kissed her tiny forehead. I'll never forget the miracle in her smile.

~ ~ ~ ~ ~ ~ ~ ~ ~ ~ ~

In all my fifty-seven years, Sophia's funeral was the cruelest experience I'd ever endured – and from the pain in Bella's eyes, she clearly felt the same.

Chapter 17

For obvious reasons, Bella and I began attending church on a weekly basis again. Although the services were very grand, I had the real sense – an intuitive knowing, maybe – that God was not only present at the altar or within the pews. Like the air we breathe, God dwelled within me, outside of me, all around me. I found God's love in nature, my grandchildren's laughter, and the sound of crashing waves near Flo's Clam Shack. *God is the sum of ALL things and there is nowhere and in nothing that His love cannot be found,* I decided.

~ ~ ~ ~ ~ ~ ~ ~ ~ ~ ~ ~

I sat wide-eyed in bed one night, as I had for a week, wrestling with a relentless affliction called insomnia. After staring at Bella for a long while and then losing another round with the toilet, I tried to work on the puzzle, but found it hard to concentrate. Though I considered the sleeplessness a curse, in many respects it was about to serve as a great blessing. While the rest of the world slumbered away, I was afforded the precious time to search my soul and question the more important things in life; issues that most daylight hours were too busy to consider. And when I prayed and asked God to come into my life to help me, I was starting to realize that God was closer than ever.

Looking back on my life and the brief future ahead of me, I also realized there could only be two roads to take: The first, for which I saw no end, was that of bitterness, sorrow and misery. The second, for which I was going to pursue with each remaining breath, was that of compassion, hope and the determination to make a positive impact upon others. Regardless of the circumstances or my withering body, I stood at the same crossroad as every other human being. This truth was humbling.

Compared to some, I knew I had nothing to complain about – like that story of an elderly man who lost his daughter, son-in-law and three grandchildren in a fatal car crash. When asked how he planned to go on, the old-timer simply replied, "God knows what He's doing. It's a matter of faith."

Faith – somehow, the answers to life always come back to faith. My mind flashed to my mother. "People speak of blind faith," she'd say, "but the heart is not blind. Those people are misguided and rely on senses that can fail them at any time. Not me. I believe it is the heart that sees. It is the heart that knows. In my life, things have happened for which there were no logical explanations. In time, as events from the past were brought into the light, I understood and thought, *Now I see!* But again, it was not with my eyes. Everything happens for a reason. I did my best with the purest of intentions each and every day. The rest was up to God – for His will was always stronger than my own. Just like an innocent child believes in Santa Claus, I know my Lord is always with me. As the years have rolled past, it's been harder for me to believe in the things I can see with my eyes than the things that can only be seen with my heart. Every day I awake, I've been truly blessed. All I have to do is have faith."

Those simple words moved me like no others and I remembered feeling sorry for others who did not have the benefit of a mother's gentle wisdom. On that very day, I adopted my mom's faith. I also hoped I'd be able to pass it on someday.

Faith – I pondered my current place in the world and wondered where my faith stood. I'd found God after Vietnam and until I found Him, I couldn't find myself. Since then, I'd lived the American Dream. I'd been blessed with a wonderful wife, a beautiful daughter and two healthy grandkids...not to mention the two cars, the house and a comfortable salary.

I decided that through the years of difficult trials and harsh experiences, my mother's hopeful beliefs had evolved. Fortunately, our shared faith had not been lost but strengthened. With nothing left to lose, I decided to share all that had been revealed to me. I wanted to shed light on my deepest beliefs. A quiet, familiar voice in my heart was telling me that the chance was *Now!* I eased out of bed and grabbed a pen and pad of white lined paper. I absolutely needed to capture all that filled my heart and mind, and I needed to do it fast. Thanks to my cursed insomnia, I purged my soul and wrote:

> I used to believe I was a religious man, but I've since learned that I am not. As my mom once put it, 'Religion is a competition for God – the selling of faith. And I'm not buying. I have plenty!'

I love God because God is love. To me, God is like the air – completely surrounding me, deep inside me, nourishing me. Without Him, I no longer exist. God is all things. He is everything.

God is always with me. He is my constant companion. Each day, I attempt to do the best with what He gives me. I can't imagine that when we finally speak face-to-face, He'll chastise me for that.

We create our own experience or existence through free will or an endless series of choices. The outcome already exists. It's just a matter of experiencing it as we choose.

This leads me to perspectives or attitudes. In my simple estimation, both decide the amount of joy and sorrow we experience in life. To be happy, we must choose happiness – circumstances aside. Perspectives also show the same truth in different lights. Understanding this makes it easier not to judge – as perhaps the world is many different shades of gray, dependent upon what an individual chooses to experience.

Albert Einstein once said that in our purest form we would be light, as we are merely energy. Energy doesn't die. It can't. It merely transforms. So I have no doubt that there is another dimension awaiting me after this experience is complete. Personally, I like to call it heaven or home.

Heaven – beyond the stars – this is where my soul came from, although my mind's eye has struggled to remember. There is no need for material objects here; all that is needed is unconditional love. It is where the past, present and future become one and one brief moment is like a billion years. All the secrets of the universe are revealed and there is no want for anything. Dark shadows do not exist in this dimension; peace and serenity replace all pain. All that is beautiful and kind and righteous dwells here, sent into the world we know if only to experience and appreciate all that was created. Our spirits – no more than parts of the whole – spend their human lives stumbling around in search of answers. However, the truth is not meant to be discovered but simply remembered… each of us, remembering who we are, the love that sent us to light up the world and the home that awaits our return.

In the end (of this place), I expect we'll review all that we did, all that we said, and the way we made others feel. Then, I believe we will have to reconcile that.

> Life is meant to experience who we are.
> It's merely a matter of going within – to
> where God is.

I put down the pen and read over my work. A smile spread across my tired, jaundiced face. I picked up the pen and finished:

> I suppose in the end, my mom was right.
> We are each a single ray of light. In the
> eyes of other people, I have seen God's
> love; in their friendship, His mercy and
> compassion; and from the mouths of
> ignorance, the wisest words have been
> spilled – for He has spoken to me. Mine
> is not a blind faith, for the Lord is the
> light of the world. Believing that His
> spirit dwells within me, I become a sin-
> gle ray of that light to be shed upon oth-
> ers. There is no shadow large enough to
> conceal this single ray of light, because
> the Lord is bigger than any church –
> and faith is greater than any religion.

With a single yawn, I felt an enormous weight lift from me and fly away. I'd finally gotten it out. Within seconds, I was peacefully snoring alongside my wife.

~ ~ ~ ~ ~ ~ ~ ~ ~ ~ ~ ~

For a few mind-numbing weeks, I contemplated my path to heaven when I saw a road sign, reading: "Hon-oring Elders – Pow Wow this weekend! Inter-tribal In-dian Council hosted by the Massasoit and Wampanoag

Tribes." I wondered if there were any answers waiting for me there. "Wanna bring the kids?" I asked Bella.

She nodded. "Looks like fun."

~ ~ ~ ~ ~ ~ ~ ~ ~ ~ ~ ~

Since I'd never been, I called Russell, an old friend, and asked, "Is there anything the grandkids and I need to know before we go to this weekend's Pow Wow?"

"When at a Pow Wow, do as the natives do," Russell said. For the next half-hour, he detailed the proper etiquette for visitors and newcomers. "Bring your lawn chairs. Don't sit on the benches around the arena; they're reserved for the dancers only. And be sure to donate some money to the drum when they lay a blanket on the ground. If you don't want to dance, ask one of the dancers to place the money on the drum for you."

"Okay," I said, baffled.

"The drum has probably traveled a long way," he explained, "and donations help with expenses. Oh yeah, and always stand during special songs: Grand Entry, Flag Songs, Veteran Songs."

"Wow," I said, "there's a lot to it, huh?"

"Make sure you remove your hat, too. And listen to the emcee. He'll tell you everything you need to know," he added.

"Great, Russell. Thanks. I appreciate it."

"No problem, Don. Just make sure the kids realize that this is a religious ceremony. They should extend the same respect that they would in church."

"Like they have a choice," I said.

That night, on bended knees, I prayed, *God, we both know I'm at the end, but I sense that this experience is one I should share with the kids before I go. Please give me the strength tomorrow.*

~ ~ ~ ~ ~ ~ ~ ~ ~ ~ ~ ~

As we pulled up to the Pow Wow, I gazed at an open field encircled with tents and RVs. We'd made it. *God is good!* I thought. There were license plates from across the country, most vehicles flying a flag that represented either the Navajo, Massasoit, Wampanoag, Narragansett, Pequot, Cheyenne, Dakota, Comanche, or Sioux nations. I couldn't wait to meet the faces behind the flags.

At first, it appeared to be a flea market, but there was so much more concealed within the outer circle. "This place is awesome," Pudge yelled.

"It sure is," I told him, "but let's make sure we're on our best behavior, okay?"

"Okay, Poppa," he and his sister both promised.

We strolled the fairway and spent time in each tent, browsing the wares: bear oil, deer legs, rabbit's feet, dancing sticks and war clubs had us chattering among ourselves. There were leather dresses and fringed handbags, each decorated in bright geometric patterns and designs. To Madison's delight, they sold handmade dolls. For Pudge, there were toy bow and arrow sets. Fancy headdresses, dripping with feathers, were more expensive than the jewelry made of topaz and quartz. Necklaces, bracelets and earrings forged from silver and copper caused Bella to stop and linger.

For the little kids, they carried wooden flutes and raw-hide drums. For the bigger folks, there were medicine bags, animal pelts and incense.

As we shopped, we spent time talking with the Native American vendors. For me, it was in their stories of history and tradition that the real value could be found. A middle-aged Narragansett Indian explained, "Pow Wows have always been used to drive away sickness, ensure success in battle, interpret dreams or help tribes in other ways. They have become social gatherings for our people to pray, sing, dance, trade and feast together. I hope you enjoy yourselves today."

I promised we would, thinking, *Drive away sickness, huh?* The pain in my swollen abdomen throbbed worse than ever. *A little late for that.*

He looked at the kids. "Just remember not to touch the dancers' clothing, or what we call regalia. Much of what is worn is sacred and cannot be replaced."

The kids also promised.

By the end of our second pass through the outer circle, I'd learned that historically, the Native American people only took what they could use from the land. They warred for the purpose of survival, often times to protect hunting grounds. They were a tolerant, accepting people who believed the spirits of all things surrounded them. And they loved to come together and celebrate life.

"We'll come back and bargain for what we want later," I told the kids. "Let's go find a good spot to watch. The Pow Wow's about to start."

~ ~ ~ ~ ~ ~ ~ ~ ~ ~ ~ ~

Inside the circle of traders' booths was another circle called the arena; the blessed circle where the emcee hosted the Pow Wow, the dancers danced and the drum made its magic. As a show of respect, the drum – the heartbeat of the people – was placed in the center of the arena under an arbor made of four upright posts with tree branches and leaves lashed on the top to form a roof, protecting it from the sun. The drum included the instrument – a wooden shell covered in rawhide – as well as its singers. There were eight men seated around the drum, wielding wooden sticks with padded leather handles. It was these men who sang all the songs.

The emcee's table was also at center point in the arena. Princesses from visiting tribes were seated by the emcee's table, while rows of benches circled the east opening of the arena. This was for the dancers only, folks who reserved their spots with personal Pendleton blankets; an expensive symbol of affluence. Each dancer's family sat behind them in lawn chairs.

I directed the kids to the west side of the circle, so that we could see everything head on. Once we set up our fold-out chairs, I was never so happy in all my life to take a seat.

Within minutes, the Grand Entry commenced and dancers entered the arena to pay their respects to our Creator. The center was a spiritual place blessed by a medicine man. It smoked with a sacred fire that burned brightly.

The eight men beneath the arbor began pounding the drum, while the head singer let out a wail in a haunting voice that prompted the Wolf Tail Singers to echo him. The color guard, made up of veterans, led the procession carrying the American flag, an eagle flag, the state flag, as well as the flags of every Native American nation represented. All who entered the circle did so from the east and traveled in the direction of the sun.

Everyone stood and removed their hats for the ceremonies. I nudged Madison and Pudge. "Be still," I whispered, while holding my abdomen trying to keep my poisoned organs from spilling out.

They nodded.

The emcee, a heavyset man with a big space between his two front teeth, greeted all visitors. "Please do not take any photos or videos during these ceremonies, as we believe our ancestors are present with us today and we cannot allow photos without their permission."

The Head Man and Head Lady Dancers entered the arena. No other person danced until they did and I watched as other dancers greeted them with a dollar bill given in a handshake. They were followed by the Princesses – Native American ambassadors who wore sashes bearing their names and the names of their tribes. The Grand Entry parade looped around the circle until everyone was in the arena. There was a pause and then the Flag Song began. As the drum beat loudly, the emcee ordered, "Post colors."

The color guard – Native Americans representing each branch of military service – posted their flags at the side of the emcee's table; colors that were very important to a people who still valued its warriors. I especially liked the eagle flag. It had a curved staff of about six feet with eagle feathers attached at the top.

As the dancers moved to the beat of the drum, I noticed there were many different styles of dance and pointed out their regalia to the kids.

The men, who danced mostly warrior style, wore long strings of bone hair pipe and beads, bandolier-style. A breastplate, or thin hollowed-out bones strung together in rows that hung from the neck for protection, reached many of their waists. The older ones carried dance staffs, long sticks decorated with beadwork and feathers, with an eagle's head, bull's horn or antlers attached. Historically known as a coup stick, it was the same staff carried into battle by many tribes.

The women danced more gracefully, wearing elegant bead and craftwork on their regalia. Believing that water animals such as the otter would offer them protection, some sported a drop made of otter hide that hung down the back and touched the ground. One even had the head of the otter left on so that the animal could watch her back. Most of the ladies carried fans of feathers and wore bustles arranged with turkey and hawk feathers decorated with horsehair and eagle fluffs.

Men and women alike wore clackers; sets of deer toes sewn onto a band of leather and tied around the ankles above their moccasins that produced a rattle sound. Colorful headdresses were fashioned from tied porcupine and deer hair, pinned in place by a roach pin and adorned with scalp feathers. "They're so beautiful," Madison said and she was right. They were quite a sight.

For the newcomers to the ceremonies, the emcee explained, "Everyone faces different circumstances in this world. Many are born into the circle and some come into it later in life. For those who weren't born into it, just watch and listen. The key is to make friends that will soon become family."

I looked down at the kids. They were both as entranced as I was.

"And for those of you who haven't met me yet, you can probably tell that as a kid my exercise routine consisted of chasing the ice cream truck around the reservation."

I didn't expect the humor and laughed right along with the crowd, fighting to ignore the invisible daggers that pierced my sides.

"It's true. And where I come from, graduating from elementary school is a real big deal." His timing was spot on and the crowd hushed. "They don't expect you to go much further than that."

Laughter echoed through the field.

I held my abdomen tighter and told Bella, "He's the one who should be a stand-up comedian."

She chuckled and placed her hand on my shoulder.

"But seriously, we will now commence with our Veteran's Song," the emcee said. "There are very few people in our culture who are as highly regarded as veterans. Going back hundreds of years, songs have been sung of their actions and we will continue that tradition today." He paused and scanned the crowd. "If you have served your country in the protection of its people, please honor us by joining us within the circle."

With her hand still on my back, Bella nudged me. But for whatever reason, I decided to stay put. It was a mistake.

The drum began to thump and the lead singer howled at the sun. "Ooohwaaah..." While spectators removed their hats and stood, war mothers – women who had lost a child in combat – led the procession into the ring. The hair on my arms stood at attention and I felt a chill run the length of my spine.

It was an eerie song, an ancient chant, sung with great emotion. Every time an era was called out, "World War I, World War II, Korea, Vietnam, Desert Storm or Iraqi Freedom," a woman would wail out in the background.

Goosebumps covered my body. Bella pressed the front of her body against my back. Though I stood outside the circle, I'd never felt so much a part of something in my life.

As abruptly as the song had started, it stopped. The emcee stepped up to the microphone and said, "To all the veterans who have honored us with their presence today…welcome home and thank you."

It was the first time I'd heard those words and it caught me by surprise. A wave of emotion flooded my chest and head. I felt like crying and will never understand why I fought it back. Though there was no longer any room for embarrassment or shame in my life, I still hid it from the kids. *Maybe some foolishness takes more than one lifetime to get past?* I wondered.

The emcee said, "When I went to Jump School in the Army, I was at the edge of the plane's door when I asked one of the instructors, 'How much time do I have if my chute doesn't open?' He smiled at me and said, 'The rest of your life.' Then he kicked me out the door."

I laughed again. "This guy really should be doing stand-up," I whispered to Bella.

"It's probably too stressful for him," she teased.

"I can see a few of you are confused," the emcee said, smiling so big that the space between his two front teeth looked huge.

The crowd quieted.

"When I smile at you, you don't know whether to smile back...or kick a field goal."

I laughed again. "Damn, he's good."

As the head singer called out in a high falsetto voice, we listened to a few more songs and watched a few more dances. I handed ten dollars to one of the dancers to place into the drum. Just then, Two Bears Standing, an ancient tribal medicine man with wise eyes and a scarred walking stick, entered the arena and offered a mid-day prayer. *He's got to be a hundred years old*, I thought.

As the religious man grabbed for his personal medicine from a rawhide satchel, he asked for blessings from the wind, water and earth. "This is our home together, every nation. We give thanks for smiling upon us."

I was taken aback by his obvious faith. *What if he's praying to the same God, but with a different name?* I wondered.

As the medicine man concluded his ceremonial prayer, the emcee looked over at me, or at least it seemed like he did. "The soul chooses to come to earth on a mission to reach the next level of understanding," he said. "We each come from the all-loving source, but from the moment we enter this world we begin our journey back to peace and oneness."

Bella gently squeezed my waist. She'd received the same message.

The heavyset emcee allowed for a respectful pause before he switched gears and directed the crowd back to levity. "Anybody here ever sit on a love handle?"

The crowd roared. I struggled to hold back. The pain was too much.

He shook his head. "It doesn't matter whether I wear boxers or briefs anymore…everything becomes a thong."

There was more laughter. I breathed through it — *one, one-thousand…two, one-thousand…three, one-thousand…*

He then explained the itinerary for the afternoon: "We'll have a contest song which is performed to test our dancers' skills. Then we'll have our giveaway. This is an ancient ceremony where a person is honored and in return gives away gifts to their friends. And I'll also be giving you some tips on the best place to hide presents."

Everyone stopped and waited. It was a strange statement.

"Each year, I hide my wife's birthday present in the cleaning closet and she hasn't found one yet."

Bella laughed all the way to the food vendors.

~ ~ ~ ~ ~ ~ ~ ~ ~ ~ ~ ~

At the open market, while people tried roasted corn and homemade pumpkin ice cream, Madison and

Pudge ordered hot dogs and French fries. "They're all-American kids for sure," I told their grandmother.

As they ate, we strolled back through the traders' booths. By the second tent, I picked up one of the Dream Catchers and read the label: *For pleasant dreams, good luck and harmony.* An old lady with gray braided hair and the wrinkles of a lifetime of smiles explained, "It is an old Ojibwa belief that the air is full of dreams, good and bad, and that the dream net, or catcher, sorts them out. The spirit bead guides the good ones through the hole in the center, but the bad ones don't know the way and get tangled up in the webbing where they perish in dawn's first light."

"Wonderful," I said, "I'll take two."

Madison and Pudge celebrated their bounty.

"And let me have that pink rabbit's foot as well," I added, remembering the day Riley had given me one. I'd teased her that some poor bunny was hopping around the forest on three legs.

"Who's that for?" Madison asked.

"Your mom," I said. "I'd like to surprise her with it later."

She and Pudge each nodded.

I grabbed the copper bracelet Bella had been eyeing, paid for all four souvenirs and announced, "It's time to go, guys." The window of pain tolerance was closing fast. It was so bad now it blurred my vision and made my extremities twitch.

~ ~ ~ ~ ~ ~ ~ ~ ~ ~ ~ ~

Long before the Quitting Song, we made our way back to the parking lot. At the car, I stopped to catch my breath and looked back at the field. "A different time, different place, different parents…I could have lived that life," I told Bella.

She smiled. "I know. Me too."

Though I felt physically burdened, I was spiritually relieved. As I started the car and pulled away, I looked in the rearview mirror and asked Madison and Pudge, "So, what did you guys think?"

"The hot dogs were good!" Pudge said, and Madison agreed.

I had to laugh.

~ ~ ~ ~ ~ ~ ~ ~ ~ ~ ~ ~

That night, I hung both dream catchers in the kids' windows before tucking them in. "Sweet dreams," I told each of them.

They wished me the same and I smiled, knowing I was going to sleep like a baby.

As I closed the door, I thought about Sophia, my young friend who had recently died, and a smile overtook my face. *Sweet dreams, beautiful,* I silently wished her…*and thank you.*

Before I turned in, I had a painful confession to make to Bella. "As far as Disney World, I really don't think I can do it. I just don't have it in me." I was too sick and was getting worse by the day.

She placed her head on the pillow next to mine and struggled to hold back the tears. "It's okay, Don. You've already done so much they'll remember. It's okay."

I hoped she was right, but the reality of it hit me like a sledgehammer. Tears filled my eyes as I realized, *there are a million things that will have to go undone.*

~ ~ ~ ~ ~ ~ ~ ~ ~ ~ ~ ~

Bella and I made love two nights later – for the last time. It was the slowest, sweetest, most tender experience we'd ever shared.

Chapter 18

My physical body was disappearing right in front of me. I stared in the mirror at the stranger looking back. *I've become a shadow of the man I used to be,* I decided. A skeleton wrapped in flesh, my face was gaunt with protruding cheekbones and sunken, yellow eyes with dark circles beneath. A mustard-colored pall to my skin finished off the early Halloween costume.

On the inside, even the pain medication wasn't helping anymore. *But if Dr. Rice ups the dosage again, I'm going to turn into a drooling, non-functioning buffoon.* Even with the constant exhaustion, random vomiting, dizziness, nausea, pounding headaches, muscle weakness and loss of feeling in my extremities, I decided to bear the intense agony for as long as I could.

We'd planned to take the kids camping at Strawberry Park in Connecticut, but I just couldn't do it. "No working on the puzzle tonight," I told them. "We're heading outdoors."

"I don't think it's a good idea, Don," Bella said, trying to put a stop to it.

I gave her a kiss on the cheek and insisted that we camp in the backyard. As a consolation, I told the kids, "If they get their parents's permission, your neighborhood friends can join us."

Within the hour, Audrey and her little brother Ian arrived with sleeping bags in hand. Darlene and Jenny, and Kali and Jake also joined the camping party. I had to laugh. "Any more and we won't be able to fit in the tent," I told Madison and Pudge.

Bella graciously offered up her spot and headed for the house, saying, "I'll just be a few yards away if you need me."

There was only one rule and I laid it down from the start. "No rap music!"

~ ~ ~ ~ ~ ~ ~ ~ ~ ~ ~ ~

It was unseasonably warm for the late spring. After I fumbled to get the fire lit and the sleeping bags properly aligned, I pulled out my shoebox from the bedroom closet and showed it to the kids. "When you get old like me, the things you remember aren't things at all," I told them. "They're experiences and the people you shared them with."

They nodded, but it was important that they understand.

I emptied the box in front of me for all to see. "But here are some reminders," I said and picked up a silver dollar. "In the military, there's a tradition that the soldier who gives an officer his first salute shall receive a silver dollar. Many moons ago, I got this one halfway around the world. It's a great symbol of respect."

The boys "ooohed." The girls were less impressed.

I picked up the pearl earring and the seashell earring, and told them the story about the rainy day Bella and I met, as well as the gift I'd received on my recent honeymoon.

This time, the girls did the cooing.

I showed them a Crayola masterpiece Madison had drawn of herself, Pudge and me.

"Oh, Poppa," she said and sat in my lap.

I pulled out a trophy that read, World's Greatest Dad, along with the white rabbit's foot I'd gotten from Riley.

I looked up at the kids and tried to explain what their mom meant to me, what family should mean to them.

Pudge stopped eating corn chips long enough to process the information. I was happy for that.

Skipping over the check from the *Daily Telegram*, I picked up the mysterious treasure box and Madison nearly jumped out of my lap. "There's a secret for me and Pudge in that box...something we'll get when we're older," she told her little friends.

I kissed her head. *Not much older*, I thought. "That's right," I said. "And remember what I told you guys – whatever you do, whoever you become...Poppa's already proud of you and that's never going to change."

Madison nodded and kissed my cheek.

~ ~ ~ ~ ~ ~ ~ ~ ~ ~ ~ ~

On appearance, it was the typical backyard camp out, no different from what many people do each summer. But everything felt different.

As the kids roasted marshmallows and laughed at each other's silly stories, I surfed wave after wave of pain and laughed right along with them. I remember the faint hum of streetlights playing background music to a pair of dueling crickets. The campfire danced in my grandchildren's hypnotized eyes, warming my heart. I could feel the weight of Madison lying on my chest, her breath caressing my cheek. There was a great sense of peace in it, as if it were a glimpse of heaven, reminding me that there was nothing to be afraid of. I watched as Pudge scavenged for a missing watch that never worked, the flashlight's beam searching wildly from within the dark tent. And perhaps as some primitive defensive instinct, everyone was huddled closer.

As the night grew darker and more still, Madison said, "Poppa, can you please tell us that scary story Mom talks about...the Liver and Onions Man?"

"No. Your brother will get too scared," I said, remembering my mistake with *The Blue Devil* story.

I felt Madison's hand on my arm and looked down. "Please, Poppa," she begged, "the Liver and Onions Man story?"

I thought about my grandfather's frightening tales. Even though I got scared, I still loved them. *What the heck,* I thought. *It'll give them something to remember me by.*

"Does everyone want to hear it?" I asked.

"YES!" they yelled.

"Okay," I said, knowing *it's now or never.* "I must have been no older than you guys when I jumped out of my bed and ran to my parents's bedroom. I'd spotted some psycho looking through my window again. His eyes were dark brown and the right one was lazy. And he smelled like onions...so strong it brought tears to my eyes. He looked just like a man who worked for the gypsy carnival that visited every summer. The more I thought about it, he looked like every scary man I'd ever seen. Even my dad said monsters existed and just because they weren't under the bed, it didn't mean they didn't hide amongst us. In fact, he said he'd met many of them… even a hungry cannibal once.

"The first time I saw the psycho looking through my window, I thought I was dreaming. But the nightmare was real. I woke both my parents. My mother didn't believe me, but my dad got up right away and checked the house – inside and out. But he didn't find anything and told me to go back to bed. I laid awake for a long time that night… afraid to fall asleep."

I searched their eyes. They were already transfixed on the tale.

"Suddenly, someone was knocking on my bedroom wall; three loud knocks that sounded like a hammer had made them. I sat up in bed and waited for the worst. Seconds later, there were three more knocks. I froze. Though I wanted to run out of the room, I actually couldn't move my legs. You see, my bedroom was on the second floor and the knocks were coming from outside. I pulled the covers over my head and worried myself to sleep.

"In the morning, I woke up to an army of fat, black spiders running around my bedroom ceiling. There were dozens of them; bigger than any spiders I'd ever seen. I yelled again and my father came running. As he started smashing them with an old slipper, he told me to calm down – but I couldn't. He said it had been cold out and the things had probably come in to get warm.

"*Or to get away from something that scared them*, I thought.

"That night, the local news reported a terrible crime had taken place in our neighborhood. A body was found face down in the Taunton River; the authorities claimed it was still under investigation. I overheard my dad talking about it in the kitchen. He said he'd heard that the floating corpse was missing both eyes and its liver and that the fish had nothing to do with it. I ran to my father and told him it had to be the man who'd been staring in my bedroom window. He just laughed it off."

The kids were completely hypnotized.

"Two weeks went by without the psycho peeking into my bedroom window. I think it was a Saturday. My dad and I were at the carnival, and I was taking a ride on the carousel when I looked up and saw the psycho staring right at me. I had to look twice to be sure. It definitely looked like him – only this man's eyes were blue. Then I smelled it…onions. That's when I knew it was definitely him! I tried to scream out and warn the other kids, but I couldn't. Nothing would come out. With a big smile, the psycho jumped on the carousel across from me and started to make his way toward me – slowly."

The kids squeezed closer to each other.

"While I tried to scream, he kept walking toward me – smiling. I was paralyzed in fear. Suddenly, someone jumped up alongside me and nearly gave me a heart attack. It was my dad, trying to put a good scare into me. When I finally caught my breath, I looked up. The psycho was gone.

"Once I could speak, I told my dad. Right away, he searched for the man, but he never found him.

"That night, a young man was discovered dead in a gutter, three miles from our house. His body was almost melted from the acid that had been poured over him. His eyes and liver were missing. Authorities quickly connected the murders and put out a warning: KILLER ON THE LOOSE!

"The next night, I shut the blinds on my bedroom window and pulled the covers up under my chin. I swore I could still feel his eyes staring at me, and I wondered what color they were tonight. I couldn't take it, so I slipped out of my bed and tiptoed to my parents's room where I fell asleep on the floor.

"Two days later, a young girl was found cut up – her eyes and liver completely removed from her body."

I paused for an extended moment, shaking my head – as though the memory was real and still bothered me. The kids held their collective breath for the conclusion.

"When my dad came home from work, he yelled for my mom – asking if she was cooking liver and onions.

"My mom said she wasn't; that even though she knew he liked it, she couldn't handle the smell.

"He said he thought it was strange because he could smell onions when he walked in.

"I swear I tried to scream out…but I couldn't. Instead, I stood paralyzed and waited. As I closed my eyes tight, they stung with tears. I loved my dad too much to watch…"

I stopped and didn't say another word.

Every kid, except for the little guy, Jake, was shaking in his or her sleeping bag. "But then what happened, Mr. DiMarco?" Jake asked.

"Nothing," I said, grinning. "That's where I ran out of story."

"It's just made up," Madison told him, trying to convey courage, as I'd always taught her.

For a moment, there was silence.

Jake leaned in from the campfire's shadows and smiled. "Awesome story," he said. "Awesome!"

I laughed, thinking, *It's one they'll never forget and maybe that's the real point of any story…whether it lasts fifty-eight years or twelve measly months.*

Madison and Pudge were now laying side-by-side in the same sleeping bag. *Scary stories can't be all that bad*, I thought.

Once the kids had fallen asleep holding each other, I sat by the fire in the silence. Without looking up, I felt someone sit beside me. It was Bella. She'd been sitting on the deck the whole time, watching and listening. I'd noticed her unmistakable silhouette. I turned to her and smiled. She slid her hand into mine, but not a word was spoken. There was no need for one. We held hands for hours and watched as the hungry flames licked at the black sky.

I'm not sure I ever physically recovered from that camp out, but it was worth it.

Chapter 19

It amazed me how I ended up right back where I had started. I had to wear a bulky diaper for incontinence, my head was shaved, and though I still had most of my teeth, my gums were aching as if they were just coming in. It was comical – in a cruel sort of way.

My hospice nurse, Donna, called Dr. Rice's office to have my pain medication refilled and the dosage increased. At this point, I was on morphine and would have taken as much as I could. The receptionist told her, "I'll have to get Dr. Owens to fill that order for you." While still on the phone, Donna relayed the message to me.

"Dr. Owens?" I asked. "Why?"

Donna asked, listened for a moment and told me, "Dr. Rice passed away two nights ago, Don."

I felt my knees buckle. *Oh God…no,* I thought, *she's too young!* "Was it… unexpected?" I asked.

Again, she asked – and waited. "Yes," she answered, softly. "It was."

As Donna placed the telephone back into its cradle, I realized I'd been given time to get my affairs in order, while she hadn't. *I'm actually the lucky one,* I decided.

Through my drug-induced haze, I prayed hard that night, giving God thanks for bringing Dr. Rice into my life when I needed her most. Like Sophia – and even George Cournoyer, the truck driver – she was an angel, who helped guide me when I could see no light.

~ ~ ~ ~ ~ ~ ~ ~ ~ ~ ~

On the morning of Pudge's kindergarten graduation, the sun shone so brightly I thought I'd go blind. Riley and Michael didn't think I'd make it, but they didn't understand the power of a grandfather's promise – not to mention there were enough chemicals coursing through my bloodstream to keep a horse alive. Granted, I couldn't walk and had to be wheeled in, but come hell or high water I knew I'd be seated in the first row of the auditorium when the school principal stepped up to the podium and cleared his throat. "I'd like to welcome the teachers, parents, friends and most of all the students of this year's kindergarten graduation. Please allow me to begin with a poem I read some years back." He cleared his throat again.

Hello Tomorrow

A, B, Cs and 1, 2, 3s,
the cow jumped over the moon.
While we laughed and made our friends,
this day came way too soon.

We learned to add, divide, subtract.
We learned to read and write.
We also learned to show respect
and why we shouldn't fight.

Our teachers taught us to be kind
and how to get along.
Each lesson was a guiding beat,
while we became the song.

Our chorus practiced long and hard.
We're thankful we've been led.
And though we wish for one more day,
it's time to move ahead.

So now we stand for one last song
with tears of joy and sorrow.
There are no good-byes to yesterday –
just hello to tomorrow.

~ ~ ~ ~ ~ ~ ~ ~ ~ ~ ~ ~

Bella grabbed my hand but I was okay. In fact, I was better than okay. *In a way, I'm graduating too*, I thought.

"One day you're looking forward to first grade and before you know it you'll be my age," the principal teased his young audience.

The kids laughed, thinking, *No Way! This guy's old.* He was forty – maybe.

A few more words of promise, a few more words of advice, and a flock of homemade caps scattered into the air. Pudge had made it past kindergarten. I'll never forget the size of his smile.

Beside a table of fruit punch and cupcakes, we smothered our proud graduate with hugs and kisses. During the conversation Riley commented, "If we could go all go back to the beginning…" She stopped and looked at me with such sorrow that it nearly made me lose it.

"We wouldn't change a thing," I said, hurrying to put her at ease.

Everyone was surprised by this.

"We make our own choices, plot our own paths and become exactly who we want to be," I explained.

Bella leaned over the back of the wheelchair to place a kiss on my head.

~ ~ ~ ~ ~ ~ ~ ~ ~ ~ ~ ~

More than ever I became very aware of my physical body and how my faculties were failing me, but I also became aware of how grateful I was that they'd carried me as far as they had.

I spent two hours putting in the last pieces to the puzzle and wouldn't you know it, there was a piece missing; one stupid piece that completed the whole picture. I called for Bella's help and we searched everywhere. It was nowhere to be found. I honestly couldn't believe it and looked at my wife. "You've got to be kidding me…"

She started to search more, but I stopped her. "We've looked everywhere. It's either lost or never existed to begin with." Few things have bothered me more.

That night, the pain was so bad I began to quietly sob. Without a word or any shame between us, Bella stripped me to my underwear and massaged my body – gently, lovingly. As we listened to soft ballads, I tried to breathe through each wave of pain that crashed on the shore. *One, one-thousand…two, one-thousand…three, one-thousand…* With more love than I've ever known, my beautiful wife tended to my broken body until the morphine found enough leverage to put me to sleep.

~ ~ ~ ~ ~ ~ ~ ~ ~ ~ ~ ~

It became a chore to get out of bed but when I could manage it, I started spending even more time sitting on the deck in my Adirondack chair, going through the scrapbooks and photo albums Bella and I had put together. The kids came over that weekend, but the pain was so intense I had to go to bed. I felt delirious. As I struggled to share whatever I had left, Madison and Pudge sat by my side. "We're only here for a short time," I told them. "So be happy, chase your dreams and do more laughing than worrying."

"We will," Madison said.

"Just remember, okay? If you can dream it, you can live it."

Madison kissed my cheek. "I'll remember everything, Poppa," she promised. "We both will."

I suddenly realized my biggest fear was that I'd be forgotten. I looked at Pudge.

He nodded right alongside his sister. "Leave more than you take, right, Poppa?"

"Right," I said. My eyes filled and I reached for my grandbabies. They were the finest gifts I'd ever received.

~ ~ ~ ~ ~ ~ ~ ~ ~ ~ ~ ~

I'd surrounded myself with positive people. That along with my attitude had brought me seven more weeks of life. But I was fading fast.

While death loomed nearby, my wife's gentle spirit quieted the fear. I finally initiated the discussion she'd been dreading. "Between the savings and the life insurance money, you'll be able to pay off the mortgage and help the kids into college, yes?"

She nodded, but didn't speak.

"It's important they do even better than Riley and Michael, right?"

"They will," she whispered.

"Disney World all set?"

"They don't know it yet, but they're going this February during school vacation."

I smiled. "Any left for the Tomorrow Fund?" The fund offered financial assistance to pediatric cancer patients and their families. Having cancer as an adult was terrifying, but I couldn't even imagine the torment it caused the parents of a child who suffered the same fate. I'd met many young couples that couldn't hold down jobs as well as spend their days praying at the side of their child's hospital bed. It was important to help.

"They'll be getting a check every year on your birthday."

I reached for my wife's hand and kissed it. She was more than I'd ever deserved and I'd never stopped blessing the day we'd met. "I'll always love you," I told her.

"You'd better," she said and buried her face into my sunken chest.

~ ~ ~ ~ ~ ~ ~ ~ ~ ~ ~ ~

To think about the lives I could have lived and didn't, I thought, and was so grateful for it.

I asked Michael to pick up my suit from the dry cleaner. I'd only owned one; a navy blue two-button that I called my wedding suit as a younger man and my funeral suit in my later years. It seemed appropriate that I'd be buried in it.

I made Michael promise he'd place four things into the inside pocket: a pearl earring, a seashell earring, a white rabbit's foot, and the Crayola masterpiece his daughter had drawn.

"I promise," he said, trying hard to be strong.

"I'll need you to give the box to the kids and I'll leave you instructions for the rest."

He nodded.

~ ~ ~ ~ ~ ~ ~ ~ ~ ~ ~ ~

Three or four nights later – I'm not sure, as I was in and out of it – as if I were a young boy again, I dozed off in my bedroom and could hear the voices of adults talking in the kitchen down the hall. They sounded sad and though I tried to listen, I was so tired and kept drifting off.

I looked up and found Bella, Riley and Michael standing over my bed. Each had been crying. I looked past them. The grandkids weren't there and I was glad for it. I didn't want them to remember me this way.

Bella placed two pills into my mouth and tilted the water glass so I could drink. The physical pain was blinding, but except for the few moments when I couldn't see past it nothing had changed. I was the same person – sort of like when you're forty and still feel like you're eighteen inside. And I loved just as deeply. Only now, I lived inside of a broken container and couldn't break out of it.

Michael placed his hand on mine and tried to smile.

I decided to help him. "I don't know why people fear death. It's life that should scare the hell out of everyone."

He half-laughed and then began to cry.

"Make sure you make time to run that marathon, son," I told him. "It was the best adventure I've ever known."

He nodded and wiped his eyes. "I will, Dad."

Riley sat by my side and stroked my hair. "Oh, Daddy," she cried.

"Don't cry, angel," I told her. "Love this strong can never die. It's not possible."

She placed her cheek to mine and sobbed. "So much for miracles," she whispered.

I moved my face so she would look at me. "Sweetheart, haven't you been watching?" I asked.

She locked eyes with me but didn't answer.

"This last year *was* the miracle!"

She nodded.

"Death is a guarantee for us all – just a part of the natural order of life – but not everyone can count themselves blessed with the life I've lived," I said. "When it's all said and done, Riley, we have love…and we have our stories. And I've been lucky enough to share both."

Even through the tears, she smiled.

"And Riley…"

"Yes, Daddy?"

"On the day you were born, you were given everything you'll ever need. I forgot that for too many years. Don't you forget."

She nodded. "I won't," she whimpered.

"Remember, the only path to peace and happiness is within yourself...and an Adirondack chair."

She kissed me and stood for Michael's embrace.

I looked up and saw Bella crying and grinning, all at the same time.

I smiled. "Dr. Rice was right, you know."

"How's that?"

"It was the best twelve months of my life. Think about it: I raced a stock car, drove cattle, spent a week in a tropical paradise with the woman of my dreams... and lived the life I chose." Even through the pain, I couldn't wipe the smile from my face. "I've seen some of the world, loved hard and suffered just as much. The only tragedy was that I waited until I was dying before I started living."

"That's all of us," she said. "We all do that."

"But don't, Bella. Live."

She shook off the thought of going on without me. "At least you finished most of your list."

"True, no regrets...but we did better than that," I said. "We met some truly amazing people and were able to even help a few of them. I learned more in the last year – and grew as a human being – than I did my entire life." I grabbed for her hand. "Thank you for taking the walk with me. It's really been something, hasn't it?"

"I wouldn't have missed it for the world." She kissed me. "We're still going to have that dance, you know."

"Dance?" I asked.

"The one we talked about the night of our wedding anniversary."

I remembered and winked at her. "You'd better believe it," I said.

~ ~ ~ ~ ~ ~ ~ ~ ~ ~ ~ ~

I'd always loved lightning storms, the elements in their most liberated form just passing through to remind us of our place in the universe. I suppose I was equally attracted to the raw power and beauty of it all. In either case, I really wanted to experience one last storm before I left.

It was the following dusk when the air suddenly went still; the quiet before the storm. As if chased away, the sun disappeared – replaced by a wall of dark clouds as great as any stampede of buffalo. The air temperature plummeted and the first few raindrops pelted my window. Slowly, cautiously, the black clouds approached from all four corners and gathered, creating the ideal conditions to put on the perfect show.

With a smile, I asked Bella, "Can you please draw back the curtains and open the window?"

She did.

A bolt of lightning – a bare thread of energy connecting the Earth to heaven – arched from within the shadows above, zigzagging downward. For a split second, it illuminated the entire sky and revealed the fear in my sad wife's eyes. One heartbeat later, a clap of thunder showed its appreciation.

Rolling like a battalion of tanks across the open desert, Mother Nature launched her massive offensive and shook the ground with fury. SNAP, CRACKLE, POP – several bolts fired in the distance. I waited for the BANG! It came. And then there was another, a distant echo of the first, before the howling wind brought the sweet smell of newness. CRACK. BANG. CRACK. BANG. I lay in my bed, my eyes filling with tears. *I'm going to miss it all,* I thought.

There was a pause, and then angry cascading rain soaked my window sill.

Bella watched me with curious eyes.

"You can close it now," I told her. "Thank you."

She sat by my side and held my hand. "Let's stay in touch, okay?" she finally whispered. It was the last thing she'd told me on the rainy day we met.

"Okay," I tried to say but I was drifting off again, totally submerged in a pool of tranquility. I felt as if I were six again, lying on a warm set of flannel sheets with my mother tucking a thick comforter under my chin. I shivered once, but it wasn't from the cold. It was from the joy that I felt, a sudden rush of peace.

As far as I was concerned, the list was complete. I'd said everything I needed to say. My family was okay. All in the world was good.

Though I couldn't yawn, I felt so tired – tired of traveling, tired of fighting. It was time to rest, so I decided to surrender to it. One more clap of thunder with a bright flash outside my window and I smiled. It was time to sleep. I think I took one more breath, maybe two, and exhaled for the last time…

~ ~ ~ ~ ~ ~ ~ ~ ~ ~ ~ ~

A collage of smiling photos greeted mourners at the funeral home, many of the pictures taken during the last thirteen and a half months of Don DiMarco's life. His eyes shone with life and his smile had never been brighter.

There was quite a turnout, many showing out of respect for Riley and Michael. Even Beatrice Goran, the neighborhood busybody, was seated up front.

Father Edward Principato wore a halo of hair around his shiny skull and a constant smile. His blue eyes were intent on making any situation better and he spoke with the accent of someone who'd been raised in the Bible Belt. As he offered several prayers for Don DiMarco's immortal soul, each word was sincere.

Tributes from several of the mourners made a few of the women in the back sob. Jimmy Smeaton said, "Although I only knew Don for a short time, it was clear to me why he touched so many lives. When talking with Don, you could tell how genuine and caring he was. He had a way about him that made everyone feel at ease in his company. I enjoyed his story telling and fun sense of humor. And for every conversation I had with Don – though I doubt he'd agree – he would impart words of wisdom, encouragement and support. I'll miss Don terribly. I'll miss his physical presence, but the memories of Don will live on. He was truly a special person. When thinking of Don, I am thankful for the time I shared with him."

Michael walked to the lectern next and the place went silent. "'So many people are just sitting around waiting to die,'" my father-in-law would say, "'but when you make a conscious decision to live, there's no better ride in the universe.'" He looked up. "'It's one life,' he'd say, 'my life, and when it's over I can only pray I've made a difference in the lives of others.'"

A hush of agreement rolled over the crowd.

Michael unfolded a letter. "And now a letter from my father-in-law...something he asked me to deliver on his behalf."

The silence grew thicker.

"To my friends at McKaskies: Thank you for all the laughs. I will miss each of you."

Each man bowed his head in respect.

"To my brother, Joseph: We may not have always seen eye-to-eye, but you are my brother and I have always looked up to you. I have no intentions of stopping now."

The paunchy, worn-out thug nodded.

"To Dewey, my brother – not by blood or heritage, but by choice – I have cherished every minute we shared together. Keep the faith, brother."

Dewey's swollen face lit up with a smile.

"To my son-in-law, Michael: You are the son I never had and I want to thank you for taking such good care of my daughter and grandchildren. Keep up the good work."

Michael stopped for a moment to collect himself and shot his wife a smile.

"To my daughter, Riley – you are still all the luck I'll ever need. Know that I am with you, always.

"To my beautiful grandchildren, Madison and Pudge – make sure you chase your dreams because they do come true. And please don't be foolish like me and wait until the end of your lives to start enjoying all of the magical moments waiting for you. Follow your hearts, be true to yourselves and know that no matter what paths you choose to take, I am already proud of you." He paused again. "Oh, and thank you for not peeking into the box, but it's all yours now."

Michael stood erect for one last push.

"And to the love of my life – thank you for loving me, Bella. I never needed anything more than that; wouldn't have asked for anything more. My life was blessed because of you. You are the beat of my heart and I will never be without you. Know that each night before you lie down to sleep."

With a nod, she looked toward the ceiling and let her tears flow freely.

~ ~ ~ ~ ~ ~ ~ ~ ~ ~ ~

At the reception following the funeral, family and friends ate apple pie, shared Don's many stories and laughed. There couldn't have been a more fitting celebration for his life.

~ ~ ~ ~ ~ ~ ~ ~ ~ ~ ~

When the family returned to the house, Michael fought back his emotions and told Bella, "Dad made me promise to place four things into the inside pocket of his suit coat...the pearl earring, a seashell earring, a white rabbit's foot and a colored drawing of he, Madison and Pudge." He shrugged. "He said he'd once promised to take care of the earring, so he's taking it with him."

Bella and Riley looked at each other. Neither had known. They held each other and began to cry.

Michael then produced his father-in-law's precious wooden box and turned to his children. "Poppa asked me to give this to you guys."

They stepped forward, prepared to receive their long-awaited prize.

Michael handed them the box. "Here's the thing your Poppa treasured most in the whole world." The last few words drifted on emotion.

Together, they finally opened it. Inside, there was nothing but a stack of photos. Some were instant Polaroids, others were glossy color prints. Madison pulled off the elastic band and started to look through them. The photos dated as far back as her birth. Each one showed one or both of them with Poppa, smiling. A few found them with their arms wrapped around each other. Others caught them laughing. Madison's head flew up. She looked at her parents and grandmother who were all crying, and then at Pudge. "It was the time we spent together," she screamed. "That's what Poppa treasured most…the time we spent with him!"

Once the sobs subsided and the hugs grew tired, Riley, Michael and the kids bid Bella, "Goodnight," and promised, "We'll see you on the weekend."

~ ~ ~ ~ ~ ~ ~ ~ ~ ~ ~ ~

It didn't take long for the silence to set in. It was so sorrowful. Within the hour, Bella decided to clean the house and burn off some of her nervous energy.

The roar of the vacuum cleaner was keeping her company when she spotted something sticking out from under the radiator. She shut off the vacuum and bent down to reach for it. The puzzle piece was in her hand before she realized what it was. "Oh, Lord," she said and headed straight for the dining room.

With a nod, she placed the last piece into the puzzle. "This is for you, hon," she whispered, "…the picture's now complete." And the tears came again – a new wave trying to soothe the incredible love that ached to be near him again.

About the Author

Steven Manchester is the author of *Pressed Pennies, The Unexpected Storm: The Gulf War Legacy* and *Jacob Evans,* as well as several books under the pseudonym, Steven Herberts. His work has appeared on NBC's *Today Show*, CBS's *The Early Show*, CNN's *American Morning* and BET's *Nightly News*. Recently, three of Steven's short stories were selected "101 Best" for the *Chicken Soup for the Soul* series. When not spending time with his beautiful wife, Paula, or his four children, this Massachusetts author is promoting his works or writing. Visit: www.StevenManchester.com